I0636105

Copyright 1904 by G. Barrie & Sons

The Masterpieces of Charles=Paul de Kock *NOW FOR THE FIRST TIME COMPLETELY TRANSLATED INTO ENGLISH* The Flower Girl of the Château d'Eau *BY GEORGE BURNHAM IVES*

WITH ONE WATER-COLOR FACSIMILE AND FIVE PHOTOGRAVURES AFTER PAINTINGS BY GUSTAVE FRAIPONT

IN TWO VOLUMES
VOL. II

Philadelphia

PRINTED FOR SUBSCRIBERS ONLY BY GEORGE BARRIE & SONS

COPYRIGHT, 1904, BY GEORGE BARRIE & SONS

THE FLOWER GIRL
OF THE CHÂTEAU D'EAU

XXIV

HOW IT HAPPENED

" I had fallen madly in love with Mademoiselle Lucienne Courtenay; you know as well as I that her beauty
and her charm attracted every eye. I paid my addresses
to her, she welcomed my homage. In short, I believed
that she loved me as dearly as I loved her, and we were
married.

" During the first year of our union, I was happy; but
I began at last to discover that my wife was not, as I
thought, a model of affection and sensibility. Lucienne
was coquettish, extremely coquettish; accustomed very
early to being flattered because of her beauty, she must
needs always be surrounded with homage, with compliments, with admirers! Dress was her principal, I might
even say her only, occupation. Amiable and playful when
she had her little court about her, my wife yawned and
was bored when we were alone. If I spoke to her of
my love, she would reply by inquiring about some new
fashion. Ah! Monsieur de Merval, if coquetry amuses

3

and fascinates in a mistress, it becomes very dangerous in a wife, especially if a man is jealous, and I was.

"The second year of my marriage passed, and I had already ceased to be happy; my wife desired to pass her life in parties, dissipation, balls; if I ventured to remonstrate, if I seemed disposed to decline an invitation, she would make a scene, she would call me a tyrant! You may imagine that I always ended by giving way; when one is in love, one is very weak, and I was still in love with my wife; I did everything to please her; I said to myself: 'Her taste for dissipation will pass! With time she will become more sensible, and she will give a little more thought to her husband.'

"My greatest grief at that time was that I was not a father; I prayed constantly that Lucienne might give me a pledge of her love, but my prayers were not granted. Ah! many times since then, monsieur, I have thanked God because He did not listen to me; for it is a great misfortune to have children when one cannot set them the example of domestic peace and virtue!"

Here Monsieur de Merval turned his head away, with a singular expression; but the count, paying no heed, continued:

"Now I must mention a person whom you knew, De Roncherolle, with whom I was very intimate. We had been close friends at school. Roncherolle was a very handsome gallant, and his unfailingly high spirits, his effervescent, although slightly satirical wit, fascinated almost everybody who knew him. We had lost sight of each other on leaving school; when I met him again, after nine or ten years, he was a man of fashion, famous for his gallant adventures, for his success with the ladies. He was still as jovial and clever as before; his tendency to mockery often involved him in difficulty, but, being as brave as he was sarcastic, he had already fought several duels in which he had borne himself most honorably. He seemed so glad to see me again, and manifested so much affection for me, that I did not hesitate to give him mine, and we soon became inseparable. But there was a great difference in our dispositions, in our characters. Roncherolle made fun of everything; he often laughed at or turned to ridicule the most venerated customs, the sentiments most worthy of respect, and we sometimes had lively altercations on that subject; but Roncherolle always brought them to a close by some jocose remark, by some repartee so original, that it was impossible to take anything seriously with him.

"When I married, Roncherolle naturally became one of the habitués of my house; you will be surprised perhaps to learn that with my jealous temperament, I introduced into my domestic circle a fascinating man, especially renowned for his conquests; but I believed Roncherolle to be my friend, my sincere friend; and despite his easy-going principles, he was the last man whom I deemed capable of betraying me! Alas! I believed in friendship, as I had believed in love; it is so pleasant to believe; but one suffers keenly in proportion when one is undeceived!

"I was destined to pay dear for my confidence ere long. Obliged to take a journey which would keep me away from Paris for a week, I desired to take my wife with me; she invented a thousand excuses for not accompanying me. I went away, urging Roncherolle to take care of Lucienne. I was blind, as you see; I had no suspicion of what others perhaps had already guessed.

"But when treachery surrounds us, it seems as if heaven itself undertakes to open our eyes; it arranges events in such a way as to reveal the truth to us; for I do not believe in chance, I believe only in Providence.

"As soon as I arrived at Havre, which was my destination, I found that the matter which I supposed was in litigation was settled, so that I was free the next day, and I started to return to Paris. I exulted in the thought of surprising my wife, whom I had not warned of my return. The train which took me back to Paris was delayed two hours on the way, and it was nearly midnight when I reached my house; the weather was bad, the night was very dark, but I distinguished a carriage which arrived almost at the same time as myself, and stopped a few steps from the porte cochère of my house. A secret presentiment or warning instantly took possession of my mind. Something told me that my wife was in that carriage, that she was not returning alone, and that I was on the point of discovering a shocking treachery! I cannot tell you how it was that that thought came to me so suddenly, or what was the source of the flash that suddenly gleamed in my eyes; but without hesitating a second, I quickened my pace and reached the carriage just as the driver opened the door to let the persons who were within alight. The size of the cab and the darkness enabled me to hide behind it and, unseen, to hear everything.

"Roncherolle alighted first, I recognized him instantly; then he helped my wife to alight; but imagine my feelings, when, instead of entering the house at once, I saw her walk a few steps away with Roncherolle, to whom she applied the sweetest and most affectionate names, and then made an appointment to meet him the next day. I did not need to hear any more; I could no longer doubt my misfortune. The man whom I had believed to be my sincere friend was my wife's lover! I rushed like a thunderbolt between the traitorous pair, and talked to them as they deserved. My wife uttered a shriek, and ran to the door and rang the bell. I grasped Roncherolle's arm, when he too tried to fly, and said to him: 'You know now what I expect of you; the insult you have offered me can only be wiped out with your blood; if heaven is just, I shall kill you; if not, after betraying your friend, you will have the added happiness of making his wife a widow. To-morrow morning, at eight o'clock, I shall expect you at Porte Maillot; we need no seconds; luckily, I know that you are no coward; I rely upon you.'

"Roncherolle disappeared without a word. I entered my house; I hesitated to appear before my wife, for I expected tears, entreaties, a scene of despair; but although my heart was torn, although it requires much

courage to endure a blow which shatters in a moment
the whole charm of one's life, my course was already
fully decided upon, and that is why I went to my wife's
apartment.

"Imagine my surprise, my stupefaction, when I found
her occupied in preparing for the night, almost as tran-
quilly as if nothing had happened. However, at my
approach, I saw that she trembled a little, she was afraid
of me; that was the only sentiment that I inspired in
her, that was her only remorse.

"'Do not tremble, madame,' I said to Lucienne, 'I
am too well-bred to adopt extreme measures with you,
measures which your infamous conduct would render
excusable, perhaps, but which after all would not wipe
out the dishonor with which you have covered my name.
That name I propose to abandon, and I order you also
to cease to bear it; this is the last order that you will
receive from me. To-morrow I go away, I leave you
forever. You have your own fortune, I have mine, and
thank heaven! our marriage contract was drawn up in
such a way that each of us retains the enjoyment of his
own property. I shall make no noise, no scandal; the
world may interpret my conduct as it pleases; very likely
it will put me in the wrong, that would not surprise me;
but I shall get over it; it will be much harder for me,
no doubt, to give up a happiness of which I had dreamed,
of which I was still dreaming, and which I did not think
was destined to last so short a time; but I will try, and
heaven will help me.'

"After saying this, I was silent for a few moments. I confess that I expected tears and some words of repentance. But I was mistaken again! My wife uttered a few incoherent sentences, in which, however, I understood that she was trying to make me think that I was a visionary, that I had misunderstood her conversation with Roncherolle, and finally she ended by saying that she was very unhappy with me and that we should do well to separate. I left her, I went away with death in my heart, but without a glance at that woman who had not a single tear for the unhappiness she caused me!

"The next day at seven o'clock, I had finished all my preparations for departure and had written to my notary; I was preparing to start for the place where I had appointed to meet Roncherolle, when a messenger brought me a letter; I recognized the handwriting of the man whom I was going to meet, and I hastily broke the seal; that letter has remained engraven in my memory! Roncherolle's missive was thus conceived:

"'My dear De Brévanne'—he had the effrontery still to address me so!—'I am very sorry for all that has happened. You have taken the thing too seriously! I believed that you—as everybody else did; and this is one of those things which happen every day; why in the devil did you come back when you were not expected? From the days of the famous Sultan of the Thousand and One Nights, such surprises have always brought ill luck to those who make them. Now you want to fight with me. I know perfectly well that you are entitled to, but it would be a stupendous piece of folly, which you would repent some day. Yes, if you should kill me, I will wager that later—much later probably, but at some time or other—the day would come when you would be sorry for it; for the passions calm down, and when a man reflects coolly, he is often surprised to find that he has been terribly angry for a trifle. I propose then to spare you the regret of having killed me; and as for myself, I need not tell you that I shall never aim a pistol at you. And so, as our duel cannot take place, it is useless for you to go to a rendezvous where you will not find me. You know me well enough to be aware that it is not from cowardice that I decline this duel; I have proved that. But with you,—no, whatever you may do, I will not fight; and as you will hope doubtless to meet me somewhere, I give you notice that when you receive this letter I shall already have left Paris. Adieu; I tell you again, I am sorry, very sorry for what I have done, as you are seriously offended, but if you should kill me ten times over, that would remedy nothing, for what is done is done. Adieu. He who no longer dares to call himself, but who will always be, your friend.' "

At this point in Monsieur de Brévanne's narrative, Monsieur de Merval could not help uttering an exclamation and interrupting the count.

"Upon my word," he said, "I do not believe that there ever was another letter like that. To write in such terms, under such circumstances! However, it depicts the man, and I recognize Monsieur de Roncherolle in every line; he shows himself in that letter as he was in society!—Excuse me for interrupting you and pray go on."

"I could not believe that that letter which I had under my eyes meant what it said; ten times I read it, then I went to Roncherolle's house; but he had not misled me, he had gone away at six o'clock that morning. Judging from the preparations that he had made, it was probable that he had left Paris, but where had he gone? No one could tell me. I sought him in every direction, to no purpose; for several days I made the most minute search, I could not discover a trace of the man, who, after shamefully betraying my friendship, dared appeal to it to excuse himself for not giving me satisfaction for his outrage. So I was forced to go away without my revenge. Ah! Monsieur de Merval, I confess that that was one of the most cruel torments that I suffered! I left France and travelled for some time; but on receipt of certain intelligence, I returned suddenly to Paris a year after my departure; I was assured that De Roncherolle had returned, that he had been seen; but despite all my efforts, I could not succeed in finding him. I went away again and travelled a long while; years passed, and time, that great restorer, at last restored the tranquillity which I had lost, without, however, restoring my happiness; for, from the sufferings that I had undergone, I had retained a deep-rooted misanthropy, and

almost an aversion to mankind. I was excusable, was I
not, monsieur? Betrayed in my dearest affections, at
the age when the heart abandons itself to them with the
least reserve, I no longer believed in anything that had
formerly contributed to my happiness; and it is melancholy to say to oneself: 'I have no friend; the man who
presses my hand to-day will betray me to-morrow if any
of his passions may be gratified by so doing.'"

"Oh! Monsieur de Brévanne, you must not include
all mankind in the same anathema! Believe me, there
are sincere sentiments, and there are men who understand friendship.—And so you have not seen Monsieur
de Roncherolle since the day that you were to fight?"

"As I tell you, it was impossible for me to find him.
Someone told me once that he had met him in the Pyrenees, travelling with a lady who called herself the
Baronne de Grangeville; from the portrait that was
given me of that lady, I had no doubt that it was my
wife, and that thought prevented me from going to the
Pyrenees; for I will admit that, while I desired earnestly
to meet a false friend upon whom I hoped to be revenged,
I had not the slightest desire to meet a woman whom I
had loved so dearly and who had betrayed me so out-
rageously. Much time has passed since then. A few
years ago, I bought this country house, in which I am
beginning to take some pleasure. Now, Monsieur de
Merval, you know the cause of my separation from Madame de Brévanne—tell me frankly if the world guessed
the truth, and if it judged justly in this matter?"

"Yes, I tell you again, you were not the one who was blamed; to be sure, there were, immediately after your rupture, some persons, ladies especially, who undertook to compassionate the Comtesse de Brévanne, and when they mentioned her, always referred to her as the unfortunate wife, the poor woman whose husband had abandoned her; but very soon those same persons were obliged to admit that they were wrong, for the connection between Madame de Grangeville and Monsieur de Roncherolle became so evident that it was impossible to refuse to believe in it. However, as there are women who are never willing to admit that they were altogether in the wrong, they undertook to excuse your wife by declaring that her intimacy with Roncherolle probably dated from the moment that you left her. But after that, events spoke so loud, the facts were so patent!"

"What's that? what events, what facts?" said the count, gazing at Monsieur de Merval; the latter paused, seemed embarrassed, and continued, in the tone of a person who feels that he has said too much:

"Why, I mean Madame de Grangeville's departure from Paris, her travelling with Monsieur de Roncherolle; however, you know all that as well as I do, and I fancy that it cannot be very agreeable to you that I should expatiate farther upon these details in the life of a person who no longer bears your name."

"My dear Monsieur de Merval, as I told you before I began the story of my deplorable misadventure, only a short time ago I should not have had the courage to do it, or to listen calmly while you spoke of that woman whom I loved so well; but I have seen that woman again, here—I mean in this neighborhood—only a few days ago."

"What! you have seen——"

"The person who calls herself now the Baronne de Grangeville, yes. It was at the party given by my neighbors, the people whose house you were leaving when I met you this morning. They had invited me, and I, surmounting for once my aversion to society, attended the party. In fact, I may as well confess that I had not entirely lost the hope of finding Roncherolle; I have been positively assured that he is in Paris now, and as most of my neighbor's guests were likely to come from Paris, I said to myself: 'I will go back into society, and perhaps I shall meet there the man whom I have sought in vain so long.' So I went to Monsieur Glumeau's; they were giving theatricals in his woods, and I stood apart from the others, but where I could see everybody. Imagine my feelings when my eyes met those of a lady seated beside Madame Glumeau, who very quickly turned her head aside when her glance and mine met. That glance, brief as it was, impressed me—it instantly reminded me of Lucienne. I left my place, and standing farther away under the trees, it was easy for me to observe at my leisure that person's features. I cannot describe my sensations; I could not, I did not wish to believe that it was my wife; I imagined her still young and pretty; in short, still as fascinating as at the time I parted from her."

"And you found a tremendous change! Remember that twenty years make great ravages, especially in women who were formerly very pretty; the ugly ones change much less, and it is that fact that consoles them for being ugly.—Did Madame de Grangeville recognize you?"

"I have every reason to think so; when a few drops of rain put the guests to flight, she alone remained in her seat, she seemed afraid to move; at last, however, she turned her head to see if I were still there; she saw me and her terror seemed to redouble; apparently I frightened her! As for myself, she aroused my compassion, nothing more! I was about to go away, when several young men came in search of her and escorted her back to Monsieur Glumeau's house, where, as you may imagine, I was careful not to follow her.—Now, Monsieur de Merval, explain to me, pray, how it happens that that meeting, which, by arousing all my memories, should have renewed my former griefs, has produced an absolutely contrary effect? Yes, since that moment my heart has been calmer, my thoughts have been much less gloomy; it seems to me that my mind views things in an entirely different aspect now!"

"The change seems to me very easy to explain, monsieur le comte. Before this meeting, your wife was still in your eyes the youthful beauty with whom you were in love and of whom you were jealous; your memories were the more bitter because they always recalled the treachery of a very fascinating person! To-day that same person appears before you with twenty years more upon her, and she is so changed that you have difficulty in recognizing her. You realized then that you were still in love with, and unhappy about, a person who no longer exists. For to you, who have passed nearly twenty years without seeing your wife, her beauty has entirely vanished; whereas to those who have seen her constantly, she may still appear beautiful. As a man of much wit once said: ' How do you expect that one person should notice that another grows old, when they see each other every day? '—Hence I conclude, Monsieur de Brévanne, that sentiments of regret are much less poignant when the object regretted has ceased to be what it once was."

" I believe that there is much truth in what you say. But have you seen Madame de Grangeville lately, Monsieur de Merval? "

" Yes, I too met her at the Glumeaus', in Paris, some time before the festivity in question. I had seen Madame de Grangeville more recently than you had, for I had caught sight of her occasionally at the play or at concerts; but I never ventured to speak to her; the false position which she occupied imposed that restraint upon me. At the Glumeaus', it was she who accosted me and attempted to renew our acquaintance; she even invited me to call upon her."

" And you accepted that invitation? "

" I should have been afraid of being discourteous if I failed to do so."

"And does she still make the same show, is she still as fashionable as ever? For she was a coquette in everything; she must have the most sumptuous furniture; the most trivial object in her apartments must have the stamp of the most refined elegance!"

Monsieur de Merval shook his head slightly as he re-replied:

"Oh, no! it's not like that at all now; Madame de Grangeville's household has undergone the same change as her person!"

"Is it possible that her tastes have changed too?"

"Oh, no! not her tastes! I presume that they are still the same; but it is her means that have changed; I believe that she is ruined!"

"Ruined!"

"Or practically so!"

"But she had twelve thousand francs a year!"

"Yes, but that was twenty years ago; and in twenty years, a person who loves luxury and pleasure can consume much more than that. In fact, I found Madame de Grangeville in a small and very modest apartment, on a fourth floor; and the furniture of that apartment was very far from handsome!"

"And how many servants?"

"How many servants? Why, just one; and I fancy that one was sufficient. I saw a sort of lady's maid, who doubtless does everything."

The count's face darkened. He was silent for some moments, then muttered:

" So she has spent, squandered her fortune; and at the age when illusions vanish, she will find herself destitute perhaps ! "

Monsieur de Merval made no reply, but took his hat.

" Are you going to leave me already ? " said the count; " I hoped to keep you with me all day."

" You are very kind, but it is impossible to-day; I must return to Paris."

" But at all events, you will promise to come again to see me ? "

" I will come next week, if you care to receive me."

" I shall count upon you, and long for you. as for a sunny day."

" Au revoir then, my dear count; we shall meet again soon."

Monsieur de Merval shook hands with Monsieur de Brévanne, then left the house, saying to himself:

" Poor count! he does not know all even yet! But what would be the use of telling him a thing the knowledge of which could not be agreeable to him, and which perhaps he will never know ? "

XXV

GEORGET'S TORMENTS

During the first days that he passed in the country, Georget rose at daybreak and was occupied constantly until the night arrived; he hardly gave himself time to eat his meals. He ran hither and thither from one part of the garden to another; he turned up the earth with the gardener, he felled trees, he gathered wood, wheeled the barrow, cleaned paths, transplanted shrubs, and did it all with so much zeal and vigor that his face was constantly streaming with perspiration.

In vain did his mother urge him to take a little rest; he paid no heed to her; and when Monsieur de Brévanne said to him: "Why do you tire yourself so, Georget, for heaven's sake? There is no hurry; I don't want people to kill themselves working, and you will make yourself sick, my friend;" Georget tried to smile as he replied:

"Oh, no! monsieur; on the contrary, it does me good to keep busy all the time; it diverts my thoughts and amuses me; it prevents me from thinking of something else too much."

"Poor boy!" said the count to himself; "I understand; he does all this to enable him to forget that young woman whom he loved; he is trying to fly from himself; and he has much difficulty in doing so." ·

"Friend Georget, him a squirrel!" said Pongo to Mère Brunoy. "Him no stay a minute in one place. Him no sit down a minute in the shade to rest and talk! So nice when you hot, to rest in the shade! Friend Georget, him melt away with sweating. If him work like that in my country, him die right away in two days!"

However, there were times when the young man stopped, compelled to wipe away the perspiration which streamed from his face; at such times he would look about to make sure that he was alone; and when he was certain that no one could see him, he would let his head fall on his breast, and sit for some minutes absorbed in thought; and often great tears would mingle with the perspiration on his cheeks.

One evening, Georget went to his mother and asked: "Do you still like it here very much, mamma?"

"Do I like it, my boy? Why I should be very hard to suit if I wasn't happy here; a pretty house, a lovely country, pleasant work, all the good things of life, and such a kind master, who keeps asking me if there is anything I want! Aren't you happy and content to be here yourself?"

"Forgive me, mother, I am perfectly contented. We have been here a long time already, haven't we?"

"A long time! Only nine days, my dear."

"Only nine days! That is strange! It seems to me as if it was more than a month!"

" Poor boy! Are you so terribly bored? Do you regret Paris? "

" Oh, no! I don't regret Paris, mother! I don't
·think of Paris at all! But, although I have said that I
would never step foot in Paris again, if you should
happen to need anything, if you have left anything at
our rooms that you miss, you must tell me so, mother;
because it would take me only a short time to go and
get it for you; and I will return at once, I won't stop
an instant. It is such a little way from here to Paris,
that I am sure it wouldn't take me three hours to go and
come back! "

" Thanks, my child, but I have no need to send you to
Paris; I haven't left anything at home that I need; you
won't have to take that trip."

Georget said nothing more, but his face betrayed his
disappointment; however, he dared not insist, for he
feared that his mother would read what was going on
in his heart. A few days later, Georget accosted Pongo,
who was busily engaged in a dispute with a superb
dahlia.

" Whom are you talking with, Pongo? "

" Who me talking with, Monsieur Georget; why, you
see, with this fine flower, this lovely dahlia, with the
little pink and white edges; but him naughty, not willing
to stand straight, always hang his head. What a bad
trick to hang his head, like a fox! You hear, flower?
Hold up your head and look at the sun, or me will have
something to say to you."

"It seems to me that it's a long time since you went
to Paris, Pongo! I thought that Monsieur Malberg used
to send you there now and then?"

"Yes, Monsieur Georget, master he send me to Paris
when him have errands for me.—Oh! see little red
flower over there hold his little head straight! Do you
see, great coward, the little one stands better than you!"

"And you have no errands in Paris just now?"

"No, Monsieur Georget, and me very glad to stay
here, where it's cool, not get tired travelling; though
master, him always want me to take the carriage; but
me not like the carriage; too crowded, dirty folks, not
polite, make faces at Pongo! One day me going to fight
a nurse who stuck out her tongue at me! Then driver
come and make me get up on top with all the bundles!"

"But that wasn't right, Pongo! What! you were
going to fight with a nurse,—a woman!"

"Why, she stuck her tongue out at me and call me
gingerbread man."

"So, Pongo, you don't like it when you have to go to
Paris?"

"No, no! And then when me leave Carabi, him always
scratch me when me come back; for him forget me, and
not mind me any more; but me go there all the same."

"Well, my dear Pongo, if you choose, the first time
that Monsieur Malberg gives you an errand to do in
Paris, I will undertake it, I will go in your place; and
you need not be afraid but that I will do exactly as you
tell me."

"Oh! thank you, Monsieur Georget, you very kind; but me can't accept."

"Why not?"

"No, no, me no do that!"

"It would be a favor to me too, because then I could take the opportunity to buy some things in Paris that I need."

"No, Monsieur Georget, me not send you in my place, because, when master, him tell me to go there, if me no do it, he says: 'Pongo he no more my servant, Pongo he make others do his work'; and he turn me away. No, Pongo always do master's work himself!—Just wait, you flower, me take a cane to you, fine Zima like master's, and then you have to stand straight."

Georget walked sadly away from Pongo; the poor boy was burning with longing to go to Paris, though it were to stay there but a moment; but he dared not admit it either to his mother or to his patron; for after swearing so often that he would never go there again, that he held Paris in horror; after having earnestly begged that he might never be sent there, how could he now have the face to ask permission to go there? Would it not be equivalent to an admission that he was still thinking of Violette, that he could not succeed in forgetting her, that, in short, he would give ten years of his life to see her for an instant? At eighteen, years seem such a trifle; if a lover's wishes could always be gratified, he would often squander in a few days the best part of his youth.

Monsieur de Merval had kept the promise he had given to the Comte de Brévanne, and had gone to Nogent to pass a day. That day had been employed in walking about the country, talking confidentially all the while. Monsieur de Brévanne had questioned his guest again concerning Madame de Grangeville's present position, and without making it apparent that he attached much importance to the matter, he had inquired her address. He had also asked Monsieur de Merval if he had not met Monsieur de Roncherolle in Paris; but Monsieur de Merval was unable to give him any information upon that subject.

During that day, employed in that confidential conversation, that outpouring of the heart, in which one often reveals one's most secret thoughts, Monsieur de Merval had been more than once on the point of disclosing a secret of the greatest interest to him whose confidence he received. But, always held back by the fear of causing him pain, he had not spoken, and had left Monsieur de Brévanne, saying to himself, as after his first visit:

"What is the use of telling him that? Perhaps he will never know it."

On the morrow of the day that he had passed with Monsieur de Merval, the count in the morning informed his servant that they would go to Paris about noon.

Pongo began at once to make his preparations, which consisted, first of all, in stuffing Carabi with cake and bits of meat, in order, he said, that the cat might not commit larceny during his absence and so call for punishment.

The mulatto had hardly finished with his friend Carabi, and was about to beat *flonflon,* which was the name he gave to his master's travelling coat, when Georget passed him.

" What are you doing there, Pongo? " said the young man, stopping.

" Me beat *flonflon,* Monsieur Georget, me make *flonflon* very fine and clean; him like to be beaten, for him go to Paris! "

" What? are you going to Paris, Pongo? "

" Yes, me go with master, he tell me we go soon, at noon; you hear, *flonflon?*—There! oh! you be all clean! "

" You say that Monsieur Malberg is going to Paris to-day? "

" Yes, Monsieur Georget, with me; he take me, so me put on Mina, my pretty new cap."

Georget stayed to hear no more, but set about searching the house for the count; at last he found him seated under a lilac bush, where as usual he seemed to be deep in meditation.

" Pray forgive me, monsieur, if I disturb you," said Georget, approaching the count; " but I have just learned that—that monsieur is going to Paris to-day."

" Yes, that is true; but what does it matter to you, my boy, so long as I do not take you, as you begged me not to do? Never fear, I don't need you; I shall take nobody but Pongo."

"Mon Dieu! monsieur, you see, I have reflected—I
have realized that I was wrong to say that to monsieur,
for I ought to be at his service, I ought to be always
ready to do what he wishes; and then—you see—I had
no right to ask monsieur not to take me to Paris when
he went there; and that is why—if monsieur would like
me to go with him—why I will be ready whenever monsieur says, I won't keep him waiting."

The count watched Georget closely while he was speaking, and replied gently:

"I thank you, Georget, for the effort that you make
to please me, but I tell you again, I will not subject
you to such a severe trial; you have a horror of Paris,
I know, and I can understand it; you might meet someone there whom you wish never to see again, whom, on
the contrary, you wish to forget entirely; I will not
expose you to dangers which you are wise enough to
avoid. Besides, I have no need of your service in Paris;
so calm your fears, my friend, you shall remain here."

The poor boy was struck dumb; he did not know
what to say; he turned pale and staggered, and at last,
finding that he had not the strength to conceal longer
what he felt, he fell on his knees in front of Monsieur
de Brévanne, stammering in a voice broken by sobs:

"Oh! take me, monsieur! Take me, I beg you! It
isn't my fault, but I can't stand it any longer! I won't
speak to her, monsieur; I won't speak to her, that I
swear to you; but if I can see her for a moment, just a
moment; if I can know that she is still there in the place

where I used to see her, then I will come right away, I
will come back calmer and more at peace, and I will
work even better than ever, for my head will not be
in a whirl as it is now."

"Rise, my poor boy! At all events, you are honest
now, and I prefer that. What is the use of disguising
what you feel? Moreover, my poor boy, you do not yet
possess the art of dissembling; stay as you are; it is
more rare, but it is much better. Well, as you can't live
without seeing her, you may go to Paris with me."

"Oh! how kind you are, monsieur!"

"But be careful! be prudent! remember the past!
Ah! if twenty years had passed since you had seen the
object of your love, I should have less fear for you; but
after only a fortnight, it's very dangerous!"

"I won't speak to her, monsieur; I swear to you that
I won't!"

"Very good. Go and get ready, and tell Pongo that
I am taking you in his place, that he need not go to
Paris."

Georget, drunken with joy, ran like a mad man through
the gardens; he longed to tell everybody that he was
going to Paris. He told the gardener, who was water-
ing his vegetables; he shouted it at his mother, who was
working in front of the house, and who thought that
she must have heard wrong; but when she attempted
to ask her son for a word of explanation, he was already
far away. He hastened up to his room to dress; he
finished his toilet in a moment; then he started out to

find Pongo, whom he found still brushing and beating *flonflon;* he tried to take possession of the coat, which the mulatto refused to give him.

"Let me have it, Pongo! let me have it!" said Georget; "you are not going to Paris, I am going to take your place. Give me the coat, I am going to take it to monsieur; it is beaten enough."

"What! what you say, Monsieur Georget,—me no go to Paris? Oh! you joking! you make fun of me!"

"I tell you, Pongo, that your master himself just told me that he would take me in your place; you can stay here with Carabi, that ought to please you."

"Me no believe you! Let *flonflon* alone."

"But I want to carry the coat to monsieur, as he is ready to go."

"You no touch *flonflon!* Me carry him to master alone, no need you."

"Then take it at once——"

"You won't give orders to Pongo. Let *flonflon* alone!"

"Ah! you tire me!" and Georget, in his impatience to be gone, leaped upon the coat which the mulatto held by one sleeve; each insisted upon the other's letting go, and as neither of them would give way and as they continued to pull, the subject of the dispute fell upon the gravel, deprived of both sleeves, which remained in the hands of the two disputants for the honor of carrying that garment to their master.

At that moment Monsieur de Brévanne arrived upon the scene of conflict; he saw his coat upon the ground, sleeveless, while Georget and Pongo, with an equally confused and sheepish expression, gazed piteously at the portion of the garment which had remained in their hands.

"Well! I am waiting for my coat!" said the count, who found it hard not to smile at the bearing of the two persons before him.

"Coat—*flonflon*—there, there!" said the mulatto, passing his master the sleeve that he held.

"What's this you are giving me, Pongo? a sleeve?"

"Oh! me put on the rest afterward, master, me stitch up all what's torn, me fix it nice. It's Monsieur Georget's fault, him want to take the coat, him say me no longer monsieur's servant; me no believe him, he try to take *flonflon* by force."

"That is true, monsieur," said Georget; "it is my fault that your coat is torn, I admit; I was in such a hurry to bring it to you, and he refused to give it to me."

"If he take my place to wait on master, then Pongo discharged, turned out! Poor Pongo! very unhappy! he go bang his head against the wall."

And the mulatto began to utter noises that would have frightened an ox. Not without much difficulty did his master convince him that he had never had any intention of dismissing him, and that if he did take Georget to Paris that day, it did not mean that Georget had any desire to take his place.

Georget himself embraced Pongo and begged him to forgive him for the pain which he had involuntarily

caused him; the mulatto became calm, he picked up the
pieces of *flonflon,* and Monsieur de Brévanne, having
donned another coat, started for Paris with Georget.

XXVI

A GOOD FRIEND

On reaching Paris, the count said to Georget:

"I don't need you at this moment, my boy; go about
your own business; but be on the boulevard, opposite
Rue d'Angoulême, at five o'clock; I will take you up
there as I pass, I shall have a cab, and we will come back
together."

"Very good, monsieur; but if monsieur needs me, if
he wishes me to go with him——"

"It isn't necessary; be at the place I have mentioned
at five o'clock."

The count walked away, and Georget did not hesitate
long as to what he would do. In a few moments he was
on the boulevard, and he walked in the direction of the
Château d'Eau. It was flower market day in that quarter,
the weather was magnificent, and there was a great con-
course of dealers and promenaders. Georget congratu-
lated himself upon that circumstance, which would enable him to keep out of sight in the crowd, and not be
seen; for he wished to see Violette, and he wished also
to see her without her suspecting it.

On approaching the place where the pretty girl kept her booth, Georget felt his legs tremble and give way under him. His heart beat so violently that he placed his hand against it, trying to suppress its throbbing. The poor boy had never been so intensely agitated. He longed, yet dreaded, to turn his eyes toward the place where he used formerly to stop so often. At last, taking advantage of a moment when many people were between him and that spot, he raised his eyes and looked; he saw Violette, and after that his glance remained fastened upon her. At that moment indeed, the flower girl, being busily engaged in making bouquets, was looking at her tray and was paying no attention to the passers-by.

Violette was as fascinating as ever; but the rosy tinge of her complexion had almost entirely disappeared, her brow was careworn, and all her features bore the stamp of melancholy; far from impairing her beauty, however, it gave a new charm to her whole person.

Georget instantly observed the change, the pallor which had replaced the roses that formerly adorned Violette's cheeks; and in a second, twenty thoughts rushed through his mind.

"Why that sad, downcast expression?—Why this change, this pallor?—Why, even while arranging her flowers, does her brow remain pensive and careworn?— Is she sick?—Is she unhappy?—Who can make her so? —What is she thinking about at this moment?"

Georget asked himself all these questions in less than a minute. But the last was the one of all others which he would have given everything in the world to be able to answer! Of what was she thinking at that moment?

Is not that always what a lover asks, when he can observe his mistress unseen, and when he sees that she is thoughtful? But it is also the question which most frequently remains unanswered.

Quite a long time passed and Georget was still in the same spot, with his eyes fixed upon Violette, who did not see him. More than once the young man was pushed aside and jostled by the passers-by, by people carrying flowers.

"Look out!" they would shout at him; "stand out of the way! let us pass! Is the fellow stuck to the concrete?"

But Georget did not stir, he did not even hear, he did not even feel the jostling; it seemed as if his whole being were concentrated in his eyes, and as if he only existed through them.

But he had no choice save to emerge from his trance and to reply, when he suddenly felt a pair of wiry arms thrown about him, and someone began to dance up and down in front of him and embrace him, exclaiming the while:

"Ah! so here you are, my poor Georget! You're not dead, or melted! How glad I am! I thought you must be in the canal or in a well, or caught in a slide in the Montmartre quarries! Let me embrace you, *saperlotte!* You villain! you brute! to disappear like this and leave your friends in despair! Let me embrace you!"

Georget recognized his former comrade, and he felt touched by the joy Chicotin showed as he gazed at him.

" Yes, it is I, Chicotin; thanks; so you have not forgotten me? "

" Forgotten you! what a stupid you are! What does that mean? why should I have forgotten you? weren't we friends? I should like to know if friends part like an old pair of breeches, which you never expect to put on again? Forgotten! why, I've hunted for you in every corner of Paris! I've been to your house, after asking Mamzelle Violette for your address, for I didn't know it! "

" You asked Mamzelle Violette for my address? "

" To be sure; I had to ask her, to find out."

" And what did she say when you mentioned me? "

" Pardi! she told me that you lived on Rue d'Angoulême. I went there, and I found a tall, thin brute of a concierge who was as drunk as a fool and fighting with a woman—she must have been his wife, for she called him a blackguard! "

" Didn't she say anything else? "

" The old woman said: ' They've gone away, and we don't know where they are.' "

" But Violette—Violette——"

" The flower girl? Oh! I don't know what's the matter with her, poor girl, but for sometime past she's been as sad as can be; she never laughs now, she has changed completely! But bless my soul! perhaps she was unhappy because she didn't see you any more; you, who used to pass your days with her, all of a sudden you drop her, without even bidding her good-bye, so it seems! That's a very nice way to act! If I'd behaved like that, why it would have been all right! Nobody would have been surprised, but they'd have said: ' Oh! that Patatras! that's just like his tricks! Appear and disappear! like Rotomago in the marionette show.'—But you, Georget, a fellow as polite as you, with the manners of a solicitor's clerk! Really, I shouldn't have expected it of you."

While listening to his old comrade, Georget kept his eyes fixed on the flower girl, who was still arranging her flowers. But there came a moment when the girl raised her head and turned her eyes in Georget's direction. He was convinced that she had seen him, and instantly, dragging Chicotin away, he forced him to leave the boulevard, saying in a choking voice:

"Come, come! Let's not stay here; she may have seen me, and I don't want her to think that I still take pleasure in looking at her, in thinking about her; she would make sport of me again, and I won't have it. Come, Chicotin."

" But, for heaven's sake, look out! How you go! You are dragging me in front of the omnibuses! If you want to get us run over, I beg to be excused! I prefer something different! I say, haven't we gone far enough?— But what is it that you have against Mamzelle Violette? You run away from her, you who used to be so dead in love with her! I don't understand it at all! What on earth has the girl done to you?"

"What has she done to me? She deceived me, she let
me believe that she was virtuous and honest, that she was
worthy of my love, in short; but it wasn't true; and she
listened to one of those fine gentlemen who made love
to her, and she went to his room!"

"She! the pretty flower girl a hussy! Nonsense!
It isn't true; I don't believe it! it's all talk!"

Georget was impressed by the assurance with which
his friend contradicted him, and in the depths of his
heart, he was conscious of a thrill of the keenest pleasure;
then it was his turn to embrace Chicotin for what he had
said; but he simply pressed his hand hard, as he muttered:

"You don't believe that of her. Ah, I was like you, I
would not believe it; but if, in your presence, she had
refused to deny such statements, you would be forced to
believe! Listen, listen!"

And Georget gave his friend an exact account of what
had happened the last time that he was on Boulevard du
Château d'Eau.

Chicotin listened, shaking his head from time to time
like a person who still doubts what he hears, and when
his friend had ceased to speak, he cried:

"What does all that prove? That little squint-eyed
villain,—and I'll smash him one of these days,—says a
lot of nasty things about a girl who won't have anything
to do with him! If he blackguards like that all the
women who send him about his business, he will have
his hands full."

"But that Jéricourt, that fashionable young man,—alas! he is not ugly, and you know very well that he made love to Violette!"

"Well, what then? He wasn't there, was he? He didn't say anything, confirm anything?"

"But Violette! Violette! When the little man told her that he had seen her go into his neighbor's room and come out rumpled and excited, she didn't say to him: 'You are a liar!'—If it hadn't been true, do you think that she wouldn't have contradicted that evil-tongued fellow and confounded him?"

"Oh, bless my soul! I don't know! You should ask her to explain it all to you."

"Ask her to explain—so that she could lie some more to me! Oh! I didn't need any explanation. Besides, she saw my grief, my despair, and she let me go away, she didn't say a word to justify herself. Come, Chicotin, do you still believe her innocent now?"

"Bless me! yes."

"Yes? Ah! if I could only think like you! I have been so unhappy since I have been unable to say everywhere that I love her! She is pale, she is sad, she is changed, and how can I find out what causes her sadness?"

"Wait! wait! I see someone yonder who can tell us better than anybody else the truth of the matter. Look, do you see that young man crossing the boulevard?"

"Monsieur Jéricourt! It is he! Let me go, Chicotin, I am going to speak to him."

" Not much! What will you say to him, I should like
to know? "

" I don't know; but I will force him to tell me if he is
Violette's lover."

" Force him! Can one force people to tell the truth?
It is necessary that that should come natural to them.
Come, let's follow Monsieur Jéricourt, let's not lose
sight of him. When we are in a place where there are
fewer people, I'll go to him and speak to him; he knows
me. He don't suspect, however, that on two occasions it
was him that I tried to throw down in front of the flower
girl's booth; but then, that was a joke!—As I have told
you, I often used to do errands for him—I haven't done
any for some time, I fancy that the funds are low—to
his friend, the young lion Saint-Arthur. There's a fellow who's allowing himself to be stripped bare by little
Dutaillis! What a number one canary he is!"

" Let us walk along faster, Chicotin; you must speak
to him."

" Never fear, we won't lose sight of him. When the
time comes, I'll ask him, as if it was a matter of no con-
sequence, to tell me the truth about Mamzelle Violette;
I'll tell him that I had an idea of marrying her. Then
why shouldn't he tell me the truth? What interest would
the man have in deceiving me? "

" What an excellent idea, Chicotin! Yes, yes, you
must speak to him; I will keep out of the way, so as
not to seem interested. Oh, go at once! go and speak
to him! "

"I can't now; he's met someone, he's talking with a gentleman!"

"What a pity!"

"It only means a little delay; we will wait, we have plenty of time."

Monsieur Jéricourt, the dramatic author, had in fact fallen in with one of his confrères, and the gentlemen talked together, sometimes walking a few steps, then stopping, but continuing their conversation all the time. This lasted a long while. Georget was in despair, and Chicotin said:

"It must be that they are writing a play together; there's one of them who seems to be acting it, he gesticulates when he talks as if he was on the stage."

"They don't act as if they proposed to say good-bye."

"Well! if it's a play in five acts that they're composing, and if there's any tableaux in it——"

"Oh! mon Dieu! now they're going into a café! That is the last straw!"

"What do you expect? We can't prevent those gentlemen from wanting to take something. Suppose we go into the café too and take a *petit verre?*"

"No, Monsieur Jéricourt might notice us, and then he would see that we have followed him."

"You are right, and he wouldn't answer my questions; indeed, it's better that he shouldn't see you. Well, let's do sentry duty; it's a bore, but after all, in our business we often do it for others, and we can afford to be bored on our own account once in a way."

Jéricourt remained more than an hour in the café with the person whom he had met; then they came out, talked again a long while in front of the café, and finally separated.

"At last!" cried Georget, as they walked along Boulevard Beaumarchais, which Jéricourt had taken. "This time, Chicotin, you mustn't wait before speaking to this gentleman, until he has met somebody else."

"No, no; but still, I must choose my place. There are some places where one can talk better than others. Ah! he is turning into Rue Pas-de-la-Mule. I'll tackle him on Place Royale.—Yes, he's turning to the left. Wait here for me, Georget."

Chicotin ran after his customer, and Georget remained on the boulevard. Five minutes passed, which seemed an eternity to the young lover; then, as his comrade did not return, Georget went down the street to Place Royale, looked about in all directions, and finally discovered Chicotin under an arcade, talking to Jéricourt, who listened with a most contemptuous expression. Georget would have liked to hear what was being said; he walked a few steps toward them, but Chicotin saw him and made a very energetic sign which meant: "Clear out."

Georget took up a position farther away; he leaned against a pillar, and waited, putting his head out from time to time to see if his friend was coming. At last he saw Chicotin walking slowly toward him, his troubled expression denoting anything but good news. Georget ran to meet his comrade, crying out:

" Well! what is his answer? Tell me at once; I have
been dying of impatience for an hour!"

" His answer? It wasn't worth while following him so
far to listen to that!"

" Ah! I understand; Violette is guilty!"

" Well! according to what that gentleman says, he
triumphed over the flower girl. When I said to him:
' Be kind enough, monsieur, to tell me something about
Mamzelle Violette's virtue, because I know someone who
desires to marry her,' he began to laugh in a sneering
way, saying: ' Her virtue! the flower girl's virtue! Ah!
this is charming! delicious! ' and then a lot of stuff that
I couldn't understand at all. However, I think he saw
you, for he added: ' It's for your little friend that you
are asking these questions.'—I replied: ' No, monsieur,
it's for myself.'—At that he began to laugh again! How
mad that made me, and how I would have liked to hit
him, but that wouldn't have helped matters at all! Then
he said: ' Only idiots believe in the virtue of these girls
who make such a parade of prudery and cruelty. Violette came to my room of her own free will, and when
a pretty girl comes to my room, everybody knows what
that means; my reputation is established. Say that to
the clown who is in love with her.'—And with that he
turned on his heel and began to sing. Ah! that fellow
is a miserable villain all the same, and I don't advise
him to give me any more errands to do, or I'll take pains
to make a mistake! I'll carry his notes to the husbands
instead of giving them to their wives, and we'll see if that

will make him laugh!—Well, Georget, you are unhappy,
you long to cry! Come, come! deuce take it! Everything hasn't come to an end! You must be a man, you
must show that you are no longer a little brat! As if a
man should pass his life whining about a girl who has
deceived him! Why, if we should cry every time a
woman plays tricks on us, men would have red noses all
the time, and that wouldn't be pretty. And then, after
all, the girl never made you any promise, you told me so
yourself; she was free to give her heart where she
chose!"

Georget wiped his eyes, faltering:

"Yes, you are right, Chicotin. Violette was free, and
I have no right to blame her. I am a great fool to
grieve so, for after all you have told me nothing new;
but you see, when I saw this morning how pale and
changed she was, I imagined—oh! a lot more foolish
things; and then you yourself told me that I was wrong
to suspect her."

"Why, I would have put my hand in the fire over
that girl's virtue! That was my idea of her!"

"Oh! I don't blame you, Chicotin; on the contrary,
I love you for it."

"And where are you living now? You've left Paris."

"Yes, I am at Nogent-sur-Marne, on a beautiful place,
belonging to Monsieur Malberg, a man who has been
very kind to my mother and me. We want nothing
there; on the contrary, we are very fortunate."

"Do wipe your eyes; come, don't cry like that!"

"I am done, I won't cry any more; I am going back to Nogent, and I shall never come to Paris again; it makes me too unhappy to see her, and to think that I mustn't love her. No, I shall not come here again. I swore that I wouldn't, when I went away before; but I will keep my oath now."

"And you will do well. I will go to see you at Nogent —that ain't against the law, is it?"

"Oh, no! do come; but you mustn't mention her to me, you mustn't tell me anything about her; I don't want to know what she is doing."

"Never fear! *bigre!* I won't be the one to tell you things again that make you feel so bad. Come, wipe your nose and don't think any more about her. Mon Dieu! there's no lack of pretty girls, they're a kind of seed that grows everywhere, like weeds; you can find them in the suburbs as well as in Paris; I'm sure that there are plenty at Nogent, but I'll bet that you haven't looked for them yet?"

"No, I haven't thought of it."

"We'll look for them together, and I will hunt up one able to make you forget all the flower girls in Paris."

"Yes, I will love another, I will love several others!"

"That's the talk; you must love 'em in bunches! In that way, if there's one of them who plays tricks on you, you can console yourself right away with another."

"You will come, won't you, Chicotin? you promise to come? But not to talk to me about her. What difference does it make to me now whether she is pale or red,

whether she is sad or merry? Mon Dieu! it's a matter
of indifference to me now; I snap my fingers at her,
I don't propose to take any further interest in her.
When a girl behaves as she has done, she doesn't deserve
anybody's interest, does she, Chicotin?"

"No, no! blow your nose again. I'll go to see you,
that's agreed; you see, I'm my own master; to be sure,
I have my gouty gentleman, who gives me something
to do sometimes, but not every day; I haven't been able
to find the Baronne de Grangeville, but that isn't my
fault. By the way, some time ago weren't you also looking for somebody for your Monsieur Malberg? It was
Violette who told me that one day when——"

"Violette! Violette! Did she mention me to you?"

"Ah! what a stupid turkey I am! Here I am talking about her now! I wish I'd bitten my tongue out!"

"Mon Dieu! it isn't a crime, after all, Chicotin. Besides, it must have been long ago, when she loved me a
little, when she was fond of me; for she was, I am perfectly sure of it."

"Well, it's all over now! You were looking for
somebody, that's all! and that was why we never met."

"That is true, but I looked in vain, I could not find
that Monsieur de Roncherolle in Paris."

"Monsieur de—what name did you say?"

"Monsieur de Roncherolle."

"Well, on my word! that is a good one! Is that the
man you looked for so long in vain?"

"Yes, can it be that you know where to find him?"

"Do I know! why, it's my gouty gentleman; he set me to find a lady. Ah! he looks to me like an old rake! but swell, and generous, though it seems he's ruined."

"And this gentleman's name is De Roncherolle?"

"Exactly; and I had a bouquet to carry from him—indeed, he bought it of Violette."

"Of Violette?"

"Confound it! I am getting to be as talkative as a magpie, and as stupid as a kettle!"

"Does that gentleman know Violette too?"

"Why, no, he knows her just as everybody may know a person who sells flowers; he bought a bouquet of her and paid for it, that's all."

"And his name is De Roncherolle?"

"Yes, yes; how many times must I tell you that?"

"And he lives——"

"In a small furnished lodging house on Rue de Bretagne, in the Marais; I don't know the number, but you can find it easily enough."

"Thanks, Chicotin, thanks! At last I am going to be able to be of some service to Monsieur Malberg; he was so anxious to find that gentleman; I must go at once and tell him. But mon Dieu! it just occurs to me—what time is it now?"

"The clock on Saint-Paul's just struck six."

"Six o'clock! and monsieur told me to be at the corner of the Boulevard and Rue d'Angoulême at five."

"It will hardly be possible for you to be there."

"No matter, we must run; come, Chicotin, quick!"

The desire to please his benefactor had banished from his mind for a moment the pretty flower girl's image. He ran at the top of his speed to the place which the count had appointed, and Chicotin followed him, saying from time to time:

" Sapristi! we are going at a lively pace! If a horse dealer should see us, he would enter us for the races on the Champs-de-Mars; we would beat all the ponies! "

The two young men arrived at the place appointed, but Georget could not see his master.

" Wait here," he said to his friend; " I am going to our house, and I shall be able to find out there if Monsieur Malberg has gone back; wait."

Georget went to the house where he used to live. He found Baudoin's wife, who by an extraordinary chance was sober, and who said to him:

" Monsieur Malberg came here to ask if you were here, but it was three-quarters of an hour ago; he was in a cab, and he didn't even get out; he probably started for Nogent right away."

Georget returned to his comrade.

" Monsieur went to the house to look for me, then he went away; of course it wasn't his place to wait for me. So I must start at once, and I will soon be there."

" Are you going on foot? "

" Yes, I can go faster than the public carriages."

" I will be your escort as far as Vincennes, but on condition that we don't run so fast as we did just now. Now that your master has gone ahead, it won't make

any difference whether you arrive half an hour sooner
or later; and if he scolds you, you have something to tell
him that will restore his good humor."

"Oh, he never scolds.—Come, Chicotin, let us start."

"What on earth are you doing? We are on Boulevard
du Temple, and you are starting off toward Porte-Saint-
Martin to go to Vincennes!"

"Ah! you are right; I was thinking of something
else, and I made a mistake."

"All right; come, file left, and let's shake out our legs;
it's lucky I'm here to start you on the right road."

XXVII

A RESEMBLANCE

The Comte de Brévanne had a reason for going to
Paris, but he did not wish to confide to anyone the purpose of his journey; having completed his visit, he was
driven, about five o'clock, to Boulevard du Temple, near
Rue d'Angoulême, and there he looked about for Georget, who, intent upon following Monsieur Jéricourt, had
forgotten his appointment with the count. The latter,
without alighting from his carriage, drove to his city
home, where the concierge informed him that Georget
had not called.

" I can guess where he probably is, and what has made him forget the appointment," thought Monsieur de Brévanne. "Driver, take me to the flower market on Boulevard Saint-Martin."

The driver whipped up his horse and the count said to himself:

" Here is an opportunity to see this girl who is so pretty, and who has turned my poor Georget's head; I will wager that he is within a few steps of the flower girl's booth, and that he can't make up his mind to go away. A boy loves so earnestly at eighteen! and this poor fellow's heart is too soft; he will be unhappy for a long while if I do not succeed in curing him. But how? First of all, I must find out whether this girl is really a bad girl."

The count left his carriage at the corner of the boulevard, and entered the flower market, saying:

" How shall I know Mademoiselle Violette? Why, of course, from Georget, whom I shall probably see hovering about her booth."

And Monsieur de Brévanne walked along, examining all the flower dealers. He saw some who were old and others who were not pretty. Beauty is a rarer thing than is generally supposed. Go into a theatre, and turn your opera glass in all directions: sometimes out of six hundred women in the audience, you will not find a single one who is really beautiful. Let us not be surprised at the vast number of conquests that pretty women make, for their number is very, very small.

The count walked on, not surprised at not seeing
Georget, as there seemed to be no fascinating flower
girls. But as he drew near the Château d'Eau, a lovely
face instantly attracted his eyes. It belonged to a flower
girl, and she was probably the one he sought. Georget
was not there, however; but the girl was so lovely that
it was impossible that there could be another among the
dealers in flowers that could be compared with her.

Monsieur de Brévanne stopped in front of the flower
girl, and gazed at her with an interest which became
deeper with every moment; as he scrutinized her features, he was conscious of an emotion which he could not
comprehend at first; the girl reminded him of someone;
he searched his memory for a moment, but it did not
take long to decide whose portrait he saw in the girl.

"What an extraordinary resemblance!" said the
count to himself, his eyes still fastened upon Violette's
face, for it was her booth at which he had stopped.
"This girl has all Lucienne's features, but Lucienne's
features when I was paying court to her, when she
was not my wife; only, Lucienne had a merry expression, a smile always on her lips, and this girl has
a melancholy look, her brow is careworn; but probably
she is not always thus. Is it a delusion of my senses?
No, that profile, that nose, the outlines of the face—it
is impossible for two persons to resemble each other more
closely. And is this the Violette with whom Georget is
in love? It must be she; but no matter, I must make
certain."

Copyright 1895 by J. Selwin Tait

The count walked to the flower girl's booth, picked up a bunch of roses and asked the price. Violette replied, and her voice made a profound impression upon the count, for that too was his wife's. He bent so piercing a glance upon the girl that she was confused and lowered her lovely eyes.

"I beg pardon, mademoiselle," said the count, as he paid for his roses; "but perhaps you can assist me in finding the person for whom I am looking; it is a young flower girl named Violette."

"Violette—why, I am Violette, monsieur."

"Ah! are you she?"

"There is nobody else of that name in this market."

"Oh! I believe you; indeed, I suspected that you must be the one."

"What do you wish of me, monsieur?"

"It will seem strange to you, mademoiselle, but I was looking for you in order to find another person."

"I don't understand you, monsieur."

"I will explain myself: I have with me now, at my place in the country, a young fellow who used to be a messenger, and whose stand was on this boulevard."

Violette, who instantly flushed crimson, exclaimed:

"You must mean Georget, monsieur."

"Yes, his name is Georget."

"In that case, monsieur, you must be the gentleman of whom he has told me so much good: that Monsieur Malberg, who was so kind to him when his mother was ill, who gave him money, and——"

"I am Monsieur Malberg," replied the count, hastening to put an end to the girl's eulogium; "but it's Georget, not I, of whom we are speaking; he came to Paris with me to-day, and he made an appointment with me at five o'clock, to return to Nogent, where my country house is. I am surprised at his lack of punctuality, and I thought that I might find him at this market. You have not seen him, mademoiselle?"

"I beg pardon, monsieur, I did see him for a moment, but it was more than two hours ago. He was over there, opposite me; I don't know whether he had been there long, but when I looked at him, when he saw that I saw him, he instantly disappeared, and I haven't seen him since then."

"And he didn't speak to you?"

"Oh, no! he doesn't speak to me now, monsieur."

As she said this, Violette's voice changed, she heaved a deep sigh, and her eyes filled with tears.

The count was touched; as he listened to the girl, he did not tire of gazing at her with a close scrutiny which would have alarmed her if she had not been at that moment engrossed by the thought of Georget.

"Is your mother still living, mademoiselle?" the count suddenly asked; and Violette, surprised by a question which had no connection with Georget, faltered:

"No, monsieur, no, I have no mother.—Did Georget tell you that he knew me, monsieur?"

"Yes, yes, he told me that.—Is it long since you lost her?"

"Why, monsieur, it is several weeks now since I have seen him; so he is in the country with you, is he, monsieur?"

"Georget? yes, he is with me. But I was talking about your mother; I was asking you if you lost her when you were young?"

"My mother? why, I never knew her, monsieur; I am a poor girl, deserted by her parents; and I owe the position that I have to-day to a kind-hearted woman who sold flowers on this same spot."

"Ah! I understand," replied the count, thinking that the girl had been brought up at the Foundling Hospital. "I beg your pardon, I am sorry that I asked you that question; I should be terribly distressed to cause you pain; I must seem very inquisitive to you, but your features remind me strongly of someone whom I once knew very well."

"Oh! you haven't offended me, monsieur; I ask nothing better than to answer you; I was so anxious to know you, since I knew how kind you had been to Georget."

"How old are you?"

"I am eighteen and a half, monsieur; I shall be nineteen in three months, I believe."

"That is strange!"

"Is Georget very happy at your place in the country, monsieur? Does he never come to Paris, he who formerly could not pass a day without walking on the boulevard? To be sure, in those days he used to speak to me, he used to talk with me, and I had to scold him very often, to make him go to work; and now he never looks at me, or else he has such a contemptuous expression, and all because someone told him something about me—as if he should have believed it! Ah! if anyone told me that Georget had stolen, or that he had done anything mean, would I believe it?—I beg your pardon, monsieur, but does he ever speak to you of me? Do you think he has forgotten me altogether?"

For several moments the count had not been listening to the flower girl; he was preoccupied, absorbed by his memories, and he did not hear what she said to him. At last, abruptly driving away the thoughts that beset him, he exclaimed:

"I am a madman! just because of a resemblance, such as nature often produces, I must needs imagine—Adieu, mademoiselle, adieu! once more, pray excuse my curiosity."

And the count hastened away, without answering the last questions of the pretty flower girl, who was more depressed than ever, as she looked after him, saying to herself:

"He wouldn't answer what I asked him about Georget; perhaps he told him not to. To be despised, when one has nothing to blame oneself for! that is horrible! and yet, I feel in the bottom of my heart that the main thing is to have one's conscience clear. I have nothing to reproach myself for, and some day they will reproach themselves for having made me so wretchedly unhappy."

The count entered his carriage and started for Nogent. But on the way, his mind was full of that extraordinary resemblance, and the young flower girl's face constantly returned to his thoughts.

In vain did Georget make all possible haste, he did not reach Nogent until fully two hours after the count. Chicotin left his comrade on the outskirts of Vincennes, panting for breath, exhausted and dying with thirst, because his friend would not consent to enter a wine shop for refreshment, as that would have delayed them. He shook hands with Georget, saying to him:

" My dear boy, I am very glad I came with you, but I've had enough; if I went any farther I should have the pip, and I believe I should break in two. Deuce take it! you have a way of walking that leaves cabs and omnibuses nowhere. Au revoir; I'll call and say good-day to you at Nogent, but I shall go all alone, and take my own time walking; I prefer that way."

Georget presented himself before his master, decidedly shamefaced; he was afraid of being scolded because he was not on hand punctually at the place which his patron had appointed; but the count simply said to him:

" As I didn't find you at the place I mentioned, I concluded that you had forgotten the time at the flower market, with the pretty flower girl, and I went there to look for you."

" You went there, monsieur? Did you see Violette? "

" Yes, I saw her and talked with her."

"You talked with her? Ah! I didn't speak to her! With one of my old comrades, named Chicotin, who wouldn't believe that Violette had behaved badly, I followed that Monsieur Jéricourt, the man to whose rooms she—she went; and as Chicotin knows that man, he begged him to tell us the truth about the flower girl. As I expected, he confirmed what I had already heard."

"It's a pity, for that girl is very interesting, and I discovered in her features a resemblance to a person who was very pretty also—long ago!"

"Oh! isn't Violette lovely, monsieur? I told you so! And—excuse me if I ask you a question—but what did she have to say to monsieur?"

"She talked about you, my boy."

"About me! about me! why on earth did she speak of me, when she doesn't love me and has made me so unhappy? Why does she think of me, when another man has her love, when she did not care for mine, which was so true, so sincere? Is it to make me unhappy again? is it to make me still more desperate, that she speaks of me? I don't want her to talk about me, I will tell her not to!"

"Come, come, be calm, Georget; you are not reasonable, my friend; and I think that I shall do well not to let you go to Paris again."

"Forgive me, monsieur; you are right to scold me. —Mon Dieu! to think that I hurried back so fast, because I had good news to tell monsieur, and here I have forgotten all about it and haven't told him! It is all

Violette's fault, you see, monsieur; she upsets my wits, she makes me forget everything; it is worse than sickness, monsieur!—And she talked about me?"

"Well, Georget, as you have thought of it at last, what is the news that you have to tell me?"

"Monsieur, I haven't forgotten that sometime ago you employed me to find the residence in Paris of a person whom you wished to find; it was a Monsieur de Roncherolle, wasn't it, monsieur?"

At the name of Roncherolle, the count's face instantly lighted up, and he seized Georget's arm, exclaiming:

"Yes, yes, it was he! Well, go on—what do you know?"

"I know that gentleman's address, at last."

"You know it?"

"Yes, monsieur.—Mon Dieu! if I had happened to mention it sooner to Chicotin, my old comrade, I should have known it a long while ago. He is that gentleman's messenger, he works for him."

"And his address?"

"Monsieur de Roncherolle lives on Rue de Bretagne, in the Marais, in a furnished lodging house. He doesn't know the number, but as the street is short, it will be easy to find."

"Rue de Bretagne, in the Marais,—a furnished lodging house?"

"Yes, monsieur, that is right."

"So I have found him at last!" murmured the count, intensely excited.

"If I should go this evening—but no, it is too late. He would not admit me perhaps. But to-morrow morning—yes, I will see him to-morrow."

"What could Violette have had to say to you about me, monsieur?" faltered Georget, walking toward his master; but he simply pointed to the door and said: "Leave me," in a tone which permitted no reply.

Poor Georget left the room, disconcerted, and saying to himself:

"It is strange! I thought I should make him very happy by giving him that gentleman's address; but it seems to have produced a contrary effect."

XXVIII

THE EDUCATION OF A PARROT

Let us return to Monsieur de Roncherolle, whom we left in his little lodging house in the Marais.

When the gout left him at rest, that gentleman usually left his room about noon, and did not return until midnight, sometimes later; always cursing the dimly-lighted staircase, his wretchedly-kept apartment, and the servants who performed their duties inefficiently; and he ordinarily finished his complaints by saying:

"But, after all, as I can't hire any better lodgings, I must make the best of it, I must be a philosopher. I can no longer attract women, I have squandered my money, and with what little I have left I still manage to lose at cards. Such infernal luck! Louis XIV was right when he said to the Maréchal de Villeroi: 'At our age, a man has no luck!'—Ah! ten thousand devils! what would he have said if he had had the gout?"

But one morning, Monsieur de Roncherolle, finding that he was unable to put his left foot to the floor, was compelled to remain in his room, reading a great deal to pass the time away, and sleeping when the gout would allow.

Stretched out in the so-called armchair *à la Voltaire,* with his diseased foot on a cushion and wrapped in flannel, Monsieur de Roncherolle had been sleeping a few moments when a shrill, piercing shriek and a number of words uttered in a voice like Mr. Punch's, woke him abruptly. Then an ordinary human voice, much too loud for that of a neighbor, however, uttered these words:

"Very good, Coco, very good; you have plenty of voice, my friend; I know perfectly well that you can talk, for I heard you at your owner's café, and that is why I bought you. Now the question is to learn what I want you to say, and you will learn it, won't you, Coco?"

"Good-day, Monsieur Brillant!"

"Good-day, my friend, good-day! you say that very well; but I am not Monsieur Brillant, I am Saint-Arthur, De Saint-Arthur."

"Good-day, Monsieur Brillant!"

"Come, come, Coco, that isn't it; now listen: Dutaillis is lovely! applaud, clap Zizi!—There, that's what you must say; it's a little long perhaps, but you can learn it half at a time. Attention: Dutaillis is lovely!"

"Good-day, Monsieur Brillant!"

"*Sapristi!* you will make me angry, Coco."

"Cré coquin! you make me sick! oh! what a fool!"

"Aha! he swears; you swear! all right; that is quite amusing, but it isn't enough for me. Dutaillis is lovely."

"Oh! what a fool!"

"Applaud, clap Zizi!"

"Good-day, Monsieur Brillant!"

"Corbleu! morbleu! I will swear, too, if you make me angry."

"You make me sick, Monsieur Brillant!"

"Dutaillis is lovely!"

"You make me sick!"

"Applaud, clap Zizi!"

Roncherolle, who had been obliged to listen to this dialogue, not without cursing and swearing at his new neighbor, interposed at this point by striking the partition with his cane, and shouting at the top of his lungs:

"Ten thousand thunders! ten thousand millions of devils! is this going to last much longer? Haven't you nearly finished, my dear neighbor and Master Parrot? Monsieur Coco and Mademoiselle Dutaillis! do you know that I am the one who will clap you, if you go on braying as you are doing? and I should have done it long ago if I could have moved!"

These words imposed silence upon the dandified little Saint-Arthur and his parrot; for it was in fact the young dandy, Jéricourt's friend and the lover of the little actress of Boulevard du Temple, who had become within a few days Monsieur de Roncherolle's neighbor; the young man's extravagance had forced him to leave very abruptly a charming little apartment on Rue de Bréda, which he had furnished in the very latest style. But because he gratified every day the expensive whims of Mademoiselle Zizi, Saint-Arthur had forgotten to pay his furniture dealer and his upholsterer; those gentlemen lost patience, demanded their money, then set the bailiffs to work; whereupon our former travelling salesman consulted his wallet, and found that he had only eight thousand francs remaining, whereas he owed eleven thousand. He said to himself: "If I stay in this apartment, they will take my money away from me; I prefer to abandon my furniture to my creditors; they can almost pay themselves with it, and I shall still have what remains to enjoy myself with. I will tell Zizi that I have moved to the Marais for family reasons, in order to be nearer an aunt whose heir I am. However, it makes little difference to her where I live, provided that I still take her to dinner at a restaurant, and provided that I am generous to her."

As a result of this reasoning, Beau Saint-Arthur had hired an apartment in the house on the Rue de Bretagne.

It was on the same floor as Monsieur de Roncherolle's, and it was three times as large; and as the young dandy retained there, as everywhere, the habit of making a show; as he dressed three times a day; as he ordered dainty breakfasts, drank champagne, and carried a cane made of an elephant's tusk, the people of the house had the highest esteem for him, looked upon him as an important personage, and would gladly have exchanged a dozen tenants like the gouty gentleman for a single one like Monsieur de Saint-Arthur.

"He has shut up at last! that's very lucky!" said Roncherolle to himself, stretching himself out in his reclining chair. "Parbleu! I seem to have a new neighbor as to whom I must felicitate the master of this house. If that had gone on, I couldn't possibly have stood it. The man must be an idiot to try to teach the parrot such stuff. —I shall meet him soon enough."

And Roncherolle yawned, closed his eyes, and was dozing again when suddenly the noise began anew beside him.

"Dutaillis is lovely! Come now! Dutaillis is lovely!"

"Good-day, Monsieur Brillant!"

"You beast!—Applaud, clap Zizi!"

"Zi—Zi—Zan—Zan—Monsieur Brillant. You make me sick!"

"And so do you me, you beast!"

"Par la mordieu! and you're a beast yourself!" cried Roncherolle, sitting up in his chair and grasping his cane again and hammering on the partition and on the floor.

"Ah! you have the effrontery to keep on with your parrot lessons! Dare to begin again, and I will twist your pupil's neck, and throw his master out of the window! What a house! What service they have! Here I've been pounding and ringing for an hour, and no one comes! I say there! waiter! chambermaid!"

Again Saint-Arthur and his parrot held their peace. But the little dandy also jerked all the bell-cords that he could find in the three rooms of which his apartment consisted.

At that jangling of bells, the waiter and the chambermaid hastened up to their tenants on the third floor. The chambermaid no longer entered Roncherolle's room, because he had several times told her to go and wash herself, and then to go to the scrubber's. The waiter, who was called the "young man," and who had worked in the house for more than twenty years, was probably quite fifty-five years old. He was a man of medium height, but endowed with a very coquettish *embonpoint,* and a prominent abdomen, which, however, did not prevent him from having a wrinkled face, and a small wig which did not come down to his ears, and which he was constantly occupied in jerking to the right or to the left. Having never worn any other costume than a pair of short trousers and a small round jacket, like the waiters at restaurants, Beauvinet—that was the "young man's" name—always wore a white apron, one half of which he turned up to conceal the other half, when it had ceased to be spotlessly clean. All in all, Beauvinet was more presentable than the chambermaid and it was he who answered Roncherolle's bell when he rang.

So Beauvinet presented himself before the gouty gentleman, his apron turned up, and pulling his wig over his right ear, which necessarily caused the left side to rise; but one ordinarily obeys the most urgent need, and it was only on extraordinary occasions that Beauvinet pulled both sides of his wig at once; even then he dared not do it except with great precaution, because one day when he indulged in that manœuvre, he had heard an ominous cracking on the top of his head, as if his wig were about to be transformed into a crown; and the perquisites of his position were too small to allow him to purchase a new wig.

" Monsieur rang, monsieur knocked, monsieur called, I believe? " said Beauvinet, showing his bloated and wrinkled face.

" Sacrebleu! yes, I did ring and I did knock; I would have set the house on fire if there had been any fire on the hearth."

" Fire! mon Dieu! is monsieur very cold? Why, it is warm——"

" Hold your tongue! and answer."

" Why, monsieur——"

" And try to let that shocking wig of yours alone; it annoys me to see you always jerking that sorry thing."

" Why, monsieur——"

" Silence! Who is it that lives here, in this apartment next to me? Is it a new neighbor that I have there? "

"Yes, monsieur, that fine apartment has only been let a week."

"To whom?"

"To a very fashionable, a very distinguished young man, who dresses as if he went to the opera every day, and who spends money——"

"Ah! I understand why you call him very fashionable; what is the man's name?"

"Monsieur Alfred de Saint-Arthur."

"*Bigre!* that's a magnificent stage name! no one ever has such names except in farces or at the Gymnase."

"Beg pardon, monsieur, I don't understand."

"You are not obliged to. Listen, Beauvinet: your Monsieur Saint-Arthur, or Saint-Alfred, no matter which, has behaved very well for a week, as I didn't know that I had a neighbor; but why in the devil has he taken it into his head to have a parrot to-day, and to teach him to talk?"

"Beg pardon, monsieur, but it isn't a parrot that the gentleman brought home this morning, it is a caca—a cato—mon Dieu! he told me the name——"

"A cockatoo, no doubt?"

"Yes, monsieur, that's the name; he is a fine creature, I tell you, with a thing on his head so that you'd swear he's a turkey with his comb."

"It belongs to the family of parrots. Well, this fellow and his bird make a frightful racket, which prevents me from sleeping; and when one has the gout, when one is in pain, one has no comfort except in sleep. I lost my

temper too much just now, perhaps, but do you go from
me and tell my neighbor that I am confined to my room
by this infernal disease, and that I beg him, out of regard
for my plight, to be kind enough not to give lessons to
his bird so long as I am obliged to keep my room; he
can be certain that I shall go out as soon as I am able
to walk, and then he may pour out his heart to his bird
at his leisure.   If this Monsieur de Saint-Arthur is a
decent man and has any breeding, he will comply with
my request; if not—we will see.— You understand,
Beauvinet?   Now go, and let your wig alone."

While this was taking place in Monsieur de Roncherolle's room, Joséphine, the chambermaid, had answered
Saint-Arthur's bell.

"What does this mean, girl?" he asked her; "isn't
a man free to do what he pleases in his own room, in
your house?   When I pay cash, and I believe I do pay
cash, can't I amuse myself by teaching sentences, droll
remarks, to my cockatoo?"

"I should say so, monsieur! who would prevent you,
pray?   Certainly, monsieur is master in his own room;
and he can do whatever comes into his head, without
having anyone else interfere; and we are too flattered to
have monsieur for a tenant, and monsieur must see that
we come at once as soon as he rings."

"In that case, girl, why does a person, who evidently
lives on this same landing, venture to knock on the wall,
to yell like a deaf man, to swear and to threaten, when I
am teaching Coco to talk?   I bought the bird with no

other purpose; as soon as he can talk well, I expect to present him to an actress, a friend of mine who adores me; and I do not propose to stop educating him because of a neighbor."

"What, monsieur! that gouty old fool in the next room had the face to call and knock? Oh! that don't surprise me, that man ain't afraid to do anything. Such a wretched tenant! how I wish he would leave us! he complains of everything in the house. To listen to him, you would think that he had always lived in châteaux; but you mustn't pay any attention to him, monsieur; and above all things, don't put yourself out. In the first place, you hire an apartment three times dearer than his, consequently you have the right to make three times as much noise."

"That reasoning strikes me as mathematical; but what sort of man is this neighbor of mine?"

"What sort of man? Bless my soul! he's the kind that has the gout; he growls and swears and yells; he's mad because he can't go out; and I have an idea that he'd like to raise the deuce still, although he's too old for that now; but he can't move, and that makes him angry."

"What! this neighbor of mine is old and helpless, and he dares to threaten me! Upon my word! that is too funny; it is really amusing! I believe that the wisest way is to laugh at him."

"Oh, yes! monsieur; but if you want me to go and speak to the old grumbler——"

"No, no, my dear, it isn't necessary; I don't need any intermediary in this sort of thing; I know how to handle it myself. Go, go; we will arrange matters with the neighbor."

And the dandified little Saint-Arthur, overjoyed to learn that his neighbor was old and ill, drew himself up and dismissed the chambermaid, pacing the floor of his room with a lordly swagger.

The servant had not been gone two minutes when Beauvinet knocked lightly at the door, then opened it and entered Saint-Arthur's room, saying:

"May I come in?"

"What is it now? what do you want of me?" asked the young dandy, scrutinizing Beauvinet's wrinkled face.

"Monsieur, it's me, Beauvinet."

"You! I don't know you."

"No, because Joséphine asked the privilege of blacking monsieur's boots; but I also belong to the house."

"In the first place, my dear fellow, nobody blacks my boots, because I only wear patent leathers; and they are never blacked; that was a stupid remark of yours; go on."

"I was saying to monsieur that I belonged in the house."

"What are you in the house?"

"I am the young man, monsieur."

"Ah! you are the young man, are you? how long have you been the young man?"

"More than twenty years, monsieur."

" You are an old young man then?"

" Yes, monsieur."

" Well, what do you want of me?"

" Monsieur, your neighbor in the next room, Monsieur de Roncherolle, sent me."

" Aha! it was the old fellow in the next room who sent you? Indeed! I am interested to know what message this gentleman who doesn't like parrots sends me. He sent you to apologize to me, I suppose?"

" Yes, monsieur, yes; the gentleman told me to tell you that he knew he lost his temper too much just now, that it was the fault of the condition he's in."

" Ah! he admits it; that's lucky; it was time!"

" And then, as he has the gout, and as he would like to sleep all the time, the gentleman told me to ask you not to teach your cockatoo so long as he's sick; but as soon as he goes out, then you can play with your bird some more."

" Upon my word, this is too much! I say, is this old fellow a downright idiot? I mustn't teach Coco to speak during the day, because my gentleman wants to sleep! Why, when a person wants to sleep all the time, he should go and live with mountain rats. And he thinks that I am going to gratify him——"

" You understand, monsieur, I am simply repeating what he told me to tell you, being the young man of the house. What shall I say to the gentleman from you?"

" Nothing. I will take my answer myself; yes, this gouty old fellow shall see me, he shall know whom he is dealing with; for it is time to put an end to all this nonsense."

"Ah! monsieur means himself to see his neighbor?"

"Yes, young man. I will teach the fellow a thing or two! So I must not instruct my parrot except when that gentleman has gone out! that is delicious! it is worth putting on the stage! I will tell it to Zizi, and she will have a good laugh.—Go, young man; I have no further need of you."

Saint-Arthur cast a glance at his mirror, to see that nothing was lacking in his costume, strove to assume a martial air, and when he had achieved it, took his pretty ivory cane and went to his neighbor's room. Roncherolle was trying again to sleep; he was on the point of succeeding, when he heard the door on the landing open and close violently; he always left it unlocked, so that people could come in without his having to get up.

"Who's there? Who in the devil is making that racket?" cried the sick man, jumping up. "Everybody seems bent on preventing me from sleeping to-day! Is that the way to shut a door?"

"Apparently it is my way of shutting one," said Saint-Arthur, entering the room with his hat on, and walking toward Roncherolle without even bowing to him. The invalid opened his eyes and began to scrutinize the personage who had entered his presence in that unceremonious way.

"You stare at me with an expression of surprise, Monsieur le Dormeur! To be sure, you don't know me.

I will begin by telling you that my name is Alfred de Saint-Arthur, and that I live here beside you, in a very pretty apartment, which does not resemble this; in fact, that I am the master or the owner of the cockatoo which you heard just now."

" I suspected as much; just from looking at you, I could have guessed that you were the master of the parrot; for master's the word, as you teach him his tricks."

" Ah! very pretty! monsieur is pleased to jest, I believe. Well, we will have a laugh; I came for that purpose. I say, Monsieur de la Marmotte—for a man who wants to sleep all the time may properly be classed with the marmottes—I say, old fellow, you sent someone to me to tell me not to teach to talk the rare bird that I possess; the nasal tones of that creature bore you, fatigue you; he prevents you from going to by-by. That is most distressing, and I am really distressed by it. But, instead of ceasing my lessons to Coco, I propose to give them to him from morning to night, if I please. I have a right to do it! I am in my own apartment; and if you venture to hammer and knock on the partition again, to make me stop, I warn you that it will end badly for you, *sacrebleu!* because, deuce take it! I am not patient, and *morbleu!* and——"

Here Saint-Arthur paused, because his neighbor was eyeing him in such a peculiar way that it began to take away his self-possession.

" Have you finished?" asked Roncherolle, rolling his chair nearer to Saint-Arthur.

"Why, yes, I believe that I have said all that I had to say."

"Then it is my turn. In the first place, where did you think you were going, when you came in here?"

"Where did I think I was going? that's a funny question! Why, I thought that I could not have made a mistake; I knew that I was going to my neighbor's room."

"No, monsieur, when you came in here, you evidently thought that you were going into a stable, for you didn't bow and you kept your hat on your head."

"Oh! that is possible, monsieur, and——"

"When anyone comes into my room, monsieur, I propose, I demand that he shall take off his hat. Come! take yours off at once!"

"What! take my hat off? But suppose I——"

"Suppose you don't choose to? Well, in that case I will just take it off myself, and it won't take long!"

Roncherolle grasped his cane, raised it quickly, and aimed at his fashionable neighbor's head; but he, seeing the gesture, very quickly snatched off his hat, while a shudder of ill augury ran through his frame.

"Now I am going to answer your nonsense, for you haven't said anything else since you came in. I didn't send word to you that you mustn't teach your parrot. In the first place, I am too well-bred, monsieur, I know too much, to employ such terms to a man whom I suppose to be well-bred also; I sent to you a request to suspend your lessons while I am suffering from the gout,

because that terrible disease often forces me to pass whole
nights without sleep; so that it is very natural that I
should wish to enjoy a little repose during the day; and
instead of acceding to my request, which a courteous
man would have done, monsieur enters my room as if it
were a public square, he calls me his 'old man,' and a
marmotte, and threatens me with his wrath if I venture
to complain again!—Do you know, monsieur, that it is
doubly cowardly to insult an old man who is ill and
cannot defend himself?"

Little Saint-Arthur, who felt very ill at ease, and had
lost all his swagger, replied in a faltering voice:

"But, monsieur, I don't know whether—I don't understand—I——"

"Well, monsieur, I will tell you something, and that
is that you were not such a coward as you thought.
That surprises you, doesn't it? But this is how it is:
in the first place, I am not so old as I look; misfortune
and disease age a man very rapidly, monsieur; and
secondly, although caught by my one leg, I am in a
condition to demand satisfaction for an insult, and you
are going to have a proof of it."

Thereupon, rolling his chair to his desk, Roncherolle
opened it and took out a pair of pistols, which he handed
to his neighbor, saying:

"Look you, with these, we will sit, each at one end of
the room, and blow each other's brains out as nicely as
possible. Come, monsieur, take one; they are loaded;
I am a far-sighted man, you see!"

Saint-Arthur had turned as pale as a turnip; he leaned against a piece of furniture to hold himself up, and glanced toward the door. But Roncherolle continued, raising his voice:

"Come, monsieur, take one and let us have done with it; you came to my room to laugh, you say; well, it seems to me that we are going to enjoy ourselves. What makes you look at the door like that? Can it possibly be that you would like to deprive me of your company? I warn you that that will not do you much good, for I will have my chair rolled to your room, I will roll it there myself if necessary, and I won't stir until you have given me satisfaction."

"Why, this old fellow is evidently an inveterate duelist!" said Saint-Arthur to himself, supporting himself on whatever came under his hand. Soon, seeing that retreat was impossible, he formed a heroic resolution, and going up to Roncherolle, he bowed humbly before him, saying in a voice which fright rendered almost touching:

"Monsieur, I am really ashamed of what I did; I am confused beyond words; I behaved like a hare-brained boy, like a poor—I may as well say it, like a blockhead. I can't imagine what I was thinking of; that is to say, yes, I do know,—I had wine at my breakfast, which I am not used to, and it must have gone to my head. I realize how badly I behaved, and I regret.it; I withdraw the absurd remarks which I may have made to you, I withdraw them; in fact, I offer my apologies for all that has taken place; pray accept them and do not be offended with one who henceforth will devote all his efforts to be agreeable to you."

Roncherolle looked at the young man for a moment, then shook his head and said:

" Is it true that you were a little tipsy?"

" It is true that I was a good deal so; I drank six *petits verres,* and then I drank champagne."

" And you are not strong at that game, perhaps?"

" Not very strong."

" Ah! I could give you lessons in that."

" You know how to drink champagne?"

" I should say so! I know thirty-three different ways of emptying one's glass."

" Thirty-three ways! ah! that's the sort of thing I would like to know. So you are not angry with me any longer, neighbor?"

" I cannot be, as you have apologized."

" I repeat my apology."

" And if you had told me sooner that you were tipsy——"

" True, I should have begun with that when I entered the room. As for my parrot, never fear, my dear neighbor, you won't hear from him any more. I have a dressing room beyond my two rooms; that is a long distance from you, and if I close all the doors, I think that you will not be able to hear him talk."

" Very good, and on my side, I hope not to be confined to the house long. Then, as I seldom come home

except to go to bed, you can teach your parrot to talk at
your ease."

" My dear neighbor, I am overjoyed that this little
discussion has afforded me the pleasure of making your
acquaintance. I see that you are a man who has lived
—when one knows thirty-three ways of drinking champagne ! "

" Yes, it is true, I have lived, and very well—too well
apparently, as they say that that's the cause of my gout."

" As soon as you are cured, I hope to dine with you;
will you do me the honor to accept an invitation? "

" Why not? I have never refused an opportunity to
enjoy myself, and I don't propose to do so now."

" I will take you to dinner with a fascinating woman,
an actress on the boulevard. That will not offend you? "

" Offend me? far from it! in the old days, I would
have invited you to dine with four."

" Bravo! bravissimo! I see that we are made to get
along together; you are very jovial."

" I am much more so when I am not ill."

" Wait—just wait three minutes, if you please; I am
going to make an experiment with Coco."

Saint-Arthur hastily left Roncherolle and went to his
room where he was heard to close several doors. After
a few moments he returned and asked:

" Well, did you hear? "

" What? "

" Did you hear my bird talking? "

" Not a sound ! "

"Ah! victory! I took him into the little dressing room, beyond the two rooms, and there he will stay. I made him talk a great deal, in fact."

"Did he say: 'Dutaillis is lovely?'"

"No, he said: 'Good-day, Monsieur Brillant!' but I will teach him, I will persist, and so long as it doesn't inconvenience you——"

"I can't hear it at all now."

"Then it will go all by itself. Au revoir, my dear neighbor; overjoyed to make your acquaintance. You will allow me to come and inquire for your health?"

"Whenever you please."

"I shall please often. Au revoir then; at your service; don't move."

"Oh! there's no danger of that!"

"To be sure; I keep forgetting your gout; what a thoughtless creature I am!—Your servant."

Saint-Arthur bowed to the ground this time, then left the house, saying to Beauvinet, whom he passed on the way:

"I have seen the gentleman who rooms beside me, and he is a delightful man, a man of the greatest merit, a man whom I expect to see a great deal of; and *sapristi!* no one had better speak ill of him in my presence; whoever does so will have me to reckon with!"

The young man of the house was thunderstruck at these words, and in his effort to recover his wits, he pulled his wig over his left ear.

XXIX

A HIGH FLYER

Thus Saint-Arthur became, as to Monsieur de Roncherolle, a zealous, courteous, obliging, and above all, a very neighborly neighbor. The little dandy, seeing the gouty gentleman frequently, was astonished to find him possessed of much intelligence and joviality, with a piquant, original way of telling a story, and a memory abundantly supplied with comical, entertaining and sometimes rather risqué anecdotes; but in Saint-Arthur's eyes this last quality doubled their merit; he tried to remember some of the tales that Roncherolle had told him, and went off to repeat them to his mistress, who was greatly amused and said to him:

"My word! why, you know any number of funny stories now! it's amazing, my dear; do you know that you are really getting to be amusing; can it be that you have some wit of your own? Oh! how well you have concealed your capacity!"

"Why, yes, I have concealed it," replied Saint-Arthur, stroking his chin; "I'm concealing lots of other things, too."

"Oh! you surprise me more and more, my dear."

Roncherolle, being forced to keep his room, was not sorry someone should come to visit him; the nonsense

of his little messenger made him laugh; the story of
his new friend's *bonnes fortunes* diverted him mightily;
and when Saint-Arthur said to him: " Don't you think
that I am a fortunate mortal with the ladies? " he would
reply with a slight shrug: " It's a fact that the ladies
are very fond of men like you.".

Saint-Arthur asked his neighbor several times to
teach him some of his methods of drinking champagne;
but Roncherolle simply smiled and replied:

" Those things can't be taught except at the table."

At last the gout entirely disappeared, and one day
Saint-Arthur failed to find Roncherolle in his room; he
was sorely disappointed, for his neighbor's witty conversation had become necessary to him; he retained some
scraps of it now and then. It is always well to frequent
people of intelligence, they allow themselves to be robbed
so readily!

The little dandy rose early the next day, in order to
find his neighbor before he went out; he caught him as
he was leaving his bed and said to him:

" You are better, I see, as you go out now? "

" Thank God! did you expect me to remain in that
old easy-chair forever? "

" No, of course not; I am delighted that you are
better; but I missed you yesterday, because, when I talk
with you, I always remember some of the funny little
stories that you tell so well, and I amuse Zizi with them.
Yesterday, I had nothing at all to tell her, and she called
me stupid; that's just a way of speaking, you know——"

"I understand perfectly.—I am very sorry, but your charmer may find you stupid again to-day, for I have no inclination to keep my room, in order to tell you stories."

"And that isn't what I came to ask you to do, .but something much better. Will you do us the honor to dine with us to-day?"

"Where?"

"At Bonvalet's, corner of Rue Charlot."

"Oh! I know Bonvalet's! I have often dined there."

"Well, does it suit you to-day?"

"It suits me very well."

"Ah! you delight me. There will be Zizi Dutaillis, you know."

"Yes, you have already told me that. I shall be enchanted to make her acquaintance; I have always been very fond of professional ladies."

"There will also be a friend of mine, an author— Monsieur Jéricourt; do you know him?"

"I never heard of him."

"He's a fellow of great talent, who will go a long way."

"Who says so? himself?"

"No, a newspaper that he writes for."

"Oh! that amounts to the same thing. However, I will give your friend credit for as much talent as you choose; I am of an obliging disposition."

"We will dine at half-past five; I know that it's bad form to dine so early, but it's on Zizi's account; she acts in the last play, and there is no fun in hurrying."

"All right! I promise to be punctual."

"Very good! By the way, you will teach me the thirty-three ways of drinking champagne, won't you?"

"You won't be able to learn all thirty-three at one sitting. That would be too great a risk to take. But we will do our best."

"That's right; we will learn as many as possible.—Until to-night."

At precisely half after five, Monsieur de Roncherolle, having donned his least threadbare coat and the one which fitted him best at the waist, a tight pair of trousers, a snow-white waistcoat, patent leather shoes, a black satin cravat tied in a dainty knot, and with his hat a little on one side, arrived at Bonvalet's, leaning not too heavily on his cane, and asked for Monsieur de Saint-Arthur's private room. A zealous waiter escorted him and opened the door of a pleasant room, just large enough for four people to be neither too crowded nor too much at their ease.

Mademoiselle Zizi Dutaillis was three-fourths reclining on a divan, toying with a lovely bouquet which her lover had just given her, and taking a flower from it now and then to put in her fair hair, after which she glanced at herself in a mirror. The young actress wore a bewitching pink and black costume, a medley of silk, velvet and lace, which strikingly resembled those of the famous Spanish dancers who were kind enough to come to Paris to introduce us to the charms of the genuine dances of their country. That costume was very becoming to the young woman, who, with her black eyes, her tiny mouth, her very dark eyelashes and her very light hair, was the most coquettish and saucy little minx that it was possible to find in the boulevard theatres.

Saint-Arthur, who was at the window, ran to meet Roncherolle.

"Ah! how good of you!" he cried; "you are a punctual man!"

"I never knew what it was to keep ladies waiting," said the newcomer, saluting Mademoiselle Zizi; she had not quitted her horizontal position when she saw the guest enter, and gave him an unceremonious little nod and said:

"Bonjour, monsieur."

"Mademoiselle Dutaillis," said the little dandy, taking his neighbor's hand and assuming a solemn expression, "I have the honor of presenting Monsieur de Roncherolle, my neighbor, who has been pleased to accept the invitation which—in your name as well as in mine—to have the pleasure——"

"Bah! that's enough! have you finished? You tire us with your speeches! Monsieur will present himself all right; we're here to have a spree and get a little tight. There's no need of making a lot of fuss to say that, is there, monsieur?"

"Bravo! that's the kind of a speech I like!" said Roncherolle, taking Zizi's hand and patting it; "and if I were more active, I would say also: this is the kind of woman I like!"

"Listen to that! you're not shy! You're an old rounder, you are; anyone can see that right away. You have made a fool of yourself for women, haven't you?"

"I glory in it; I have but one regret, and that is that I can't do it any more!"

"Do you hear, Alfred? Take monsieur for your model. Let his cane be your oriflamme! You will always find him on the path of glory!"

As she spoke, Zizi had taken possession of Roncherolle's cane; she thrust it into a mustard pot on the table and waved cane and mustard pot in the air. Roncherolle sank on a chair, laughing till the tears came; but Saint-Arthur cried out, because she had spattered him with the mustard, which he had received in the eye and on his waistcoat.

"*Sapristi!* take care, Zizi; see what you've done; you're spattering mustard on my waistcoat."

"What a calamity! Waistcoats can be cleaned, my friend."

"But you have also thrown some into my eye!"

"Eyes can be cleaned too."

"It stings me horribly."

"That will make your sight clearer; and perhaps you are going to see things you don't expect, which will dazzle you! So don't cry, but attend to the important business that brings us together—the grub! Have you given your order? I'm very hungry myself; and you, monsieur?"

"I am well disposed to vie with you."

" With a fork only ? "

" Ah! be careful; your eyes are the best remedy for the gout, I believe."

" Oho! if I was sure of that, I'd apply for a patent for my eyes.—By the way, Frefred, what about that rare bird, that miraculous bird, you were to give me? When will he appear? Are we going to eat him roasted ? "

" I should think not! That would be a great shame, for he is magnificent. But I am perfecting his education; I'll give him to you when he is able to say pretty things."

" I am sure that you are not teaching him anything at all."

" Oh! ask my neighbor; he'll tell you that it was my cockatoo's education that led to our acquaintance."

" That is the truth, *belle dame;* oh! you will possess a very knowing bird."

" That will be a change for me, as I have never had anything but canaries.—Come, Frefred, is the dinner ordered? I am to act to-night, you know—in the last piece luckily. I don't go on till half-past ten, but I must have time to dress first; and when you have just dined and have to hurry, it swells you out and you can't get into your dresses."

" The dinner is served; I am glad to believe, my diva, that you will be content."

" I flatter myself that I shall be; besides, it's the first time you have entertained monsieur, and you ought to make it a point of honor to let him see that you have

some skill in ordering a little Balthazar. Ring for the
waiter, my dear boy."

" But, you see, I—I asked Jéricourt to come, and he
promised." ·

" Bah! I don't care a hang for your Jéricourt, who
always keeps us waiting. Why did you have to invite
him? I've had my fill of your Jéricourt for some time
past! He puts on airs and calls everything detestable
that others write. And sweet things his plays are, too!
people stand in line to get tickets."

" Why, Zizi, I thought it would please you; formerly
you were never satisfied if Jéricourt didn't dine with us."

" Oh! formerly—that may be! but formerly and to-
day—there's half a century between the two.—Say, monsieur, ought we to wait for his friend, who's always loaf-
ing, but always keeps people waiting, to give himself
importance? Just exactly like the people who are slightly
known in art or literature, and who, the first time a new
play is given, never come till they're sure it's begun, because then everybody has to move to let them get to their
stalls. And they're convinced that everyone says: ' Ah!
that's So-and-so; that's the famous author! that's the
celebrated artist! see—he combs his hair in a way that
shows his genius! '—But instead of the exclamations of
admiration that they think they call forth as they pass,
if they had sharper ears, they'd hear: ' Oh! what a nuisance! what a bore! to disturb everybody in the middle
of an act! The devil take the fellow! He must be very
anxious to show himself! but he isn't much to look at!

It's just a little bit of self-advertising! And then!'—isn't that so, monsieur?"

"Why, do you know, fascinating Zizi, that you are a keen observer?"

"I don't know what I am, but I know that I have a tremendous appetite, and that I want to dine. It's five minutes to six. We have waited a long while already."

"I agree with you, a lady should never wait for a gentleman."

Saint-Arthur rang and the waiter served the dinner. They attacked the oysters, which they watered with an excellent chablis. From time to time the host exclaimed:

"I don't care, I'm surprised that Jéricourt doesn't come; I told him that he would dine with my honorable neighbor."

"You should have announced a neighbor of the other gender," said Roncherolle; "that would have been more likely to attract the gentleman."

"Never mind! never mind! let's go on eating! He'll come for dessert and we'll give him some nuts and raisins," said Zizi.

But just as the soup was served, Jéricourt appeared; and he scowled slightly when he saw that they had not waited dinner for him.

"I say! come on, you miserable slow-coach!" cried Saint-Arthur; "don't you ever mean to be punctual?"

"What difference does it make—when you don't wait for me?" retorted Jéricourt, with a bare salute to the company.

"Wait for you!" cried Zizi; "on my word! I think not! Catch us having pains in the stomach for monsieur!"

"My friend," said Alfred, "let me present Monsieur de Roncherolle, my neighbor."

Jéricourt bent his head slightly, with a patronizing glance at Roncherolle, whose costume probably seemed to him far behind the fashion of the day. The old gentleman, observing the arrogant air with which the man of letters saluted him, made haste to say to Saint-Arthur:

"I beg pardon, my dear neighbor, but I did not ask you to present me to monsieur. Present him to me, if you please—that is all right; but that I should be presented to him—that I don't like."

Saint-Arthur was dumfounded; Jéricourt compressed his lips and the little actress began to laugh, saying:

"You don't seem to be very strong in the matter of etiquette, Alfred; you'll never be appointed an ambassador, my boy!"

Jéricourt, observing that the strange guest was of a punctilious temper and familiar with good society, decided to take the thing jocosely; and he rejoined, bowing to Roncherolle:

"In truth, it was my place to be presented to monsieur, for he has the advantage of age."

"A melancholy advantage, is it not, monsieur? But one must needs accept it when it comes."

"Will you have some oysters, Jéricourt? I'll ring for the waiter."

"No, thanks, I don't eat oysters; I don't care about them any more."

"The deuce! you don't care about oysters! Why, I've seen the time when you adored them!"

"What a donkey you are, Alfred," cried Zizi, "to be surprised because tastes change!"

"Well! my tastes never change so far as food is concerned; I love oysters, I shall always care for them."

"Perhaps it's the oysters that care for you," said Jéricourt, helping himself to soup.

"Hum! this begins well," said Roncherolle to himself, filling the actress's glass with madeira, while she glared savagely at Jéricourt. That gentleman, as he ate his soup, glanced at the gentleman opposite from time to time, and said to himself:

"I know that man; this certainly isn't the first time that I've seen him; but where in the devil have I met him?"

Roncherolle, for his part, having recognized the man of letters at the first glance, smiled slyly as he submitted to be stared at, and continued to be most attentive to his fair neighbor, who said to him, eating for four all the while:

"You please me, you do! you're a good fellow! you're worth a deal more than all these youngsters! you're as young as they are, only you've been so longer!"

At last Jéricourt, unable to contain himself, said to his vis-à-vis:

"Mon Dieu! monsieur, it seems to you perhaps that I stare at you rather persistently."

" That flatters me, monsieur; I assume that you find
me pleasant to look at."

" That is not just the reason, monsieur; the fact is
that it seems to me that this is not the first time we have
met."

" True, monsieur; and I recognized you instantly,
when you entered the room."

" Be good enough then to remind me where it was."

" It was near here—at the Château d'Eau flower
market; you were bargaining for a bouquet, as was an
exceedingly ugly little fellow—a friend of yours, I think
—and you did not make up your mind; whereupon I
arrived and put an end to your hesitation by buying the
bouquet;—do you remember now?"

" Yes, monsieur, I remember very well."

And Jéricourt pressed his lips together again and
scowled, because that reminder recalled no agreeable
memories.

" Then there was a *gamin* who threw the ugly little
fellow down, and as he fell he tore his trousers."

" Where?" queried Mademoiselle Zizi.

" Only on the knees."

" Bah! that isn't amusing enough!"

" There was also a young flower girl—a very pretty
girl, on my word!"

" I know her," said Saint-Arthur; " she supplies me;
it's Violette."

" What does she supply you with, you big monster?"
cried Zizi, raising her fork to her lover, as if to stab him.

"Mon Dieu! it's simple enough, my angel; a flower girl supplies me with flowers, naturally."

"Hum! you would be quite capable of going to her for other supplies."

"O Zizi! for heaven's sake, don't be jealous like this. Besides, this flower girl is one of Jéricourt's conquests; one of his victims."

"I don't deny it, I committed that sin; and monsieur here will bear me out in saying that the little one is worth the trouble."

"I will bear you out in saying that the little one is pretty, monsieur, but that's all; for, on the day that I saw you in her company, you did not have the air of having made a conquest of her!"

"This old fellow is decidedly antipathetic to me!" said Jéricourt to himself.

XXX

MANY WAYS OF DRINKING CHAMPAGNE

"Come, Alfred! some champagne—right away! I want some champagne—and I want it frappé."

"Here it is, my siren; it's behind us, cooking in the ice.—Ah! now is the time when Monsieur de Roncherolle is going to teach us a lot of pretty things.—Jéricourt, monsieur knows thirty-three ways of drinking a glass of champagne!"

" Monsieur is quite capable of it."

" For my experiments," said Roncherolle, " I must have cups, not goblets."

" Here are some; I ordered two kinds of glasses."

" I fill my glass—this is the first way; attention! "

Roncherolle coolly emptied his glass and said:

" First of all, there's that way—to drink as everybody else does."

" Oh! I know that."

" It's lucky that you know one," said Zizi; " otherwise it might be thought that you had to be driven to water."

" Let us go on to the second way."

" You will allow me to eat a little sweetbread first? "

" That is only fair."

" Otherwise," sneered Jéricourt, " one might think that you invited monsieur to dinner for the sole purpose of learning to drink."

" And if that were so," rejoined Roncherolle, " I should not bear my neighbor a grudge; that would prove that I am still good for something, and one so often entertains people who are good for nothing! "

" The second way, my dear fellow, the second way! " said Zizi, with a playful tap on Roncherolle's cheek.

" At your service, *belle dame.*—Look—this glass is full; I put it on this plate, and the point is to drain it without touching it with the hands or spilling a drop."

" Oh! that must be extremely difficult—I will go farther and say that it seems to me impossible," said Saint-Arthur.

" Not at all—look."

Roncherolle took the plate on which the glass stood, lifted it, put the glass to his lips, then tipped it toward his mouth, still holding it steady with the plate, and swallowed all it contained.

" Ah! charming, delightful!" cried Alfred.

" I have seen that done before, but I had forgotten it," said Zizi; " wait; I believe that I can do it."

The young actress did exactly as Roncherolle had done, and succeeded perfectly.

" It's your turn, Jéricourt."

" Do that! why that's the ass's bridge!" replied the man of letters, with a shrug.

" Well, do it then."

" No, I didn't come to dinner to play tricks."

" That's a pity," said Roncherolle, " for I am sure that monsieur must know some that we do not."

" In that case," said Saint-Arthur, filling a glass to the brim with champagne and putting it on a plate, " it's my turn; now that I have seen the thing done twice, I don't see why I shouldn't do it too; I am no more of a fool than other people."

" That's too bad, my dear; if you were, it would be a way of attracting attention!"

" Hush, Zizi! don't say nasty things, but watch; I am going to begin."

The pretty youth succeeded in raising the glass to his lips, but just as he was about to drink, he lifted the plate too high, and all the contents of the glass fell on his shirt and his cravat. Alfred cried aloud in dismay, while his three guests roared with laughter, that incident having restored Jéricourt's good humor.

"*Sapristi!* I am done for. I was on the edge of success, for I certainly should have drunk it all without spilling a drop."

"But you didn't spill a drop," said Roncherolle; "the whole business went."

"I am wet through, my shirt is drenched and my cravat; what shall I do? I can't show myself in this condition."

"Well then, don't show yourself, my friend, keep out of sight. At all events, it will be dark when you leave here, and you'll only need to button your coat military fashion; that will give you the air of a hero, it will change you completely."

"But I am all wet, I am——"

"Nonsense! take a napkin and wipe yourself, and above all things don't be sulky; we came here to enjoy ourselves, and you still have to learn thirty-one ways of drinking champagne."

Saint-Arthur made no reply; he stuffed three napkins into his bosom and began to eat again.

"Deuce take it! my dear man," said Jéricourt, drinking his wine slowly, "that is what comes of trying to learn original things in order to make yourself agreeable in society; you don't always succeed."

"In fact, there are some people who never succeed," observed Roncherolle.

"I request a suspension of the lessons in drinking champagne," said Alfred; "I must dry myself before attempting anything else."

"We consent," said Zizi, "on condition that it is not to interfere with our drinking."

"It seems to me that you are doing very well," said Jéricourt; "you will be rather gay in your play to-night!"

"So much the better! The play lacks gayety, and I shall do well to impart a little to it."

"I came near acting once," said the host, still sponging himself. "Do you remember, Jéricourt, that place in the country you took me to some weeks ago—at Nogent-sur-Marne?"

"Yes, it was very amusing."

"There was one thing that I didn't call amusing, and that was being obliged to escort that lady back to Paris —an ex-pretty woman."

"Why were you such a fool as to tell her that we had a coupé waiting? She instantly caught the ball on the bound and asked us to give her a little room in our carriage."

"Little was hardly the word; that lady may have been thin once, but she isn't now."

"Ah! I never heard of this lady that you brought home!" cried the young actress, with an American glance at her lover. "That has rather a crooked look!"

"Oh! really, my diva, when I tell you that she was on the decline!"

"It seems to me that you too were on the decline—with her."

"However, she was a woman of great distinction, a baroness!"

"Listen to that! monsieur must have baronesses now!"

"The Baronne de—de Grangeville—that's the name."

"De Grangeville?" said Roncherolle, who, on hearing that name, replaced on the table the glass that he was about to put to his lips. "Did you say that the lady you brought home was the Baronne de Grangeville?"

"Yes, my dear neighbor; do you know her?"

"No—that is to say, her name recalled a person whom I used to know."

Roncherolle had become thoughtful; Zizi tapped him on the knee, saying:

"Well, well, tell us what you're dreaming about, my Knight of the Round Table? Is that baroness's name going to spoil your spirits? I don't propose to have that! Don't let me hear any more of your great ladies; I call for a third way of drinking champagne."

"Here! present!" said Roncherolle, resuming his playful air. "See, my dear girl, here is a third way: we put the glass on the plate like this just now, didn't we? Well, now we are going to stand this second glass on the first one; that is easy enough; but then we fill the glass that is on top, and drink the contents by lifting the plate as we did just now, without touching either glass."

"Oh! that must be terribly hard!"

"Look—here goes."

Roncherolle performed the feat he had described, without spilling a drop of wine. Saint-Arthur was lost in admiration, but Jéricourt muttered as he tipped back in his chair:

"I have seen clowns on the boulevard do that."

Roncherolle glared at Jéricourt with a half-angry, half-bantering expression, saying: "In truth, monsieur, I was a clown a very long while! And with the permission of the company, I will undertake to make you as flat as this knife blade in a very few moments."

Jéricourt did not know what reply to make. Zizi, who, with the tact which all women possess, divined a quarrel on the point of breaking out, made haste to say to Roncherolle:

"Come, my dear gallant, since you are so obliging and are willing to instruct us in your science, show me again what you have just done, and I will try to copy you; I will be your assistant."

"I shan't try this third way of drinking," said Saint-Arthur, "except in my own room and with unsophisticated water."

"You will do well, my boy, for you would break too many glasses here."

The young actress did what Roncherolle had just shown them, and did it with equal success.

"Bravo! bravo!" cried the host. "Honor to Zizi! You know three ways already, dear love!"

"And I don't propose to stop at that."

" " These ladies succeed in whatever they choose to undertake," said Roncherolle.

Jéricourt, with a curl of his lip, muttered:

" Madame Saqui could do no better! "

" Oh! you always look as if you were sneering! " said Zizi; " but you would be hard put to it to do as much. It's easy to criticise, my dear man! "

" This much is certain, that I shall not venture to contend with you."

" Because you realize your inferiority."

" But I am waiting till you come to the thirty-third way. I fancy that you will do some very extraordinary things then! "

" Oh! my boy, we're not such fools. We mean to have some fun, to get a little screwed, but we don't propose to get drunk. We will learn one more way and that will do for to-night; what do you say, my gallant? "

" As you command, *belle dame.*"

" Why, do you know that you're a hard-headed party? Champagne doesn't seem to affect you at all. You drink more than we do, and you don't seem to notice it."

" That is the result of my long studies—another advantage of age! "

" Look at Alfred; he hasn't drunk half as much as you, I'll bet, and his eyes are in curl-papers already; anyone would think he was going to sleep."

" I—oh! I haven't any desire to sleep; I was engaged in thought."

" Of what? "

"Of the baroness whom he escorted home, no doubt!"
said Jéricourt, with an ironical glance at the gentleman
who aroused his displeasure, and whose emotion at the
mention of the baroness's name he had noticed.

"Are you going to stuff us some more with your titled
lady?" cried Mademoiselle Zizi; "bah! what a tease this
Jéricourt is!"

"That subject bores you, my sweet angel; forgive me,
I won't mention that lady again. However, I believe that
this Madame de Grangeville is nothing more than a
counterfeit baroness."

"What makes you think so, monsieur? By what right
do you insult that lady?" demanded Roncherolle, in a
tone in which there was no trace of jesting, and with a
by no means amicable glance at the man of letters.

"What! I insult her? Why do you set yourself up as
the lady's champion, monsieur, if you don't know her?"

"I do know her, monsieur, and I have a right to defend her. The Baronne de Grangeville is more noble
than you are eminent in letters; but perhaps that is not
saying overmuch for her nobility."

"You are attacking me now, monsieur; do you mean
to insult me?"

"Come, come, messieurs! upon my word! how is
this? do you propose to quarrel now?" murmured Alfred, whose mouth had become dry and sticky. "I won't
have it; I——"

"Hold your tongue, Bibi!" cried Mademoiselle Zizi.
"Don't you see that it's a joke? It would be pretty,

wouldn't it, to come to dinner with a lady and take to squabbling in her presence!—In the first place, I believe monsieur is too well bred for that; and as for Jéricourt, he knows well enough that it doesn't pay to make me angry; I have ways of revenging myself! Come; let's have no more talk about it, and our dear neighbor will show us the fourth way to drink champagne; and everybody must try to imitate him this time. What do you say, my dear friend?"

"I told you just now, *belle dame,* that I am always at your service."

"Good! now you are agreeable again."

While Roncherolle filled his glass, Jéricourt rose, took his hat, and said, bowing coldly to the company:

"It is eight o'clock and I have an appointment at that hour; I am distressed that I cannot stay longer."

"What! leaving us so early?" faltered Alfred.

"Liberty! *libertas!*" said Zizi; "all sorts of good wishes, monsieur!"

When Jéricourt had left the room, the young woman sprang to her feet and began to dance a sort of *cachucha* in front of the mirror, singing:

> "Il est parti
> Ce cher ami!
> Ah! ça m'enchante!
> J'en suis contente!
> Traderi dera la la
> Traderi deri! Biribi!"

"Faith!" said Roncherolle, "I must tell you frankly, my dear Monsieur Saint-Arthur, that Monsieur Jéricourt doesn't attract me at all, and that I ask you as a favor not to invite me to dine with him again!"

"Nor me; I won't dine with that ill-licked fellow any more; do you hear, my dear?"

"I hear.—But let's see the fourth way."

"Attention!—You must sing: 'When the bells of the village ring the hour of work, *eh bon, bon, bon!*' I have my glass full, I drink after your three *bons,* and I answer *bon.* You repeat *eh bon bon bon* three times; I answer *bon* every time, after drinking; and when I say *bon* the last time I must have finished my glass."

"*Fichtre!* that's rather complicated!"

"Not at all; it's simply a matter of emptying your glass in three swallows; you mustn't begin till after the *eh bon bon bon,* and you must finish it before you say the last *bon.*—Sing, fair Zizi."

"Here goes!

> "When the bells of the village
> Ring the hour of work,
> Eh bon bon bon!"

Roncherolle, after drinking:

"*Bon!*"

Zizi:

"*Eh bon bon bon!*"

Roncherolle:

"*Bon!*"

Zizi:

"*Eh bon bon——*"

"*Bon!* and you see, it's empty!"

"Ah! that's a very pretty way!—It's my turn; fill my glass, old fellow, and sing; I'm ready."

Roncherolle sang and Mademoiselle Zizi drank, answered *bon,* and swallowed her wine at one gulp.

"You went a little fast," said the professor; "but never mind, you'll do it all right."

"My turn!" cried Alfred, lifting his glass in a hand that was far from steady. "Sing, and you'll see; I'm sure of succeeding at this method; I am waiting at the post."

Mademoiselle Zizi sang the ballad. At the first *bon bon!* Saint-Arthur spilt his wine on the floor; at the second he struck his nose with his glass; and at the third he swallowed the wrong way and strangled; they were obliged to pound him on the back and make him look at the ceiling, in order to bring him to life.

"My dear boy, I think that you have done enough for to-day," said Zizi; "you are not adroit to-night, and I don't want you to learn any more ways.—Great heaven! it's nine o'clock! I must go and dress—I wear a costume that it takes a long while to put on.—I say, I'm a little dizzy; but no matter! it will pass off on the stage.—Adieu, monsieur; I hope to see you again."

"Are you going away alone?"

"I have only to cross the boulevard. Alfred, you will come to my dressing-room for me at half-past eleven, not a minute earlier; I forbid you."

"Yes, dear angel.—Isn't she enchanting, neighbor, with that little demoniacal expression?"

"And he'd like me not to love anybody but him, the idiot!" whispered Zizi in Roncherolle's ear; "can you imagine such conceit?"

"That certainly would be a great pity."

Mademoiselle Zizi disappeared. Alfred paid the waiter, doing his utmost to stand erect on his legs.

Roncherolle took his arm, to help him to go downstairs, and before leaving him on the boulevard, said:

"Do me the favor to give me the address of the lady whom you took home—the Baronne de Grangeville."

"Ah! the Baronne de—you want to know her address? Villain! monster! you have criminal designs!"

"Perhaps so—but her address."

"Wait—I know it perfectly."

"Well then, where is it?"

"Ah!—Rue de—what do you call it—you know it well enough!"

"If you should tell me the name, I should know it better."

"Rue—parbleu! Rue Fontaine-Saint-Georges; number 21 or 24—it's in the twenties."

"Infinitely obliged."

"Au revoir, my dear friend! I'm going to the Café Turc for a game of billiards; I feel in condition to make fifteen cannons in succession."

"Much pleasure to you."

And Roncherolle walked away, saying:

"I know her address at last! To-morrow I will carry her a bouquet myself."

XXXI

THE EFFECTS OF TIME

But our plans are traced on sand; and then too, sad as it is to admit it, champagne is not really good for the gout.

On the day following that dinner party, during which Roncherolle had given instruction in such pleasant matters, instead of going as he hoped to pay a visit to the Baronne de Grangeville, he was obliged to keep his bed; his gout had returned, more obstinate and more painful than ever; the poor invalid lost his temper, complained, swore like one possessed, because it seemed to him that that relieved him; and finally he said to himself:

"I won't give any more lessons in drinking champagne."

At the end of three days, all that Roncherolle could do was to lie at full length in his reclining chair, with his foot on cushions; then, as he could not hope to leave the house for some time, he sent the young man of the house, Beauvinet, to bring his usual messenger; and Chicotin soon appeared before him.

"Look you, my boy," said Roncherolle, "I have been shrewder than you—I have discovered Madame de Grangeville's address."

"The deuce you have! however did you do it? You can hardly walk!"

"I could walk a few days ago, and if it hadn't been for an infernal dinner—but faith, I guess I won't curse that dinner, for I enjoyed myself hugely; and after all, if I suffer, I suffer for something; let us return to the lady; the Baronne de Grangeville lives on Rue Fontaine-Saint-Georges, number 21 or 23; I am not quite sure of the number but it's in the twenties."

"Oh! that's enough, bourgeois; that's all I need; if necessary, I will try all the houses in the street."

"Very good; now take this five-franc piece; you will go and buy a bouquet for which you will pay three francs, no less, understand; don't try to cheat me."

"Oh! never you fear, bourgeois, that's all right; if the flower girl should ask only forty sous, I would give her three francs."

"But I should prefer that the girl should ask three francs; the bouquet will be finer."

"It's all right; never you fear, the bouquet will be a good one."

"When you have got it, you will take it to Madame de Grangeville from me, and you will tell her that Monsieur de Roncherolle sends his respects and that he will come to see her as soon as he can go out."

"I will say when you get over your gout."

"No, don't mention my gout, that isn't necessary. Say to her that I am indisposed; that is all, do you understand?"

"Yes, bourgeois, never fear; it will all go as if it was on wheels; and shall I come back and tell you what answer the lady gives me?"

"Naturally."

"I am off. By the way, bourgeois, perhaps you don't know, but no doubt you will soon receive a visit from a friend of yours; that happens just right; you are sick and it will amuse you."

"What do you mean?"

"I mean that yesterday, no longer ago than that, I saw my old comrade Georget, a good fellow, who's in the dumps all the time because he's in love. But that's another story; it would take too long to tell you."

"I will excuse you from telling it, but come to the point at once."

"Well, while we were talking, I mentioned your name; it happens that his master at Nogent knows you and would like to see you; he didn't know your address, so I gave it to Georget."

"What is the name of this gentleman at Nogent?"

"His name is Monsieur Malberg."

"I don't know anybody by that name; your comrade must have made a mistake and taken one name for another. But go about your errand to Madame de Grangeville, and above all things buy a pretty bouquet."

"I should say so! if I didn't get a fine one for three francs, it would be funny."

Chicotin took his leave. Roncherolle stretched out his leg, made a wry face and uttered a hearty oath, because of the pain; then he laid his head on the back of his chair and tried to sleep.

Five minutes passed; the hall door opened again, and a gentleman appeared in the doorway; it was the Comte de Brévanne, who said as he glanced into the chamber:

"Monsieur de Roncherolle, if you please?"

Receiving no reply, the count decided to enter; he saw a gentleman dozing, who had not been shaved for several days, whose head was covered with a huge fur cap, which fell almost over his eyes, and who was wrapped in an old dressing gown of which it was not easy to tell the color. He shook his head, saying:

"That boy must have directed me to the wrong door, this can't be the place. Roncherolle would not live in such a wretchedly furnished room; besides, this sick old gentleman in the chair must be at home. I must try elsewhere."

Brévanne was about to go away, when Roncherolle opened his eyes and seeing a stranger in his room, cried:

"What is it? What do you want of me? Why are you here, monsieur?"

At the sound of that voice, which had not changed so much as the person to whom it belonged, the count stopped, shuddered slightly and repeated in a loud voice:

"I want Monsieur de Roncherolle."

"Well, I am De Roncherolle! what do you want of me?"

The count stepped forward; he scrutinized the man before him, and he wondered if that pale, sick creature, whose face had grown thin and indicated long suffering, who seemed to be at least sixty years old, and whose costume was far from denoting prosperous circumstances, could possibly be Roncherolle, formerly so dandified and magnificent, who was cited as a model for men of fashion, and whom all the women admired.

As for Roncherolle, for some moments he had been looking attentively at his visitor; the more he looked at him, the more keenly did his features betray the emotion which he felt; and at last when the count exclaimed:

"Is it really true that you are De Roncherolle?" he instantly replied:

"To be sure, and you are De Brévanne!"

The count recoiled, exclaiming:

"You dare to use intimate terms to me, monsieur!"

"Oh! I beg your pardon, that's true; I should not address you so; I forgot, it was the old habit; but hereafter I will be more careful. Pray sit down, monsieur le comte; I knew you at once, for, except that your hair is turning gray, you are but little changed; whereas with me it is very different; you could not believe that it was I. I have grown old rapidly, I crumbled all at once; add to that all sorts of annoyances, the change in my position, and people turning their backs upon me because I can no longer oblige them, and others because I did oblige them formerly, like Beaumont, De Marcey and De Juvigny! But I am chattering away and you are still standing; pray take a seat and be good enough to tell what brings you here."

"You ask me what brings me, monsieur!" retorted De Brévanne, still standing in front of De Roncherolle. "You ask me that! you mean that you do not divine?"

"Faith, no!"

"When you see once more the man whom you shamelessly outraged, and whom you have eluded for so many years, you do not divine that he comes to demand the satisfaction which you refused him so long ago?"

"Bah! do you really mean it's for that? What! after so long a time, after twenty years, you still think of that business?"

"There is no limitation in matters relating to honor."

"Ah! that makes a difference; you are obstinate about it. I am sorry for that; but did not I admit my fault? Didn't I ask your pardon long ago? Come, Brévanne, come, does not heaven say: 'mercy for all sins?' We were such good friends once."

"Hush! do not appeal to the memory of that friendship, which makes your conduct even more odious. But let us not waste time in useless talk; for twenty years I have been looking for you, to fight with you; I have found you to-day, and I trust that you will no longer refuse to give me satisfaction."

"Since you are bent upon it! Mon Dieu! men are supposed to become reasonable when they grow old; the fact is that they are never reasonable.—Honor! honor! oh! how right Beaumarchais was!—All this is infernally stupid, on my word!"

"Well, monsieur?"

"Well, I will do whatever you wish; arrange it for —for—ah! ten thousand million thunders! how I suffer! how I suffer!"

A violent attack of pain seized the invalid; he turned pale, his voice died away, great drops of perspiration rolled down his cheeks, the contraction of his features proved the violence of the pain that he felt, and the count was deeply moved at sight of his suffering; he looked all about the room in search of something to help him. He saw on the mantelpiece a phial filled with a liquid; he took it and offered it to Roncherolle.

"Here, perhaps this is what you take when you have such attacks. Drink."

"No," replied Roncherolle, pushing away the phial. "Let me suffer; I have well earned it; you see what I am reduced to; if you kill me, instead of punishing me you will do me a favor."

"Monsieur," said the count, "the duel cannot take place while you are in this condition, I appreciate that; I must wait until you are cured, in order that I may have an adversary worthy of me. I leave you, and I will come again a fortnight hence to learn how you are."

"Oh! as you please. Are you going?"

And with an involuntary gesture Roncherolle put out his hand to the count; but he contented himself with a slight inclination of the head, saying:

"I will send somebody to you, monsieur, to help you."

Then he took his leave, still upset by what he had seen, saying to himself:

"What a change! he is unrecognizable. Ah! he is in a still worse plight than she!"

"If he waits until I get over the gout to fight with me," said Roncherolle to himself, "I fancy that our duel is indefinitely postponed. What a devil of a man!—Ah! that attack is passing away; that is lucky.—Poor Brévanne; he has hardly changed at all; and in the bottom of my heart I was secretly glad to see him, we used to be such good friends, and I should have been so happy to renew our friendship! He would not have turned his back on me, like all those others whom I obliged long ago, and who will have nothing to say to me now, because I lent them money and they don't want to repay it. But what is done is done. Oh! these women! they are the cause of all the follies that we commit."

Beauvinet opened the hall door and put his head in, saying:

"The gentleman who just went out said that monsieur had a bad attack and needed attention; so I came——"

"Clear out and leave me in peace!" retorted Roncherolle, striking the floor angrily with his cane.

The young man did not wait for that invitation to be repeated; he disappeared like a stage shadow-figure, and slammed the door behind his back.

"But he will come again in a fortnight," reflected the invalid after a moment. "He is a man of his word, he won't fail to come; and if, as I must hope, I am in condition to walk, I shall have to meet him.—Fight with him! well, if he is obstinate about it, I will be equally obstinate.—Who is coming to disturb me now, ten thousand devils?"

"Why, it's me," said Chicotin, entering the room; "I did your errand, bourgeois, and I did it well, I flatter myself; in the first place, I bought a superb bouquet; oh! it was A No. 1; it was worth four francs rather than three. I didn't buy it of Mamzelle Violette, just to make her mad; I don't mean to buy anything more of her. But you don't care anything about that.—I went to Rue Fontaine-Saint-Georges, and I found Madame la Baronne de Grangeville, not in the twenties, but at 19, but that don't make any difference. They let me in, and I found the lady sitting in a great machine. To cut it short, when I said to her: 'Madame, it is Monsieur de Roncherolle who sends you this bouquet, with all sorts of messages;' if you had seen what a jump that lady gave on her—her divan, just like a carp in the frying pan; then she said: 'Monsieur de Roncherolle! what, is he in Paris? Tell him to come and see me right away, as soon as possible; I shall expect him impatiently.'— I answered: 'Madame, certainly, to be sure—that's what he means to do; he will come as soon as he can stand on his pins '—oh, no! I didn't say pins, I said legs; and then I bowed and left, and she didn't give me anything."

"Well, keep the rest of the money I gave you."

"Thanks, bourgeois, thanks; and did your friend from Nogent come to see you?"

"Yes, yes, he came, my friend. Do you know, Chicotin, that you're a wretched chatterbox, and that I ought to pull your ears for giving anyone my address without finding out whether I wanted you to?"

"Mon Dieu! did I make a fool of myself? Isn't your friend your friend any longer?"

"Yes, you did make a fool of yourself; but I hope that you won't do it again; meanwhile, you are responsible for my having to leave this house, which, however, I hardly regret."

"Are you going to move?"

"Yes, in a few days, as soon as I can walk. But I don't propose to take furnished lodgings again; he would find me, he would visit them all. I mean to hire a room in some quiet house, and furnish it myself. That won't take long; a bed, a table, two chairs and a bureau, that is all that I need. Listen, Chicotin, while I am unable to go about, you must find those things for me, so that I shall simply have to move in as soon as I am cured. Do you understand,—just a small apartment, as neat and clean as possible; a bedroom and a study, that will be enough for me."

"All right, bourgeois, I understand; I'll look about for you. In what quarter?"

"I don't care."

"Oh! then I can find something easier. How much do you want to pay for your lodgings?"

"Hum! as little as possible; the funds are decreasing every day, my boy!"

"Do you want to go as high as eighty francs?"

"A quarter?"

"Oh, no! What next! I mean for a year."

"You can get nothing better than a garret, a kennel for that price. You may go as high as two hundred francs,—two hundred and fifty."

"In that case, bourgeois, I'll find you something fine, a little palace; I propose that you shall be more comfortable than you are now."

"You won't have much difficulty about that; try not to make me go up too many stairs."

"Pardi! for two hundred and fifty francs you ought to be able to obtain a magnificent lodging on the first floor."

"I don't think it. However, attend to it at once."

Three days after this conversation, Chicotin entered Roncherolle's room with a triumphant air; he found him getting better, and walking about the room.

"Here I am, bourgeois, I've found what you want. I think you'll be satisfied; but lodgings are dearer than I thought; I couldn't find a lodging on the first floor for your two hundred and fifty francs."

"Well, what have you found?"

"I have found two pleasant little rooms, for two hundred francs, no more; fresh paper, not colored, but you can put one on; and a view—oh! such a view! as good as if you was on the Arc de Triomphe; and all the conveniences right at your door; and a waxed staircase, not up to the top, but as far as the third floor."

"What floor is this apartment on?"

"Why, on the fifth, bourgeois!"

"Sacrebleu! I am not surprised that there is a good view; is that what you call getting me a lodging near the ground?"

"There ain't any to be had, master; but the stairs are as easy as can be; you can go up without moving your legs; and then there is a concierge who is willing to do the housework for all the tenants, at a very moderate price, and even to make the coffee."

"There are many advantages, and no mistake; where is this jewel of an apartment situated?"

"Not very far from here, monsieur, on Rue de Crussol; it's near the boulevard, near that handsome round theatre for horses, that's just been built."

"I don't know Rue de Crussol."

"If monsieur is able to walk, I will show him the way there."

"Go and fetch a carriage, and you may take me to see the lodgings."

"Right away, bourgeois."

Chicotin went out to fetch a cab, and climbed up behind when Roncherolle was inside. They stopped on Rue de Crussol in front of the house which Chicotin pointed out. An old concierge, very dirty but very polite, made repeated reverences to Roncherolle, and bustled upstairs before him, while Chicotin said to the old gentleman:

"If you don't want to go up, bourgeois, because it tires you, why I will take you on my back. I am strong and I won't drop you; I would carry you that way through the streets if you wanted."

" Thanks, my boy, but that new style of locomotion does not attract me, and I doubt whether I could make it the fashion. Besides, they say that one must walk about and exercise with the gout. So I will go up on my feet."

" If you must exercise, you see that it is much better that you should live on the fifth floor."

Roncherolle inspected the lodgings, heaved a profound sigh in spite of himself, and reflected:

" After all, what can one expect to get for two hundred francs? It's all I can afford—in fact, rather more."

He gave the concierge her earnest money, informing her that he relied upon her to do the housework and to make his coffee; whereupon the old woman redoubled her reverences and her politeness, crying:

" I hope monsieur will like our house; I shall always be ready to wait on him; whenever he needs anything, all he has got to do is to put his head out of the window and call Mère Lamort, and I will go up in a second."

" What did you say that I must call you, madame? "

" Mère Lamort."

" Ah! your name is Lamort, is it? "

" At your service, monsieur."

" You are very good; you have, I won't say a devil of a name, but a singular name, at least; an almost terrifying name."

" Mon Dieu! monsieur, that don't prevent me from being as well as can be, or from having had twelve children, who are all as well as you or I."

" For their sakes, I hope they are as well as you."

"And monsieur will see that my name don't prevent me from having a good foot and a good eye; and he'll be satisfied with my services."

"I don't doubt it; we shall meet again soon, Madame Lamort."

Roncherolle returned to his cab, and Chicotin climbed up behind again, saying to the driver:

"I am in monsieur's suite, in his suite, I say." *

Two days later, Roncherolle, having purchased just what he absolutely needed to furnish his new lodgings, paid what he owed at his quarters, and announced that they might let his room.

"Ah! monsieur is leaving us?" said Beauvinet, pulling at one side of his wig. "If anyone comes to ask for monsieur, what address shall I give?"

"You may send them to Passage I-don't-know-where, the first door to the right as you enter Paris by the Barrière de l'Etoile."

When Roncherolle had been gone a long time, the young man was still pulling at his wig, saying to himself:

"Passage I-don't-know-where! that's funny; I know all the passages in Paris except that one."

* An untranslatable pun: 'Je suis de la suite de monsieur; de sa suite, j'en suis.'

XXXII

A BUNCH OF VIOLETS

Since the Comte de Brévanne had spoken to Violette, and since she had seen Georget look at her from a distance, and then walk hastily away, with a glance of contempt at her, the young flower girl felt every day more depressed and discouraged. So long as Georget had been near her, so long as she was able to see him morning and evening, and read in his eyes the love he felt for her, the young girl had looked upon that love as a mere childish freak, and had refused to admit to herself that she shared the sentiment which she aroused.

But now that her young lover had left Paris in order to avoid being near her, now that he had fled from her, and when he met her manifested no other feeling than that of contempt or hatred, poor Violette realized how dearly she loved Georget; and, what was even more cruel, how dearly she still loved him, despite the grief he caused her.

When she learned that the gentleman who had questioned her concerning Georget was the young messenger's patron, the pretty flower girl had felt a thrill of joy, and hope had returned to her heart; she flattered herself that through the medium of Monsieur Malberg, she could convince her lover that he had done wrong to suspect her. But the abrupt way in which the count left her dispelled that hope.

However, as hope does not quickly leave a young heart, especially that of a young woman who knows that she is pretty, Violette flattered herself for several days that Georget would return to Paris, that he would pass her booth, and that he would not have the courage not to stop; then she said to herself also that this Monsieur Malberg, who had asked her so many questions concerning her age and her mother, would probably want to see her again. But the days passed and no one came, neither Georget, nor his patron. A single man passed now and then in front of the booth of the flower girl, at whom he cast insulting glances, glances which seemed to enjoy the grief that he could read on her face. That man was the author of all the girl's trials; and once even he had dared to approach her and had tried to make love to her; but thereupon Violette had risen, so indignant and so threatening, and the flashing eyes which she turned upon Jéricourt denoted such a determined resolution, and her right hand had grasped so quickly several bunches of thorns which were among her flowers, that he had walked rapidly away, and had never again attempted to enter into conversation with the flower girl.

It was ten o'clock in the morning, and Chicotin had just left Roncherolle, who was living in his new lodgings on Rue de Crussol, and, feeling that his left foot was not yet in condition to descend the five flights, had again employed his regular messenger to carry a bouquet to Madame de Grangeville and to inquire for her health. But as the unfortunate victim of the gout saw his resources diminish every day, he had told Chicotin to buy a bouquet for one franc instead of three.

The ci-devant lady-killer was still gallant; but his fortune no longer permitted him to be gallant in the same measure as of yore.

Chicotin walked along Boulevard du Château d'Eau, with his franc in his hand; and as it was not flower market day, there were very few dealers in evidence; and the flower girls who were in their places had very few violets, which doubtless were also scarce at that moment.

The pretty flower girl who bore the name of that flower was the only one supplied with them; she had some large and fine bunches.

"*Sapristi!*" said Chicotin to himself, as he turned over some miserable little bunches at two sous which another flower girl offered him; "this isn't what I want; I can't carry such things as these to the lady on Rue Fontaine-Saint-Georges; for when one buys only one kind of flower for a franc, one ought to get a fine bunch."

"You think so, do you, sonny? Perhaps you don't know that violets are out of season just now. See, I will tie these four little bunches that I have left all together and they will make a very pretty bouquet."

"Not much! I don't want 'em; your bunches are all withered; they look as if they had been used before."

"What a stupid little animal!"

Chicotin walked away from her, saying to himself:

"It's no use for me to look, there's only one flower girl who has any real good bunches of what I am looking for, and that's Violette; but I have sworn not to buy anything of her since I knew that she deceived poor Georget. However, I must do my errand, and I don't know whether I shall find violets anywhere else. After all, you buy of a person and pay her and that's the end of it; that don't make you friends; and then, she don't ask so much as the others; I'll go to her."

So Chicotin walked to the girl's booth and examined her bouquets.

"Ah! is it you, Chicotin?" cried Violette, as she recognized Georget's friend. "It's a long time since I've seen you; it's a strange thing how all my old acqaintances have gone away, I don't know where. Have you done like your friend Georget? Have you stopped standing on the boulevard?"

"How much do you ask for this bunch, mamzelle?"

"I say, Chicotin, do you ever see your friend Georget? for of course he must come to Paris from time to time."

"This big bunch of violets, mamzelle, I ask you how much it is."

"And I ask you if you ever see Georget? It seems to me you might answer me."

"Mamzelle, I came here to buy some violets and not for anything else. I buy them of you, because you're the only one that's got any good ones; if it wasn't for that——"

"If it wasn't for that—well, what? Come, finish what you were going to say."

"Well! I was going to say that if it wasn't for that I wouldn't have spoken to you."

"What, you too, Chicotin? Why, has it gone so far that I must receive insults from everybody? that everybody is going to insult me? Ah! that's a shame! what have I done to you, that you should say that to me?"

"To me—you haven't done anything to me personally, but you have to somebody else, somebody I'm very fond of, who's my friend; you've made him unhappy, and when anyone treat my friends bad, I always take a hand in it."

"Ah! Georget has told you too——"

"Yes, mamzelle, he has told me—mon Dieu! you know well enough what he must have told me,—that he couldn't love you any longer, because you—but no matter —How much for this big bunch, mamzelle?"

"And you believed all that too; you are convinced that I am a girl without honor, without shame?"

"Mamzelle, I give you my word that I didn't believe it right away; no, indeed; and that I didn't want to believe it at all; but when you are certain of a thing—look you, just consider that Georget and I followed that dandified Monsieur Jéricourt a whole day, to make him speak; I begged him to tell me the truth about you."

"Monsieur Jéricourt—well?"

"Well! he called me a fool; he said that when a girl went—How much for this bunch, if you please?"

"Ah! the coward! the villain! but he lied, Chicotin, I swear to you that he lied!"

"Oh! mamzelle, everybody knows that women never admit such things; if only nobody had seen you; but as someone did see you, nothing you can say will make me believe—Well, if you're not crying now! I'm sorry for it, I don't like to make anybody cry; but it ain't my fault; I didn't say a word about this; it was you who would talk about it; it worries me to see you cry, and I'll go away, as you won't tell me how much this big bunch of violets is."

"Whatever you please," faltered the girl, holding her handkerchief to her eyes.

"Mon Dieu! I can't pay more than twenty sous, mamzelle."

"All right, that's enough; take it."

"Yes, mamzelle, I will take it; here's the twenty sous. Adieu, mamzelle."

Chicotin took the bouquet and walked away very fast, because he felt that if he remained longer with the flower girl he would be quite capable of crying with her.

Violette wiped her eyes and tried to keep back her tears; but this fresh blow had wounded her heart too deeply; she felt too unhappy, and was absolutely determined to extricate herself from that position. Throughout the day she cudgelled her brains trying to think whom she could apply to for good advice; she felt that she must have a friend, a protector to defend her, to assist her to justify herself. But in vain did the poor girl cast her eyes about; fatherless and motherless, she was also friendless since Georget believed her guilty. At last, an idea, a last hope presented itself to her mind; despite the haste with which Monsieur Malberg had left her, it had seemed to her that he had felt some interest in her; the questions he had asked, the extreme attention with which he had gazed upon her, everything led her to suppose that something spoke to him in her favor; moreover, all the good that she had heard of that strange man, and the benefactions which he had heaped upon Georget and his mother, finally confirmed her in her determination. She decided to go to Nogent, and to appeal to Georget's patron for aid and protection; and she flattered herself that he would not turn her away. Somewhat tranquillized by this hope, Violette went to sleep less unhappy, saying to herself:

"To-morrow morning I will go to Nogent."

XXXIII

DISAPPOINTMENT.—CERTAINTY

On the fifteenth day after his visit to Monsieur de Roncherolle, the Comte de Brévanne did not fail to return to the furnished apartment on Rue de Bretagne. As he was starting upstairs, Beauvinet stopped him, saying:

"Whose room is monsieur going to?"

" To Monsieur de Roncherolle's; I know that it is on the third floor!"

" Yes, it was on the third floor, but as the tenant has left, it ain't worth while for monsieur to go up."

" He has left?—He has gone out, you mean, don't you?"

" No, monsieur, no; he has gone away, he has left our house."

" Left your house! when, pray?"

" About ten days ago."

" And where does he live now? He must have left you his address?"

" His address—yes, monsieur; he lives on Passage I-don't-know-where, first door to the right when you enter Paris by Barrière de l'Etoile."

The count, who was in a very bad humor already, administered a hasty kick on the young man's posterior, and left the house in a rage, saying:

" Let that teach you to make such idiotic answers to me!—Gone! gone! he has escaped me again!" said Monsieur de Brévanne to himself as he went away; " he has sworn that he will not fight with me! Gone! but he could not stand on his legs; so he must have been carried, and it is impossible that he can have left Paris; a man doesn't travel when he is helpless, and above all when he has no money. Judging from what I saw, his circumstances were not prosperous. Shall I have him hunted for in Paris again? No, I will wait until chance once more brings me face to face with him. But I am sorry not to have seen him again; I would have tried to find out—but no, I could never have asked him that!"

Monsieur de Brévanne was about to return to his estate in the country, thoughtful, and dissatisfied with himself, when he suddenly remembered that Monsieur de Merval had given him his address in Paris; so he took a cab and was driven there.

"This is a pleasant surprise," said Monsieur de Merval to the count. "I hardly expected to see you before the bad weather begins; for the autumn will soon be here, and we are having the last fine days."

"My dear sir, do not be too grateful for my visit; a powerful motive brought me to Paris to-day."

"Why, it is true, I had not noticed—you seem to have had some keen disappointment; can I help you in any way?"

"Have you time to listen to me?"

"Always."

Thereupon Monsieur de Brévanne informed Monsieur de Merval that he had found Roncherolle; he described the visit he had paid him, and told him of the useless proceeding which had been the result of his first visit.

"You see," said Monsieur de Brévanne as he finished his narrative, "he has escaped me again; he denies me the satisfaction which I have a right to expect from him; he runs away without leaving his address; he does not want me to find him! What do you think of such conduct?"

Monsieur de Merval shook his head, and after a moment replied:

"Do you desire my real opinion?"

"To be sure."

"Well, if you wish me to tell you my thought, I consider that Roncherolle has done well."

"Done well? to refuse to give satisfaction to the man whom he has insulted? done well to run away, to act like a coward? Ah! I don't understand you, Monsieur de Merval!"

"Please listen to me calmly. In the first place, Roncherolle is not a coward, as we all know; if he runs away from you, it isn't because he's afraid of death. Mon Dieu! he told you so himself; ruined, suffering torture in his bed three-fourths of the time, do you think that you would punish him by depriving him of life? No. You will kill him, for you know very well that he will never aim his weapon at you; you will kill him—you have a right to, and no one would consider it a crime on your part; but when you have accomplished this act of vengeance, will you be any happier? No, no! on the contrary, you will be much less so. I could have understood this duel in the days just after the insult, although it would still have caused you remorse in the future; but after twenty years, when the heroes of the episode are so different from what they were, when it seems that Providence has undertaken to punish the guilty, you would hunt down a miserable wretch, who for twenty years past must have cursed a misstep which deprived

him of a genuine friend, whom he has never replaced!
No, no; do not do it; leave time to act; it is inexorable;
and when we forgive those who have offended us, be sure
that every day time takes it upon itself to make them
understand how heavily they have laden their future with
remorse and regret by yielding in their youth to a guilty
passion, a guilty sentiment!"

The count listened to Monsieur de Merval without interrupting him, and seemed to reflect deeply. After
quite a long silence, he raised his eyes to Monsieur de
Merval's face, and gazed fixedly at him, saying:

"But that is not all, you have not told me all that you
know; there is something else."

"What? what do you mean? why do you suppose that
I know anything else of interest to you?"

"Because now I remember your questions. I do not
know how you were able to discover a secret which had
remained a secret to me down to this day; however, I
mean this—that of that criminal connection—between
Roncherolle and her who bore my name—there was—
there was a child born; is that true?"

"Yes, that is true."

"Ah! you knew it then, did you?"

"Chance, one of those circumstances which one cannot foresee, led to my discovering that mystery; this is
how it happened: a year after you left your wife,—observe that date, a year after, and I am certain of what I
tell you,—I had been passing a few days at the country
house of a friend at Ermenonville. Finding myself in the

neighborhood of the lovely spot where Rosseau's tomb is situated, I took it into my head to stop there; in my child-hood I had been taken to visit that village, which is overflowing with reminiscences of the illustrious author of *Emile*. But I find that one sees with more pleasure and interest at thirty years than at fifteen whatever speaks to the mind, the soul and the heart.—I had taken rooms at the best inn, which was, I believe, the only one in the village; I intended to pass two days at Ermenonville, to revisit the park, the desert, the island, in fact all those charming and poetic spots which one never tires of visit-ing. On the evening of my arrival there was a terrible storm. I was, I remember, in the common room of the inn; the rain was falling in torrents, and although it was September, it was quite cold, and I was glad to find a huge fire in an enormous fireplace.

"Suddenly we heard the noise of carriage wheels, which approached and stopped in front of the inn. Great surprise and great delight was felt by the inn-keeper and his wife, who did not expect guests so late, especially in such horrible weather. They ran to the door and I retained my seat in front of the fire. Soon the inn-keeper's wife returned and said to me:

"' It's a gentleman and lady, very distinguished folks, it's easy to see. His wife is in an interesting condition; she's afraid of the storm and wants to sleep here; but while we're getting a room ready for her, she's coming to sit in front of this warm fire, with monsieur's per-mission.'

"'Why, of course!' I said to the hostess; 'I will with very great pleasure give up this seat to the lady, which is the best one.'

"'She seems to be near her time,' continued the hostess; 'it would be lucky for us for she'd have to stay here for some time.'

"As the woman stopped speaking, the travellers entered the room, and a voice which was not unknown to me exclaimed:

"'Pardieu; here's a fire that does one good to see!'

"I had retired to the end of the room. Imagine my surprise, when I recognized De Roncherolle with Madame de Grangeville on his arm, who did seem, in fact, to be in a very interesting condition. Neither of them noticed me. Understanding how embarrassing the meeting would be to them, I made haste to disappear through a small door at the end of the room; I went up to my bedroom, which I did not leave again, and the next day at daybreak I left the inn without seeing the other guests again. That, monsieur le comte, is how I discovered a secret which, I think, has always been a mystery to everybody else; and my reason for never mentioning it to you has been that it seemed at least unnecessary to tell you of something which it could not be agreeable to you to learn, and which moreover is entirely unconnected with you, you understand,—entirely unconnected."

"Yes, I understand very well. However, I never had any suspicion of anything else. Did you return to Ermenonville?"

"Yes, I admit that I was curious enough for that; about three weeks after leaving so hurriedly at daybreak, I went back to the village and stopped at the same inn. The mistress of the house recognized me perfectly, and as we were talking of the guests whom I had left there, I asked her if the event which she desired had taken place in her inn.—' No, monsieur, no; ' she replied; ' the next day, the lady was better, and insisted on leaving, and I heard them tell the servant who was driving, to take the Paris road.'—This, my dear count, is all that I know concerning a fact which I should never have mentioned to you if you had not seemed to be informed about it to-day."

" And this child—the fruit of that guilty liaison—did you ever learn what became of it, what they did with it? "

" No, I assumed that it did not live. Otherwise, would not Madame de Grangeville have it with her, calling herself its godmother or its adopted mother? There are a thousand ways of disguising the truth when one wishes to keep a child with one."

" Well, I know more than you. I know what they did with that child and what became of it."

" Is it possible? "

" At least, I think I'm on the track of the mystery."

" And if you are not mistaken, what do you expect to do, monsieur le comte? "

" Oh! I don't know yet; it is all so shocking, so detestable! I cannot listen coolly when those events are being talked about. Adieu, Monsieur de Merval; I am

going back to the country. I need to breathe the country
air in order to restore my tranquillity, to help me to recover from the emotions of this day."

Monsieur de Merval did not try to detain Brévanne,
whose state of irritation he appreciated; and the count
at once returned to Nogent.

Pongo was waiting for his master, teaching Carabi to
pretend to be dead. Mère Brunoy was sewing, and Georget was going and coming about the garden, for the poor
fellow could not keep still. Since he had been to Paris,
and had seen how sad Violette looked and how she had
changed, her image constantly haunted him; and when
he saw his patron start for Paris that morning, he had
been twenty times on the point of asking leave to accompany him, but he had not dared; after the oath he had
lately taken, it would have been showing too little strength
of character. So the young lover had remained at
Nogent, where the day had seemed endless to him; and
he hovered about the gate, in order to see the count
when he returned, hoping that he might have seen Violette again and would speak of her to him.

Monsieur de Brévanne returned during the afternoon;
but his brow was dark, his expression more thoughtful
than usual. Without a word he passed his household,
who bowed before him; and he shut himself up in his
room at once.

"Master no want to talk," said the mulatto to Georget,
"him not nod his head and say good-day; him not in
good temper."

"Oh! I saw that too; he didn't say a single word as he passed.—I suppose he didn't see her—he has other things on his mind. Well, he won't speak to me about her, and he looks too stern for me to mention her to him."

And Georget returned sadly to his mother.

XXXIV

THE COAL BARGE

They had all returned to their duties. But hardly an hour had passed since the count's return, when a young woman appeared at the gate. The gardener happened to be alone in front of the house at that moment, and he admitted Violette, for it was she who had arrived at Nogent and had succeeded in finding the house she had sought.

"Is this Monsieur Malberg's house?" the girl asked timidly.

"Yes, mamzelle, this is the place."

"Is Monsieur Malberg at home?"

"Yes, he came back from Paris about an hour ago."

"And could I—could I speak to him?"

"Oh, yes! I think so. But come in, mamzelle, and I will go and tell monsieur."

Violette passed through the gate tremblingly; the gardener, who had taken a step or two toward the house, returned to her and said:

" Who shall I tell monsieur? What is your name?"

" My name, monsieur—but it isn't worth while; Monsieur Malberg won't remember my name; or else, perhaps then he wouldn't want to,—and in that case I would rather—oh dear! I don't know!"

" Bless my soul! I don't know either."

" Just be kind enough to tell Monsieur Malberg that it's a girl who has come from Paris, and who would like to speak to him."

" Very good."

The gardener went into the house; Violette glanced timidly about, hoping that in those beautiful avenues which she admired, in the fields which she saw in the distance, she might catch a glimpse of Georget; then she said to herself with a sigh:

" No, it is much better that he shouldn't see me, for he would think that I came here after him, and he would be quite capable of running away from this house too."

" If mamzelle will come this way, monsieur is ready to receive her," said the gardener, returning.

Violette was greatly agitated, but she followed her guide toward the house.

The count was in his study on the ground floor; all the curtains at the windows were drawn, night was coming on, and the room was dark and silent.

" Here's the young woman," said the gardener, pushing Violette before him, as she did not dare go in, and saying in her ear:

" Don't be afraid, he won't eat you!"

"Who is it who wishes to see me?" said the count, who was seated at his desk.

"Excuse me, monsieur, it is I."

Violette had finally made up her mind to enter the room; she was then close to Monsieur de Brévanne's desk, and he, as he raised his eyes, was thunderstruck to see the young flower girl before him.

"What! you? you here, in my house?" he cried, almost angrily.

"Yes, monsieur, yes; you recognize me, do you not, monsieur?"

"Recognize you? oh, yes; your features are too deeply engraven in my memory!—But once more, mademoiselle, why have you come here? Who sent you?"

"Sent me? No one sent me, monsieur; I have come of my own accord. It is very bold on my part, no doubt, but when one does not know which way to turn, when one receives fresh insults every day, which one does not deserve—for I swear to you, monsieur, that I have no fault to reproach myself with, that I can walk with my head erect, that I can look my comrades in the face without blushing; and yet I am suspected, and more than that, people say that I am a good-for-nothing, and those who ought to defend me are the first to abandon me, to despise me. Oh! I am very unhappy, monsieur. Excuse me for coming to tell you this; I know that it doesn't interest you, and yet, if you would take up my defence, monsieur, I am very sure that people would believe you; and he—he who is here at your house, with his mother,

if you should tell him that it's horrible to say unkind
things about me—for what he believes he tells to others,
to his friends, and yesterday Chicotin, who is a good
fellow, although he loafs too much, Chicotin, who has
always been friendly to me, why, even he insulted me, he
treated me with contempt! Ah! that was too much; I
felt that my courage was giving way; and to get back a
little of it, I thought of you, monsieur, who like so much
to do good; I said to myself that you would take pity on
a poor girl without parents, without friends, without anybody on earth to help her; that you would defend her;
and that is why I came, monsieur."

Violette ceased to speak and waited for the count to
answer her; but he seemed absorbed in his thoughts,
his head had fallen upon his breast, and he said nothing.

After a pause, the girl continued:

"Monsieur seemed the other day to take a little interest in me, and that is what encouraged me to come
here."

"Ah! in my house! you!" cried Brévanne, roused
from his meditations by these words; "why, you know
very well, mademoiselle, that my house is no place for
you; that you less than any other ought to come here;
that it's like defying me, like hurling an insult in my face,
to come here!"

Violette felt her strength giving way; as she was utterly unable to understand the indignation of this man
who had been described to her as so kind-hearted, she
lowered her eyes and faltered:

"Monsieur, I did not know—I did not think—God knows that I had no such intention as you suppose. Excuse me, monsieur, I see that I did wrong to come, as it makes you angry; but I thought that you would have pity on me, a poor girl, alone on earth, without——"

"Without parents? Who told you that you were without parents? I am almost certain that you have parents, for I know them."

"Mon Dieu! can it be possible, monsieur, that you know my parents, that you can tell me whether my mother is still alive? Oh! for heaven's sake, do not deceive me, do not give me a false hope! See, monsieur, as your questions the other day led me to think that you might help me to find my family, to-day, when I came here, I thought I would bring with me the only object that I have that belonged to my parents."

"Ah! you have something that proves to whom you belong—a paper, a letter, no doubt? Give it to me, give it to me; I shall recognize their handwriting."

"No, monsieur, it isn't handwriting, it's nothing but a handkerchief. It seems that it was among the things they gave my nurse to procure clothes for me; you see I had a very strange kind of *layette,* monsieur; there were trousers in it and waistcoats and cravats; probably my parents thought I was a boy."

"But this handkerchief—"

"The handkerchief my nurse thought was so beautiful, so nicely embroidered, that she did not cut it up to make me a cap, but she kept it for me. Mon Dieu! now I can't find it; but I am sure that I brought it. Ah! here it is, monsieur, here it is."

And Violette handed the count a handkerchief of the finest linen, with embroidery in each corner. The count walked to a window, examined the embroidery, and recognized his wife's monogram and his own, as well as his coat of arms and his coronet.

That proof was convincing; it removed Monsieur de Brévanne's last doubt; and although he was previously almost certain that Violette was the daughter of his wife and of Roncherolle, on recognizing the monogram, he felt a violent wrench at his heart, and a shudder ran through his veins; for, however suspicious one may be of a fact, there is a vast distance between that and certainty.

"Does monsieur see on the handkerchief anything that helps him to identify my parents, and to tell whether they are still alive?" murmured Violette, while the count kept his eyes fixed on the handkerchief.

"Yes, yes, I have no doubt whatever now, and I had rightly divined who you were."

"In that case, monsieur will certainly tell me——"

"But whoever entrusted you to a nurse must have given you some name, have told her the name of your parents, or given her their address. Tell me, mademoiselle, what name did they give? Answer; I insist that you conceal nothing from me!"

The count's wrathful expression, and the tone in which he questioned the girl, made her tremble; poor Violette

dared not meet the angry glances that were bent upon
her, and she hardly had the strength to reply:

" Mon Dieu, monsieur, I am not concealing anything;
on the contrary, I came here to find out. I don't remember my nurse, but the kind lady who took me in, and
who brought me up and took me to Paris, was careful
to write down all that the nurse had told her. That is
how I know that the gentleman who placed me in the
nurse's charge told her that my name was Evelina de Paulausky; but he didn't give any address; he said that he
would come to see me, that he would write; but no one
came, no one ever wrote, they forgot me, abandoned me;
that is all that I know, monsieur, absolutely all; for if
I knew anything else, why should I not tell it to you, monsieur, as it might help me to find out who my parents
are?"

" Evelina de Paulausky!" exclaimed the count, pacing
the floor. " At least they had the decency to conceal their
names! But Roncherolle? Why didn't he give her his?—
Because, after doing the wrong, he did not choose to take
the consequences, and they considered that the simplest
way was to abandon the child. Ah! the wretches!"

Violette waited in fear and trembling for the count to
speak to her; for she saw from his excitement, and from
the threatening expression of his face, that he was still
angry, and she dared not question him further; but, as
time passed and the count, absorbed in his reflections,
continued to pace the floor and to pay no attention to the
girl, she mustered all her courage and said to him at last:

" Since you know my parents, monsieur, in pity's name be kind enough to tell me who they are. Is my mother still alive? "

" Your parents? " cried Brévanne, halting suddenly in front of the girl; " your parents? Ah! you want to know who they are, do you? Well, learn that you are the child of crime—treachery! Your mother was false to all her duties, she was false to the oaths she had taken to an honorable man, she was obliged to lay aside the name which she had sullied. Your father! ah! your father betrayed friendship in the most dastardly way; believing in nothing, respecting nothing, mocking at all that is held sacred in the world, turning to ridicule the most sacred sentiments, he betrayed his best friend! "

" Oh! pity, pity for them, monsieur! "

" Pity! why, you see that they had no pity for you; —for they abandoned you—and now you think that I will take care of you,—of you, their child, the fruit of their adulterous intercourse!—No, no! I do not want to see you again; your presence reopens all my wounds.— Leave my house, mademoiselle, and enter it no more."

" Oh! pardon, pardon, monsieur! if I had known——"

" As for this handkerchief, which belonged to your mother, I will keep it, for there are monograms on it and a coat of arms which you have no right to retain. Go, go; I do not want to see you any more; your presence distresses me."

Violette felt as if she were dying; but the count's wrath terrified her; utterly crushed by what she had

learned, she had not the strength to say a word; she left
the study and the house; two streams of tears flowed
from her eyes, and she did not think of wiping them away.
She crossed the lawn and went toward the gate; the
gardener, who was still there, struck by the girl's suffering, called to her, asked her why she was weeping, and
urged her to stop a moment in the summer-house, observing that the weather was very threatening and that a
storm was brewing. Violette did not listen, or did not
hear, but walked on at a rapid pace, and soon passed
through the gate and left the count's residence behind.

Despairing, humiliated, distressed beyond measure at
having been so maltreated by the man who had made
Georget and his mother welcome, Violette walked for a
long time without any idea where she was going. But
what did it matter to her? She paid no heed to the road
that she was following, but she walked very quickly; not
to gain shelter from the rain which was beginning to fall,
for she did not feel it; her head was on fire, her limbs
shook with fever; but she walked on, saying to herself:

"I am a child of crime! my mother was guilty, my
father was false to friendship! ah! no doubt that is the
reason why he drives me from his house, and forbids me
to ask help and protection from him. Well, in that case,
it is not worth while to live; it was not enough to have
been abandoned by my parents; now that people know
who I am, I must expect to be turned away with contempt
wherever I go. How he treated me, that gentleman who
is said to be so kind! Oh, no! I cannot live like this,

I am too unhappy. Despised by the whole world,—I had done nothing to deserve that; and now my birth is thrown in my face! Did I ask to be born?"

Violette walked on, but darkness came on rapidly and soon she could see nothing, and kept running against trees. She had gone astray in the wood of Vincennes, and the rain was falling in torrents. The poor girl leaned against a small tree, whose foliage was insufficient to protect her from the storm; but she did not notice the water which drenched her garments, for she was absorbed by her grief. A little covered wagon, drawn by a meagre horse, passed along the road by the side of which Violette had stopped; a peasant, who was inside, saw the girl exposed to the fury of the storm; he stopped his wagon and called out to her:

"You are not in a very good place there; you are getting the whole of it; get in with me; if you are going to Paris, I'll put you down at the Barrière de Belleville."

"Thanks, monsieur, thanks, it isn't worth while;" replied Violette in a feeble voice. "I am all right here."

"All right! oh, yes! you are all right to catch a sickness; I won't leave a woman in the woods at this time of night, and in such weather as this!—Oho! you don't want to get in, don't you?—Well, I am going to make you! yes, I tell you you've got to get in!"

The peasant jumped down from his wagon, took the girl under the arms, forced her to the step, put one foot upon it and at last succeeded in making her get in.

Violette submitted like a child. The peasant seated her upon his cabbages and carrots, saying:

" You will be better in here than under that little tree, catching all the rain; you're wet through already, and I'm sure that's what made you numb. Poor girl, she can't talk nor move her legs; but the jolting of the wagon will warm her up.—Come on, get up, Blanchet! "

Blanchet started; the cart, having no springs, did in fact shake its occupants in a fashion well calculated to rouse their wits. Violette submitted to the jolting, and said nothing; she seemed indifferent to all that went on about her; she understood but one thing, and that was that she ought not to live any longer, because she would be despised by everybody; she was unhappy enough when she went to Nogent in the morning; now she was desperate, and she came away from there with death in her heart; she had hoped to find consolation and protection there, but she had found shame and contempt; she had been turned away, and she did not feel that she had the strength to endure that last affront.

The peasant who had taken the girl into his wagon did not notice her gloomy despair; as he talked all the time, as he asked questions and answered them all himself, other persons did not need to open their mouths with him; his mouth was a word-mill, which was always at work. Thus they arrived at the Barrière de la Courtille, where the peasant stopped Blanchet, and said to the girl:

" My child, this is where I stop; I can't take you any further. But here you are in Paris, and the best part of it is that the rain has stopped; indeed I believe that the weather is going to be fine again; it wouldn't surprise me. I will help you down, for you must have limbered up by now, haven't you? My wagon always produces that effect. Come, lean on me—that's the way! You see, there's Faubourg du Temple in front of you, and the boulevard's at the end of it. That's the way you want to go; all right, good luck; but you'd better dry yourself as soon as you get home."

The peasant left the young girl and entered a wine shop. Violette had not even found a word of thanks to say to the good-natured man; she was in the street, she looked at the barrier, passed her hand over her forehead as if to collect her thoughts, then entered Paris, saying to herself:

" I know where I am, the canal is over yonder ! "

Violette was no longer weeping, her eyes were dry. She walked rapidly through the faubourg, and when she reached the canal, instead of crossing the bridge, she turned to the left and walked for some time along the bank. It was ten o'clock at night, and there were few people on the path that she followed. A fatal idea had taken possession of the girl's mind—she was determined to die; she thought that she was dishonored because the man whose assistance she had implored had turned her out of his house. She said to herself that Georget could never love her again now, and she was resolved to rid herself of an existence which would henceforth be nothing but torture to her.

Suddenly she stopped and looked about her; no one was passing. She stepped over the chain which was between her and the edge of the canal. In front of her there was a large coal barge; she hesitated a moment, then she reflected that she could throw herself into the water from the barge without being seen. She crossed a plank and was soon aboard of the barge; and before jumping into the water, she fell to her knees and murmured this prayer:

"O my God! forgive me; it is a crime that I am about to commit, but I no longer feel strong enough to endure life, to be despised by everybody, although I have not committed the sins of which I am accused. He can no longer love me, for his protector turns me out of his house; but perhaps he will regret me, and will learn some day that I was innocent."

She had no sooner finished these words than she rose and rushed forward; but someone who was hidden within a few steps of her and who had heard her prayer, stepped out and stopped her, holding her in a powerful grasp, and exclaiming:

"Upon my word! jump into the water! by all that's good! you shan't do it. God help me! how glad I am that I happened to be here, and that I took Père Chiffon's place as watchman on the barge! Poor Mamzelle Violette! you—mean to die?"

"Yes, because I am despised by everyone."

"Oh! you won't be any more, mamzelle, you won't be any more! In the first place, not by me, Chicotin, for I heard you just now talking to the good Lord, and people don't lie to Him. I heard you, poor girl! you are innocent, and I understand how you must have suffered; but I will be one of the first to do you justice."

And Chicotin fell on his knees before the girl, took off his cap, and said to her in a humble voice:

"Mamzelle, I ask your pardon for suspecting you, for believing ugly things that were said about you. To-day I would swear before all the magistrates that you have never ceased to be virtuous. So forgive me, mamzelle, for suspecting you."

Chicotin's touching act, the words that he had uttered, revolutionized Violette's whole being; her tears flowed afresh, but this time they were soothing and relieved her; her heart expanded, she breathed more freely, it seemed to her that she had returned to life. She held out her hands to the young messenger, saying:

"Thanks, thanks, my friend; what you have done is well, I feel greatly relieved; yes, I no longer feel as I did; it seems to me as if you had relieved me of a heavy load that I was carrying here on my breast. Ah! I do not want to die now."

"Is that really so, Mamzelle Violette, is it really so? I tell you, that if I was still uneasy about that, I wouldn't leave you any more than your shadow."

"No, Chicotin, I no longer want to die, I swear; you have brought me back to life; and now, I will tell you that I am glad that you prevented me from carrying out my fatal design."

"Ah! that's what I call talking; but what was the cause of this attack of despair? Has somebody else been making you unhappy?"

Violette told Chicotin about her trip to Nogent, and of how she had been treated by Georget's protector.

"Mamzelle," said the young messenger, "that isn't natural; to make that gentleman, that people tell so much good about, get so angry with you, there must be something about your birth that isn't clear, and that worries him tremendously. Ah! if Georget had seen you sent away like that, I am very sure that he would have taken up your defence!"

"No, for he believes me guilty, he despises me."

"Oh, I will open his eyes, I will!"

"What I regret is that Monsieur Malberg kept that handkerchief, which was all that I had that belonged to my parents; for he said he wouldn't give it back to me."

"Oh! never fear, mamzelle, he'll have to give it back to you; I'll see to that.—But come, mamzelle, let's go away from here; I will take you home. The coal can look out for itself; besides, you live here in the faubourg, I believe."

"No, Chicotin; I have taken another room in a quieter house, on Rue de Crussol, and I've been living there a week."

"Rue de Crussol! I have a customer there. It would be funny if it was the same house. Come, mamzelle, take my arm; you are trembling and cold; I'll bet that you've got a fever."

" Perhaps so, a little; I got wet through; I have just come from Nogent, and I was out in part of the storm."

" You must go to bed at once when you get home, and try to keep very warm."

Violette took the young messenger's arm. They crossed the bridge at Rue d'Angoulême, and soon reached Rue de Crussol. The girl stopped in front of the house where Chicotin had found rooms for Roncherolle.

" This is the place," said Violette.

" Ah! what a coincidence! this is my customer's house. Which floor do you live on?"

" Oh! way up at the top, under the eaves; I believe it's the sixth floor; but the room is very pleasant, I assure you."

" That must be right over my gouty man. Is Mère Lamort your concierge?"

" Yes, a very good-hearted woman who always wants to get my breakfast."

" Well, mamzelle, take my advice and tell her to bring you up a mulled egg to-night; that will prevent you from being sick. Good-night, mamzelle; when I go to see my old gentleman, I'll ask the concierge about you. You don't bear me any grudge, mamzelle, do you?"

" Oh! no indeed, Chicotin; on the contrary, you prevented me from committing a crime, and you have brought hope back to my heart."

" Good-night then, mamzelle; I'll go back to look after the coal."

XXXV

THE VICISSITUDES OF FORTUNE

Let us turn back a little and pay a visit to Madame de
Grangeville, whom we left at the moment when she found
herself alone with her husband, in the little wood belonging to Monsieur Glumeau.

That meeting excited the lady intensely, not with
that emotion which makes the heart beat fast by re-
calling pleasant memories, for the baroness had always
been too much of a flirt to be sentimental; but the sight
of her husband had caused her anxiety, almost terror;
then, turning back for a moment to the past and com-
paring it with her present situation, she had been unable
to keep from regretting the position which she occupied
when she was Comtesse de Brévanne, and the fortune
which permitted her to gratify all her whims.

The five hundred francs which Monsieur de Merval
had handed her, on the pretence that he owed them to
her, had not lasted long in the hands of a woman who had
always been a consumer of money.

When Madame de Grangeville saw at a milliner's a
hat or a bonnet to her liking, she must have it, no matter
at what price. As for the interior of her establishment,
we have seen that she turned over the management of it

to her maid Lizida; the result was that the creditors were numerous.

On the morning after the little party given by the Glumeaus, at which the baroness was present, she rang for Lizida the instant she woke.

"Did madame enjoy herself yesterday at Nogent?" asked the maid. "Madame returned at daybreak, I believe. Was there a carriage there to bring madame back to Paris?"

"Oh! my dear Lizida, I have many things to tell you. Yes, some young gentlemen brought me back in their carriage. They were very good-looking, those same young gentlemen, and dressed in the latest fashion. But if you knew whom I met at the party! I am still all of a quiver thinking of it!"

"Some suitor, some lover of madame, who would have liked to abduct her by force, to carry her off into the country?"

"Oh, no! you are nowhere near it!—At that party I met—my husband!"

"Is it possible?"

"Yes, Lizida, and you must understand how that upset me. Luckily it was in the woods; he was not very near me, but I recognized him instantly; he has hardly changed at all; it is surprising, but I really thought that he was better-looking than he used to be."

"And of course he recognized madame too?"

"Oh! instantly; I saw that by his expression."

"He looked at madame with affection, I warrant?"

"No, there was no affection in his eyes. He is such a proud man, so absurdly proud! Just imagine that everybody else had left, and we two were all alone in the woods."

"Did madame try to have an interview with her husband?"

"No, I did not want to. But I don't know what the matter was with me; my emotion took away all my strength, and I could not move; I was afraid."

"What folly! and monsieur your husband took advantage of that moment to fall at your knees, to ask your pardon for his base conduct——"

"Oh! yes, of course! He glanced at me askance; he was leaning against a tree, and I assure you that I didn't feel safe at all. Luckily the company, disturbed at my non-appearance in the salon, sent three or four young men to look for me; they found me in the woods, and I assure you that I was very glad to go back with them."

"And after that—your husband?"

"Oh! he didn't come into the salon, and I was delighted. I didn't see him again.—Well, Lizida, what do you say to all this?"

"Faith, madame, I say that monsieur le comte certainly is not agreeable; when he found himself alone with a charming little woman like madame, after a long separation, then or never was the time to throw himself at her feet, to be reconciled, and to come together again!"

"Yes, it is certain that many husbands would have done that."

" And madame is so kind, I am sure that she would have forgiven him."

" That is very possible; but, however, that didn't happen. All the same, I am delighted that that man saw me with the dress I wore yesterday; he could not have suspected that I am short of money."

" Madame's costume was certainly magnificent."

" Just look in my bureau, Lizida, in the top drawer, and see how much money I still have."

Mademoiselle Lizida looked into the drawer and answered:

" Madame, I find twenty francs."

" What! only twenty francs! and you changed a note for five hundred only a few days ago! It isn't possible; you haven't looked thoroughly."

" I assure you, madame, that there is no more. But if madame will remember all that she has spent, she will understand that there can hardly be any more.—In the first place, we paid the dressmaker one hundred and twenty-three francs, then the grocer ten francs, and after that fifty more, because he came and made a row."

" That is true; it is hateful to have to give so much money to those people."

" And then, madame bought that lovely hat that she wore yesterday—sixty francs, I believe."

" Yes, and that was none too much."

" And then madame bought that superb silk dress with the figured flounces—one hundred and twenty francs, I believe——"

"Yes, it was as cheap as dirt!"

"All these make nearly four hundred francs; and then there were purchases at the perfumer's, gloves, and so forth; and then, we have had to live. So madame sees that she can hardly have more than twenty francs left."

"That is true. Mon Dieu! how the money goes! somebody ought to invent something else, of which one could have more. Well, I must not hesitate any longer; whatever the course of the market, I must sell my Mouzaias!"

Madame de Grangeville ordered her last resources sold; the securities that had cost her two thousand francs produced barely nine hundred. With that sum the baroness's household went on for some time; but as she still had many debts and the creditors became threatening, it was necessary to give them something on account; and with her mania for gratifying all her fancies, Madame de Grangeville was incapable of economizing. The result was that the end soon came of the proceeds of the Mouzaias, and then she was obliged to forego gratifying her caprices; then she was compelled, in spite of herself, to reflect, to think of the future; and that was appalling for that woman, who had never known how to occupy her time, even in those kinds of work which well-born women do not disdain, and which become a resource when adversity succeeds cloudless days.

Madame de Grangeville was obliged constantly to send to the Mont-de-Piété some article of clothing or some jewel, in order to obtain money. She was surprised at the very small amounts which they advanced on these objects, but Mademoiselle Lizida, who became much less amiable as the resources diminished, did not scruple to say to her mistress:

" Perhaps madame thinks that they will lend her what these cost! madame imagines that the frippery for which she has paid so much has some value. Not much! for example, a bonnet or a hat that madame paid forty francs for at the Temple, they will advance fifteen sous on. And the trouble is that madame bought such things so often; that is what ruined us."

" But that silk dress that you carried to-day to pawn, Lizida, is not frippery; it is one I bought to go to the Glumeaus' at Nogent—about two months ago; it isn't worn at all, and it cost me one hundred and twenty francs."

" True, but it's faded, and there's spots on it; madame spots her clothes terribly; the design isn't fashionable any longer, nor is the color; in fact, I shall have difficulty in getting twenty-two francs for it, and that won't carry us far!"

Madame de Grangeville heaved a profound sigh and said to herself:

" What will happen when I have nothing more to pledge?"

" Oh! you see, madame," rejoined the lady's maid, becoming more and more familiar, " you didn't have any tact! when you met your husband in the woods at Nogent, you ought to have made some advances, have smiled graciously on him. A husband who is so rich, dear me! is worth a glance; if you had made eyes at him, it would have flattered him, and he would have come back to you."

"I don't think so," replied Madame de Grangeville coldly.

"Bless me!" rejoined the lady's maid; "unless that gentleman has some reasons—well, I don't know the explanation!"

Meanwhile the summer had given place to the autumn, and already new necessities made themselves felt. Madame was cold in the morning and wanted a fire in her room; but they often lacked wood, and instead of trying to obtain some by playing the amiable with some new dealer, Mademoiselle Lizida thought of nothing but looking for a new place, having no desire to remain at a house where there were no more profits to be had. Anxiety and annoyance aged Madame de Grangeville rapidly. In six weeks she changed more than in six years. The deprivation of a fashionable bonnet or hat was to that woman a sharper grief than all the other events of her life. The wrinkles became more numerous and more visible on her face, and she was forced to go without any of those fashionable gewgaws with which a woman often conceals them. For a coquette, that was the most cruel torture; she had not the courage to endure her ill-fortune, and by worrying over it she made its ravages more rapid.

One morning, when the wind was blowing from the north and the baroness absolutely insisted upon having a fire, Mademoiselle Lizida, having no firewood, had already broken up a chair from the reception room, and several mushroom boxes, with which she was preparing to make a brisk blaze, when the concierge rang, and delivered a letter on which there was nothing to pay.

"A letter for madame," said Lizida, as she handed the missive to her mistress. "Open it, madame; perhaps it's some good news. If somebody should send you some money, how handily it would work in just now!"

"I don't expect any," said the baroness.

"An additional reason, madame; when one expects things, they don't come; when one doesn't expect them, they come; and then, see what a lovely square letter, with three wax seals."

"That is true."

"And the lovely handwriting; it is like copper-plate."

"Yes, it is probably some circular from a scrivener. However, let us see what it is."

Madame de Grangeville had no sooner torn the envelope than several bank notes fell out; she uttered a cry of surprise, while Mademoiselle Lizida began to dance about the room, crying:

"What did I tell you, madame? Bank notes! fortune is smiling on us again! oh joy!"

"One thousand, two thousand, five hundred—somebody has sent me two thousand five hundred francs!"

"Good! we can go on for some time with that."

"By the way, Lizida, don't burn the mushroom boxes."

"That's so; we may use them again."

"Ah! here's a short letter with the notes; let me see who sends me this money—'Madame, one of your old acquaintances, knowing that fortune is not propitious at this moment, begs you to deign to accept this sum. Every six months the same person will take the liberty of sending you the same amount.'—And no signature."

"Every six months as much! that is rather nice; that makes five thousand francs a year for madame.—Ah! there's an agreeable acquaintance. But still, it doesn't surprise me; for madame is so kind, so noble, so generous when she has money, that it's no more than fair that somebody should treat her in the same way. I will bet that this comes from someone whom you have previously benefited. Does madame know the writing?"

"Dear me, no! the letter is written in the same hand as the address. It is perfect writing—too good to be the writing of anyone who does not make a business of it."

"So madame does not know, does not guess, from whom this money comes?"

"Oh! I guessed instantly. It's from the same man who obliged me once before: dear De Merval! what a delicate creature! he does not want to name himself now, he is afraid that I would refuse his help. Ah! how that man loved me, Lizida! why didn't I marry him?"

"Oh! it's a gentleman who was once in love with madame, is it?"

"Yes, indeed, much in love!"

"In that case, madame, this means that he is still. He must be a fine man! to send bank notes, and not even be

willing to be thanked! there are not many friends so un-
selfish."

Thanks to this gift, which Madame de Grangeville at-
tributed to Monsieur de Merval, that lady recovered her
peace of mind. She had no more anxiety for the future,
and she could once more give all her attention to her
toilet, while Mademoiselle Lizida became as flattering
as before.

It was a few days after this event that Madame de
Grangeville received the bouquet which Roncherolle sent
her by Chicotin.

The name of Roncherolle could not fail to quicken the
beating of the woman's heart, who for that man's sake
had lost the place in society which she had occupied. For
many years she had not heard her former lover's name;
she did not know whether he was still alive; and on
learning that he was in Paris, on receiving the bouquet
which proved to her that Roncherolle was still gallant,
she fancied herself once more in the days of her love-
affairs; she persuaded herself that she had not grown
old, and she expected to find her lover still as deeply in
love as before.

But the gout had prevented the gallant from following
the bouquet; and in order not to allow the lady to think
that he had forgotten her, we have seen that he ordered
Chicotin to call upon Madame de Grangeville again and
to present to her this time a bunch of violets.

"I am deeply touched by Monsieur de Roncherolle's
souvenirs," the baroness said to the young messenger.

"But although I love bouquets, say to him who sends you that I should much prefer to see him than these flowers. Why does he not come himself?"

Chicotin did not reply: "Because he has the gout;" for Roncherolle had forbidden him to mention that. He said whatever came into his head, and returned to make a report of his errand.

But a few days later, Roncherolle, feeling able to walk, bent his steps toward Madame de Grangeville's abode.

XXXVI

TWO FORMER LOVERS

"Madame, there is a gentleman here who wishes to see you," said Lizida to her mistress one day.

"Did he give his name?"

"He would not; he says that he prefers to afford madame the pleasure of recognizing him."

"It is Monsieur de Merval, no doubt—the same gentleman who came last summer?"

"Oh, no! it's not that gentleman, madame; I should have recognized him. It's one whom I never saw before."

"What sort of looking man? Has he a distinguished appearance? is he stylishly dressed?"

"So far as being distinguished goes—yes, madame. He acts as if he was in the habit of being waited on. As for his dress, why, his clothes don't look as if they'd just come from the tailor's!"

"Arrange my cap, Lizida; does my hair look well?"

"Madame is pretty enough to paint."

"Well then, show the gentleman in; if by any chance it's the unknown friend who sends me bank notes!"

"Oh! he doesn't look like it, madame; or else he's well disguised."

The maid left the room, and in a moment Roncherolle was ushered into his old friend's presence.

Madame de Grangeville was seated on a *causeuse,* dressed in a pretty morning gown, with a charming cap on her head, beneath which great clusters of hair, curled *à la neige,* served as a frame to a face which unfortunately could not be arranged like the hair. The days of privation had left accursed traces which refused to disappear, despite cosmetics and inventions of the perfumer. Wrinkles are most persistent acquaintances; when they once visit us, they never go away.

Roncherolle had made himself as fine as possible; his linen was extremely white, his whole costume scrupulously neat. Unluckily that immaculate neatness could not prevent his coat's being threadbare, his overcoat shabby and of an old-fashioned cut, his trousers of a color that was no longer worn, his waistcoat very ragged on the edges, and his hat much too glossy from overmuch brushing.

Despite all this, however, the former king of fashion presented himself with his distinguished manners of long ago; but he dragged his left leg a little, leaned heavily on his cane, and on removing his hat disclosed a grizzled and almost bald head.

"Here I am, *belle dame!* It is I! Better late than never, eh?"

As he spoke, Roncherolle halted in front of Madame de Grangeville and scrutinized her with a peculiar expression; on her side, that lady examined closely and with an air of amazement the man before her, and tried to think where she had seen him before.

"Well! can it be that you don't recognize me?" continued Roncherolle, walking still nearer, the better to see the baroness; and he added, like a person who fears that he has made a mistake:

"Surely it is Madame de Grangeville to whom I have the honor of speaking?"

"Yes, monsieur; and you are——"

"De Roncherolle, at your service, if you will permit."

"Roncherolle; is it possible? is it really you?"

"Why, yes, it is really I, my dear Lucienne."

"Dear fellow! What a pleasure to see you again! Come and sit here, beside me."

Roncherolle limped to the *causeuse,* saying to himself: "*Bigre!* how old she is! what a ruin!"

While the baroness thought:

"How he has changed! how ugly he has grown! I should never have known him!"

"Tell me, my dear friend," said Roncherolle, making himself comfortable on the *causeuse,* "didn't you expect a visit from me? Didn't you receive my bouquets?"

" I beg pardon; indeed I expected you, and most impatiently, I assure you; but the fact is——"

" That I am devilishly changed, eh? What can you
expect? time spares no one; and then the gout—that
makes one suffer, it wears one out! "

" Have you had the gout? "

" Yes; indeed I have it now."

" That accounts for it then; I noticed in your gait
something—that you used not to have."

" I should say so; I limp like an old horse! "

" You have lost your hair too."

" I have lost a lot of things."

" You are no longer as slender as you used to be."

Roncherolle, beginning to be weary of these remarks,
replied with his ironical air, pretending to laugh:

" Ha! ha! what do you expect, my dear friend?
We aren't either of us what we were twenty years ago!
You yourself haven't that wasp-like waist that called
forth universal admiration, and those irreproachable teeth
that drove all women to despair."

Madame de Grangeville flushed and bit her lips in
anger. She tried, however, to maintain an affable manner
as she said:

" Ah! so you find me changed? That is strange; there
are people who declare that I am just the same."

" That is because those people haven't passed twelve
years without seeing you. But we two old friends, old
acquaintances, have not met to flatter each other. Bless
me! we know each other too intimately and of too long

date not to be frank between ourselves. Poor Lucienne!
ha! ha!"

"Well, monsieur! what makes you laugh like that,
pray?"

"Because I am thinking; I remember that you used
to ride like an angel in the old days; and I myself was a
very good horseman. We sat in our saddles, I like
Baucher, you like a bareback rider at the Hippodrome.
Well, just imagine us now if we should have to mount
a horse!—Ha! ha! ha!"

Madame de Grangeville made an impatient gesture and
turned her head away, saying to herself:

"Mon Dieu! what wretched *ton* he has now!"

"But let us drop that, my dear, and talk of our
affairs a little. We parted twelve years ago—on rather
bad terms, as I remember; but we were still lovers then,
and lovers often quarrel; at all events, two people can't
love each other forever—it grows monotonous. To-day
there's no question of all that; we are old friends, and
you cannot doubt the interest that I take in whatever con-
cerns you."

"Interest! it seems to me, however, that you have dis-
played very little interest in me. I have passed twelve
years without a word from monsieur; at that time my
fortune was already much impaired, and since then I have
had time to become ruined altogether, to be reduced to a
very straitened, very embarrassing position; but have
you troubled yourself about it? Not the least in the
world! And yet it seems to me, monsieur, that if you

had had any affection for me, if you had taken any interest in me, you would have had an opportunity to prove it."

"Come, come, *belle dame,* let us not lose our tempers, and above all let us not condemn without a hearing. You accuse me wrongfully. In the first place, I supposed that you were still in comfortable circumstances at least; and in the second place, I myself have not been for a long time in a position to assist my friends. I did it often formerly, —without reciprocity; but that would not have prevented me from continuing to do it if fortune had permitted. But she turned her back on me, she deserted me utterly; I treated her too cavalierly and she bore me ill-will. I was unlucky in everything—cards, bets, races, investments; it was impossible for me to retrieve myself in any direction! And what remains now of a handsome property?—some claims on which I can collect nothing, and a few wretched industrial stocks, which I am obliged to sell in order to live, and which will soon be all gone; that is where I am now; so that I can't think of others, being always compelled to think of myself; that is reasonable."

"Ah! so you are reduced to that!" rejoined Madame de Grangeville coldly, casting from time to time an inquisitive glance at the different parts of her former lover's attire. "That is very sad. I understand now. I said to myself: 'Why, Monsieur de Roncherolle, who was always so elegant, so coquettish in his dress—why does he neglect himself so?' But of course, if you can't do otherwise!"

Roncherolle bit his lips, swaying back and forth on the *causeuse,* and replied:

"Oh! that is the least of my troubles! I attach little importance to those trifles now. At our age, you see, my dear friend, coquetry serves no purpose, unless it be to make us ridiculous! When the time has come, it's no use to paint and bedeck ourselves—it doesn't take away either a wrinkle or a year!"

"He has become painfully tiresome, has this man," thought Madame de Grangeville, as she put a phial of salts to her nose. After a moment, she rejoined with a nonchalant air:

"Thank heaven! everybody hasn't deserted me; I have some friends who remember doubtless that I obliged them formerly, and one of them is giving me an allowance of five thousand francs at this moment."

"The devil! that is handsome, that is very handsome! Is it a male or a female friend who treats you in such magnificent fashion?"

"Mon Dieu! I have no idea! the person doesn't divulge his name; he prefers to remain anonymous, in order not to be thanked even. Isn't that a noble act?"

"Superb! and I regret exceedingly my inability to be the author of it. But you must certainly be able to guess, despite the mystery with which this person surrounds himself."

"No—that is to say, I have some suspicions, which I believe to be well founded."

"Indeed! but it seems that you did not suspect me?"

" Oh, no! not for one moment! "

" That is very amiable on your part."

" You see that I was right."

" But you were not aware of my unfortunate plight."

" What does that matter? as if you would ever have thought of me! "

" That is an extraordinary reproach! It seems to me that I proved to you abundantly that I thought of you in the old days."

" Yes, yes,—unfortunately.—Ah! if one could foresee what is going to happen, if one could read the future! "

" True! there are lots of things that one would not do —that one bitterly regrets having done! "

A long silence ensued. Madame de Grangeville broke it by exclaiming suddenly:

" You could never guess whom I met in the country last summer—Monsieur le Comte de Brévanne! "

" Really? "

" Yes, at a party, in a wood, where there were a great many people. I saw him at a distance in the crowd; I saw that he was looking at me and that he recognized me."

" Do you think so? "

" Do I think so! It was evident enough, for his manner was very agitated. I too recognized him instantly; he has changed hardly at all, except that his hair is turning gray; the face is still the same; he is good-looking —yes, he is a very handsome man! "

" Had you never discovered that before? "

" What an unkind thing to say to me! "

" Well! did you speak? "

" No; I am inclined to think that he was strongly tempted to speak to me; he hovered about me in the wood, and he was on the point of speaking to me, I believe, when some people came up; they surrounded me, took me away, and I lost sight of him. He must have gone away, for I didn't see him again during the evening."

" And that is all? "

" Yes, all."

" Well, madame, I too have seen Brévanne, and not very long ago."

" Is it possible? Did you meet him? "

" No, he came to the house in which I was living, expressly to see me; he had learned my address by chance."

" He came to see you—for what purpose? "

" Why, for the same purpose that led him to seek me everywhere twenty years ago—to fight me."

" To fight you! nonsense! it's impossible! "

" Why impossible, I pray to know? "

" Because men don't fight after so long a time for things—which have no present existence."

" Ah! very prettily put; I am sorry that your husband didn't hear it! But although in fact the motive for fighting is lacking now—the present existence—De Brévanne is still bent upon it—oh! obstinately bent upon it. Probably he has been looking for me constantly, for twenty years; and he had no sooner learned where I was—was perched, than he rushed to the spot, the same as ever, waving his sword, to demand satisfaction. But as I was suffering then from a violent attack of the gout, the sight of my agony convinced him that I was not in condition to stand up to him; so he granted me a respite."

"Then it is only postponed; you will end by fighting, I see."

"I admire the stoicism of your nature; you say that as if you were talking about your husband and myself going to the Opéra ball!"

"Mon Dieu! you have become very censorious, very severe! Should I weep when I say it?"

"No; indeed that is not your nature; you were never very tearful. To make you shed tears it would be necessary that your hair should be unbecomingly dressed at a large party; and that is an accident to which you were never likely to be exposed."

"You are still satirical, caustic, as always, Monsieur de Roncherolle!"

"If you find anything about me that has not changed, I am delighted beyond measure."

"A truce to jesting, monsieur; when is this duel to take place? I beg you to believe that I am deeply interested."

"Don't be alarmed, madame, the duel will not take place. I am as obstinate as De Brévanne. I have sworn not to afford him the chagrin of killing me, and I shall keep my oath."

"The chagrin! so you think that the count would regret it if he should kill you?"

"I am sure of it; and it would be even worse now than if he had killed me long ago."

"You are a surprising creature, on my word! A man who has been seeking you for so many years so persistently! You must see that he is as furious as ever against you; consequently, I fancy that he would not grieve very bitterly over your death!"

"You are wrong, madame; the count is no longer furious with me; rage doesn't last twenty years; it dies long before that time. It is nothing but the sentiment of honor that impels your husband now; and that sentiment would not stifle the regret that he would feel if he should kill a man whom he once loved with the most sincere affection."

"But whom he now holds in the greatest possible detestation!"

"No, madame, I assure you that he no longer detests me. When a man grows old, he remembers the happy days of his youth much more vividly than the troubles of his maturer years; the latter are effaced in the jolting and hurly-burly of life; the first remain and rise to the surface, to divert our thoughts, to charm our memories— and that is why I believe that De Brévanne no longer detests me.—What I say surprises you—you do not agree with me; but women do not understand friendship!"

"You have an amusing way of practising it! However, how do you propose to prevent this duel?"

"As I have prevented it for twenty years; I propose to elude the count's search. I have moved already; I no

longer live in furnished lodgings, and I should be very
much astonished if he should find me where I am now."

Madame de Grangeville said nothing more; Roncherolle seemed to reflect; and the ex-lovers were silent
for a considerable time. At last the gouty gentleman
put out his hand toward his hat, and seemed about to
go, when his former friend detained him, saying with
some hesitation:

"Monsieur de Roncherolle, I have something to say to
you on another subject of—of deep interest to us both."

"A subject of interest to us both?" repeated Roncherolle, replacing his hat on the table; "you surprise
me; I thought that we no longer had anything of interest
to say to each other. What is it all about?"

"You must have a very short memory, monsieur, since
it is necessary for me to remind you of that—that result
of our liaison—of our wrong-doing, alas!"

"Ah, yes! thrice alas!"

"Well, monsieur, that child, that little girl—for it
was a girl—tell me, monsieur, what became of her?
Formerly, when I questioned you on that subject, you
always answered: 'Don't be disturbed, I know where
she is, we shall find her again.'—But that was more than
twelve years ago, monsieur, and it seems to me that it is
high time that I should know what became of that child!"

Roncherolle moved about on the *causeuse* as he replied:

"Yes, yes, that is very true; there is the subject of the
little girl; I had forgotten about her entirely, and you

will understand in a moment why I had forgotten her;
it was because it would have done no good to think of
her, for I have no idea what became of her after I put
her out to nurse."

" You don't know what became of her! why, that is
abominable, monsieur, it is frightful; you break my
heart!"

" No fine words, my dear friend, I beg you; with me,
as you must know, they will miss their effect; I break
nothing at all of yours; for if you had chosen to be a
mother, to know and to enjoy the happiness which that
title affords, you would not have begun by begging me
to rid you of your child as soon as possible the instant
that it came into the world."

" Monsieur, that is not true; you insult me, you slander
me!"

" You are beginning again.   Come, Lucienne, stop
acting and listen to me.   When you were in an interesting condition and on the point of emerging from it, we
were journeying through the fertile pastures of Nor-
mandie; suddenly the fancy seized you to visit Ermenonville, the village that became so famous because a so-
called philosopher—for I consider that that Monsieur
Jean-Jacques had little claim as such, and that a man can
hardly call himself the friend of mankind when he constantly inflicts injury on those who have conferred bene-
fits on him—but no matter, he made the village of Ermenonville famous by living there, and especially by being
buried there.   I remarked to you that it was imprudent

to approach Paris, where your husband might be, especially in your condition; but you were always obstinate in your whims, and I have never been able to thwart a lady. We reached Ermenonville in horrible weather; very good. The next day you felt ill and insisted on returning to Paris, to be sure of having all the necessary assistance in your condition; that was another imprudence. But no matter—I yielded. We reached Paris; we had hardly arrived, when whom should we see on the street but your husband! Very good; he didn't see us; you wanted to go away again, but it was too late; you brought a daughter into the world.—In the confusion and embarrassment into which that event, anticipated though it was, cast us, you began by saying to me: 'Take the child away at once! find a nurse instantly, and let her go back to her home in the country this very day.'—I continued to do your will; I carried the little one—who was a sweet little thing, on my word!—to a room above yours, which I was occupying temporarily; and I said to my servant—I had Comtois then, a most intelligent fellow, whom I could never replace—I told him to find me a stout, healthy nurse. Comtois went away and very soon returned with the desired object: she was a peasant woman of excellent appearance—a Picard. I remember distinctly that she was a Picard. I gave her the child, and she raved over her; then she asked me for the *layette;* I confess that that embarrassed me sadly; you ought to have thought of that, madame, but you never considered it. I gave her all that I found at my hand: trousers, dressing-gown, shirts, cravats; I remember too that I gave her a handkerchief that belonged to you, and that I happened to have in my pocket. The nurse laughed heartily when I gave her all those things. I handed her a hundred francs in addition. She made a price for nursing the child, and it wasn't exorbitant. She asked me the little girl's names, but you and I had not fixed upon any. I said to the Picard: 'You may call the child Evelina de Paulausky'—yes, those are the names I gave her; I had just read a novel the heroine of which bore that name. —I then asked the nurse for her name and address, so that I might send her money and have news of the child. She gave them to me, and then she started off with her nursling. It was all arranged very quickly, as you see."

"Certainly, monsieur, I have nothing to reproach you for, up to that point—except the *layette,* which you might have bought."

"That is to say, which you should have bought before-hand."

"Oh! monsieur, when one is travelling all the time, has one any opportunity to make purchases?"

"In that case, madame, when could I have bought it, as I was travelling with you?—Besides, is that sort of thing a man's business?"

"Well, monsieur, let us drop that and return to the nurse. You heard from the child through her? you sent her money?"

"I never heard from the nurse, madame, for the very simple reason that I did not give her my address; I refrained, from prudential motives; and then too we were always in flying camp at that time, and I really don't know what address I could have given her."

" Then, monsieur, you must have written to her?"

" Mon Dieu! that is what I expected to do, and to send her some money; and then I would have given her an address, *poste restante,* so that she might answer me. But at that point difficulties arose. Imagine, if you please, that, when that woman gave me her name and address, I did not take the precaution to write them down at once; we were in such a hurry, so completely upset! What with giving my clothes for the *layette,* and the child's crying, and your sending to ask what was going on— in short, I didn't write down the confounded address at the time, feeling sure that I should remember it. The nurse went away. We had a thousand things to do: I had to obtain money to resume our travels, and we were constantly beset by the fear of being discovered by your husband.—As you will remember, we started for the Pyrenees as soon as you were in a condition to endure the journey."

" I know all that—well?"

" At last, one fine day, you asked me about the child. I answered: ' She is well; she must be all right.' But that reminded me that I had neglected to send the nurse any money since the little one came into the world, six months before. I said to myself: ' Pardieu! I must re- pair that neglect.'—I instantly wrote a few lines in haste, but when it came to writing the woman's name and

address, I could not possibly remember them! She was
from Picardie, and her first name was Marguerite; but
Marguerite what? there are Marguerites everywhere!
And the name of that wretched village—I could not remember that either!—I said to myself: 'A little patience
and it will come back to me.'—Six more months passed
and I thought again of the child; I tried once more to remember the nurse's address; but I could not recall it!"

"And you kept telling me that the child was well!"

"What would you have had me tell you? I couldn't
say that she was ill, because I didn't know.—In short, for
nineteen years I have tried very often to think of that
address, but it hasn't come back to me yet."

"And so, monsieur, by your fault, I am deprived of my
daughter forever, and the poor child is without a family!
It is shocking!"

"Pardon me, madame, pardon me; on mature reflection—in the little one's behalf first of all—I am not sure
that it is a great calamity that she has never known the
secret of her birth; she would still have been in a false
position; and then life in Paris wouldn't have been as
good for her health as the fresh country air—especially
in Picardie. That's an excellent region; they drink
cider there, which is very healthy. If she is still alive,
I am sure that she must be in good health. She lives in
the fields and woods—bless my soul! she is happier, no
doubt, than she would be here; especially as I could
never give her an establishment with the remains of my
fortune."

"But what of me, monsieur?—do you make no account of my regrets? I am deprived of my daughter's caresses!"

"I beg pardon, madame, but the longing for those caresses takes you rather tardily."

"Why, monsieur, it is twelve years since I last saw you."

"But for seven years we were almost never apart, and you were perfectly willing to leave the child at nurse; you asked me about her sometimes—at long intervals; but you never said: 'Do send for her.'—You thought that the attention you would have to give the child would disturb your pleasures; and for my part, I believe that her presence would embarrass you even more now; for the girl is nineteen years old; and a daughter of nineteen would be terribly repugnant to you; she might rob you of conquests!"

"Monsieur, you do not mean to insult me, I trust?"

"By no means, my dear friend! We have had an explanation, and I have confessed the truth. 'I had to do it!' as Bilboquet says; and now I will take my cane and my hat and return to my Marais."

"Do you live in the Marais? What a horrible neighborhood!"

"Oh, no! however, one lives where one can! I have not, as you have, anonymous admirers who make me an allowance; but I congratulate you; you can still gratify your taste for pleasure, for fine clothes. I consider you very rich now—compared with myself."

"No, indeed! no, indeed!" Madame de Grangeville replied eagerly, with an embarrassed air. "I have only what I need to live; a woman requires so many things, you know; it would be impossible for me to accommodate anybody."

Roncherolle put on his hat, leaned on his cane and exclaimed with a savage glance at the baroness:

"Did you suppose by any chance, madame, that I intended to ask you for anything, or to borrow anything of you? I hoped that you had lived with me long enough to know me. I have spent a devilish lot of money on women; they have led me into all sorts of folly, but nothing base. I have ruined myself for them, and I had a right to do it. I have made love to them much, loved them sometimes, deceived them often; but thank God! I have never accepted anything from them; I am entitled to say to them just what I think, and I avail myself of that right on occasion.—My respects, my affectionate friend!"

With these words, Roncherolle bowed to Madame de Grangeville with a mocking expression, and left her apartment, saying to himself:

"Ah! these women whose lives have been nothing but coquetry—when you search their hearts, what a barren soil you find! Sow benefactions there and you never reap anything but ingratitude."

As for Madame de Grangeville, as soon as her former lover had left her, she called her maid and said:

"If by any chance that gentleman should come again to see me, Lizida, I shall not be at home to him! The idea! a ruined man, who dresses shabbily, who drags one leg, and who has nothing but disagreeable things to say!"

"Madame is quite right. That is a good sort of man to keep out."

XXXVII

THE CONCIERGE-NURSE

In a hasty, violent, nervous disposition, wrath is quick to come; it bursts out violently, but it does not last long; the heart that feels the most profoundly the wounds that it receives, is also the most sensitive to the tears that it sees shed, and it very speedily repents of the pain it has inflicted.

The Comte de Brévanne, who had only a few hours before acquired the certainty that his wife had had a child by Roncherolle, had been unable to control his wrath and his jealousy when their child appeared before him; at the first blush, he had imagined that it was a fresh insult, an additional affront purposely put upon him. All his sufferings, all his anguish had returned to his mind and to his heart, and we have seen how, as a result of all these circumstances, he had received poor Violette.

But when a half hour had passed after the young girl's departure, the count, who had remained alone in his study, had had time to grow calm; moreover, the storm that was in the air had broken, the rain was falling in torrents; at such times nervous people always feel relieved, they breathe more freely, their brain becomes clearer and their irritation falls with the rain.

Brévanne looked about him, passed his hand over his forehead, and said to himself:

" So that girl has gone. How I treated her! why, I must have lost my reason. She came here to ask me for help, for protection, and I brutally sent her away, drove her out of doors. Poor child! is it her fault that she is the fruit of adultery? She does not know who her mother is, as she came to ask me for information concerning her parents. They shamelessly abandoned her, and I turn her out of doors! Can it be that I propose to be as shameless as they? Ah! I behaved very badly. And this storm—great heavens! the rain is falling in sheets. Can she have gone away in such weather?"

The count rang violently and Pongo quickly answered.

" Master, he ring?"

" Yes; that young girl from Paris who came just now to speak to me—where is she? Go and find her, and bring her back; I don't want her to go away."

" Yes, master."

And the mulatto, who had seen no girl, ran all over the house, the courtyard and the garden, shouting at the top of his voice:

" Young girl from Paris! come right back. Master ask for you; master want to see you. She no answer. —Oh! me find you! "

Georget spied Pongo just at the moment that he was applying to a great chestnut tree, saying to it:

" You see young lady who come to speak to master? "

" What are you doing there, Pongo? "

" Monsieur Georget, me look for someone master want, and me no find."

" And you are applying to that tree to learn where she is? "

" Oh! he understand all right; he no speak, but he understand."

" Whom are you looking for? "

" A young girl from Paris, who come to speak to master; he no longer want her to go away."

" A young girl from Paris has been here to see Monsieur Malberg? "

" Yes."

" What was she like, Pongo? Describe her to me."

" Me no see her. It was master, him tell me."

" Who let her in then? Ah! there's the gardener."

Georget ran to the gardener, and Pongo ran about the garden, talking to the trees and the flowers.

" Did you see this girl who came from Paris to speak to monsieur? "

" Yes, to be sure; it was me who let her in and took her to the master."

" What was she like? "

" Pretty as a picture, on my word; she's a fine slip of a girl."

" Did she tell you her name before you let her in? "

" No, she said it wasn't worth while."

" Did she stay long with monsieur? "

" Why, yes, quite a while."

" And she has gone? "

" Yes, as much as half an hour ago; the storm was just beginning, and when I saw that, I asked her to wait in my house; I told her she'd get wet; but she wouldn't stop; she made me feel bad because she was crying."

" She was crying? What! she was crying when she left Monsieur Malberg? "

" I should say so! big tears too! she looked as if she was in very great trouble, but she started off all the same."

Georget waited to hear no more; he ran to the count, and could hardly say what he wished to, he was so excited.

" Monsieur, the girl who came—a young girl came from Paris,—and talked with you, monsieur? "

" To be sure; well? "

" Why, she went away again, monsieur; and the gardener noticed that when she went away, she was crying, she was very unhappy."

" Ah! she was crying? "

" Yes, monsieur. I ask your pardon, monsieur, for questioning you; but this girl—was it she, monsieur? "

" She—who? "

"Violette, monsieur, the little flower girl; the one that—you know, monsieur."

"No, no, it wasn't she;" replied the count, trying to calm Georget's excitement. "Why do you suppose that that girl would come to see me?"

"Mon Dieu! I don't know, monsieur; but as you spoke to her one day, in Paris, I thought that perhaps she might have something to say to you. But it wasn't she who came here and of course that makes a difference; excuse me, monsieur."

At that moment Pongo appeared in the count's apartment, all out of breath, crying:

"Master! master! girl from Paris—I no bring her back, her gone."

"All right, I know it."

"Oh yes; but me know from Thomas,—he meet her in the country, and her out in all the storm! he call to her: 'stop, mamzelle; come, get under cover.' But her run all the time just like her not hear, and her all soaked with water. Poor girl, her get sick for sure!"

The count turned pale, but he concealed his emotion and requested to be left alone. Pongo went back to Carabi, saying:

"He want to go out too; but me no want him to get wet like the young girl; poor girl, in the fields when it storm; that not right!"

Georget said no more; but although Monsieur de Brévanne had assured him that the girl was not Violette, although he dared not doubt his protector's words, yet he

felt sad and oppressed, and he deeply regretted that he
had not seen the poor girl who had gone away weeping.

Early the next morning, without a word to anybody, the
count started for Paris; and he had no sooner arrived
than he betook himself to Boulevard du Château d'Eau.
The weather was cold but fine; it was one of those beautiful autumn mornings when the sun shines on the yellow
leaves and promises a fine day.

It was not a flower market day; but some of the
flower girls were in their places, none the less. As the
count approached, he looked about for Violette, but in
vain. The girl, who was ordinarily so faithful to her
occupation, had not opened her booth, had not appeared
in her place.

Monsieur de Brévanne waited for a long time, walking
back and forth on the boulevard; he entered a café
nearby, breakfasted, read the newspapers, and then returned to the place where the flower girl always stood;
but Violette did not come.

" She is probably kept away to-day by the necessity of
buying flowers for her trade," said the count to himself;
" I will go back to Nogent and I will see her to-morrow."

But on the next day, the young flower girl was not in
her place, and the count was again obliged to go away
without seeing her.

The girl's health had been seriously impaired by the
events and the agitation resulting from her journey to
Nogent. One does not experience a violent disappointment with impunity; one does not defy the storm and

wind without feeling the effects of it. On leaving the coal barge, Violette shivered on her companion's arm, and he noticed it; on reaching her room, the girl had gone to bed at once, and on the next day, despite her earnest desire to attend to her business, it had been impossible for her to rise.

Luckily, Mère Lamort was always at the service of her tenants. The concierge passed her time going up and down the six flights of stairs in her house. Her dog kept her lodge, and barked when anyone entered and attempted to ascend the staircase. At that signal from her substitute, Mère Lamort instantly went to the window of the floor where she happened to be, and conversed from there with the persons who came to see some of the tenants.

Chicotin, who was now deeply interested in Violette's health, finding that she did not come to the boulevard on the day following the evening when he had prevented her from accomplishing her fatal design, did not fail to go and enquire of the concierge, who replied:

"The girl's sick and in bed; I am making her some herb tea, because that breaks up a fever."

The young messenger, whom Mère Lamort's information failed to reassure, climbed the six flights rapidly and entered Violette's room; he found her in bed, with the flushed face and hollow, burning eyes which indicate a violent attack of fever. But the girl smiled at Chicotin and offered him her hand, saying in a weak voice:

" Thanks, Chicotin, for coming to see me; what you said last night was true; that shower has made me sick; but it won't amount to anything."

" Don't you want me to fetch a doctor, mamzelle? "

" No, it's not necessary; it won't amount to anything. Besides, the concierge is very kind, she takes good care of me."

" She is going to bring you up some herb tea; but I will come every day to find out how you are getting on, —twice a day rather than once."

" I don't want to interfere with your work, my friend."

" Oh! that won't interfere with me. In fact, I have a customer in your house, just below you,—a gentleman who isn't always steady on his legs; but just at present he seems to walk very well. Would you like me to tell him to come up to see you? You see, he is no fool; he talks better than I do."

" Thanks, Chicotin, I don't need any company; I am never bored when I'm alone, for I know how to read, I like to read; and besides that, I have plenty to think about."

" But not about such miserable things as you thought about yesterday? "

" No, no; that's all over."

" Good. I spoke to you about your neighbor because he ain't a young man and it wouldn't make any gossip; but if you don't want him to come—Ah! here's Mère Lamort with a pitcher in each hand. You will have something nice.—Good-by, mamzelle, I'll come again soon."

On leaving Violette, Chicotin met Monsieur de Roncherolle on the stairs, going up to his room.

"Ah! are you coming from my room, my boy?" said
the gouty gentleman when he recognized his usual messenger.

"No, bourgeois, no; I am coming from the room over
yours."

"Over mine? What, are there people perched higher
than I am? I thought that I acted as lightning rod for
the house."

"Oh, no, monsieur, there's a very pretty young girl,
who lives all alone above you."

"Ah! you rascal! I see,—this girl is your mistress!"

"No, monsieur, you don't see at all. The poor girl
is adored by one of my friends, and I should never think
of such a thing as making love to her, because, you see,
I ain't capable of being false to a friend, although I'm
only a messenger."

"You are right, my boy, you are right," murmured
Roncherolle, hanging his head, "for that doesn't bring
good luck."

"But if you knew all that has happened to the poor
girl! Just imagine, monsieur, that if it hadn't been for
me, she would have jumped into the canal last night."

"Indeed! for what reason? Desperate with love—
her lover has abandoned her, I suppose?"

"No, he still loves her, he thinks of nothing but her;
he thinks that she was unfaithful to him; he is convinced
that she has listened to a fine young dandy who makes

eyes at her, and who has boasted of having been her lover."

"And why do you think that it isn't true?"

"Why, bourgeois? Because, last night, when she went aboard the coal barge, with the intention of carrying out her fatal plan, she couldn't have suspected that I was there, hidden behind the coal; and before she jumped into the water, she knelt down, to make a last prayer to the good Lord. She asked Him to forgive her for putting an end to her life, but she said that she didn't feel strong enough to live, despised and humiliated by everybody, abandoned by everybody she loved, when she had done nothing to reproach herself for. When she said that, she couldn't guess that anyone was listening to her, and she was getting ready to die. Well, I say that at such a time she couldn't lie; ain't that right, monsieur?"

Roncherolle tapped Chicotin on the shoulder and smiled.

"He doesn't reason badly, the rascal.—But what does your little protégée do?"

"She is a flower girl, monsieur. Now I think of it, you know her; she is the one you bought a bouquet of the first time I had the honor of meeting you,—when you told me to come with you."

"The deuce! is it possible that it is that pretty, attractive girl? for she is remarkably lovely, this friend of yours."

"Yes, monsieur, yes; she's the one; Violette, they call her."

"But wait a moment—if it's she, why the young dandy who claims to be her lover must be a certain Monsieur Jéricourt."

"Just so, master; Jéricourt's his name—a man who writes plays; do you know him?"

"I dined with him a short time ago."

"Do you know him well?"

"No, thank God! Why do you ask me that?"

"Oh! not for any reason; that is to say, I was thinking that if he was a friend of yours, he might not lie so much to you, that's all."

"No, he isn't a friend of mine by any means.—By the way, you say that this girl is sick; has she enough money to be well taken care of?"

"Oh! yes, bourgeois; she ain't hard up, she sells all she wants to; and then, she has money put by."

"So much the better; who is taking care of her?"

"Your concierge, Mère Lamort."

"I don't know that one can have much confidence in her as a doctor. I will go myself to see this girl, for what you have told me has aroused my interest in her."

"I am sorry, bourgeois, but that can't be."

"What is it that can't be?"

"You can't go to see Mamzelle Violette, because she forbids it."

"How can she have forbidden it? I have never been there."

"Excuse me, but this is how it is: you see, when I was talking with her this morning, I took the liberty to mention you; I told her that she had a very pleasant neighbor."

"Ah! you say such things about me, do you?"

"That you were my customer.—By the way, bourgeois, shall I take a bouquet to Madame de Grangeville from you to-day?"

"No, no, that's all over; you won't take her any more bouquets—from me at least.—But let us return to the flower girl; you said to her——"

"I said to her: 'you have a very distinguished neighbor, who is—who is no fool.'"

"Really, you don't think me a fool?"

"No, monsieur."

"I am very much flattered that you have such a good opinion of me."

"You are joking; but I know what I'm talking about, I tell you!"

"And this girl doesn't choose to receive me because you told her that I was no fool?"

"Oh! it isn't that. I said: 'If you wish, mamzelle, Monsieur de Roncherolle won't refuse to come now and then to sit with you, and he'll be splendid company for you;' and then I added: 'you can receive him without compromising yourself, because in the first place, he ain't young, in the second place, he's gouty, and in the third place——'"

"Go on, while you are about it!"

"In short, I meant to say that you didn't look like a rake."

"It is certain that I should find it rather difficult to play that part now.—But this extravagant eulogy of my person did not make your friend disposed to see me?"

"No; she said that she didn't need company, that she preferred to think all by herself."

"In that case, my boy, we will let her alone; we must never annoy anybody, especially the sick."

Monsieur de Roncherolle entered his room, and Chicotin returned to the boulevard, saying to himself:

"Shall I go to Nogent and tell Georget all that has happened? If I do, he won't be able to think badly of Violette any more. On the other hand, if I tell him that she's sick, he'll worry and torment himself; he'll want to come back to Paris and perhaps that will displease his employer. I think that I'd better wait until Violette is well before I go to see Georget."

But the next day, the young flower girl, very far from being well, had a higher fever and was slightly delirious; she hardly recognized Chicotin when he came to see her. He said to the concierge, when she approached with several jugs in her hand:

"It seems to me that your patient ain't doing very well, Mère Lamort?"

"Oh, yes! oh, yes!"

"What's that? oh, yes? Why she hardly recognized me, and then she says things that don't mean anything."

"It's the delirium going away; but I've got three kinds of herb tea for her and—ah! there's Mirontaine barking; somebody's coming."

And the concierge put her head out of the round window on the sixth floor overlooking the courtyard.

"Who's there? Who do you want?" she cried.

An old man who had entered the house, looked up and answered in a quavering voice which only reached the fourth floor:

"Have you a Monsieur Dupuis in the house?"

"What? What's that? is there a well—*puits*—in the house?"

"He used to be an advocate."

"You say it's your trade?"

"He has several children."

"Are you looking for lodgings?"

"Aren't you coming down?"

"You say that you stuff mattresses? What a miserable voice! I wonder if the man has got a cold in his head! —Ah! there's Mirontaine barking again; I must go down.—Coming!—What a nuisance!"

The concierge went dowstairs, and Chicotin, after examining Violette again, shook his head and said to himself:

"I don't know whether it's wise to trust to Madame Lamort's three kinds of tea; I don't know much about such things myself, but I see well enough that this poor girl has a devil of a fever. No matter what happens, I shall go down and fetch the old fellow from the floor below."

Chicotin went down to Roncherolle's room, and found him all ready to go out.

"Have you come again to see if you are to carry a bouquet to the baroness?" he asked with a smile; "I told you that that was all gone by; I shan't have any more bouquets to send to anybody."

"No, bourgeois, no, I ain't come for that, but because of your little neighbor upstairs, Mamzelle Violette."

"Well, how is she to-day?"

"Not well; she's as wild as a hawk; the concierge says that that's a good sign, but I don't agree with her; I came to ask you if you would have the kindness to go to see her, because you're better able than I am to judge of her condition."

"So you think that she will be willing to receive me to-day, do you?"

"Pardi! yes, as she don't know whether there's anyone near her, and as just now she thought she was in the country, under the trees."

"I am not a doctor, but no matter, I will go to see this girl, and if I can be of any use to her, I ask nothing better; show me the way."

"Come, bourgeois, we haven't got far to go."

"I can believe that."

Roncherolle followed the young messenger, who ushered him into Violette's room. The attic chamber was not elegant, but it was neat and clean; the furniture was decent and in good condition; in short, nothing in the room indicated poverty, or made the heart ache; on the contrary, there were two large bouquets in two pretty vases.

Roncherolle approached the spotless white bed on which the sick girl lay; she seemed to be in a very agitated sleep. He took one hand which was moist and burning, he felt her pulse, then shook his head, saying:

"The fever is very high, but the skin is not dry; I am glad of that, it is less dangerous."

"You don't like dry skins?"

"I say that I don't think that this fever is dangerous. But what do I see on the mantel?"

"Those are flowers, some of Mamzelle Violette's stock."

"Such enormous bunches of flowers in a sick room! why, there's enough there to kill her, and I'm not surprised that she is out of her head; take them all away at once, throw the flowers out of the window."

"You see, Mamzelle Violette adores flowers, and Mère Lamort, instead of leaving them in a corner of the courtyard, by the pump, where Violette always keeps them, she said yesterday: 'I'll just take two big bunches, and she'll enjoy looking at them as long as she is lying in her bed.'"

"Mère Lamort seems to me too well named; if that's the way that she takes care of sick people, I must congratulate her.—Take all these flowers away, my boy, and give the girl nothing to drink except a very weak infusion of linden, with a few orange leaves: I am no doctor, but I have an idea that that will be enough, and that she will be better to-morrow. But take all these flowers away, don't leave a single one here!"

While Chicotin hastily removed all the flowers from
the vases, Roncherolle gazed at the sleeping girl and
murmured:

"It would be a pity; she is very pretty, is this child.
Where the devil have I seen that face?—Come, my boy,
we'll let her sleep; I am going down to give Mère Lamort
a talking to."

XXXVIII

THE NEIGHBOR'S VISIT

The next morning Chicotin appeared in Monsieur de
Roncherolle's apartment with a radiant face, exclaiming:

"I've come to tell you, monsieur, that you fixed Mamzelle Violette up in fine shape; she ain't out of her head
to-day, her fever is much less; in fact, she feels a great
deal better; she told me to come and thank you and tell
you that she'd come herself as soon as she gets up."

"Thank me! for what? Because I advised giving her
linden tea to drink, and because I had the flowers taken
out of her room? why, anybody would have said as
much as that. Don't let the girl put herself out for such
a trifle. However, as she is better, I will go up soon to
see her, to bid her good-morning. I fancy that that is
not forbidden now?"

"Oh, no! you're a friend of hers now, bourgeois."

"Very good; in that case, announce a visit from her friend of the fifth floor."

During the day, Roncherolle ascended the single flight of stairs which separated him from the flower girl. He found the door open, and entered the room of the sick girl, who was then alone, the concierge having just gone down because she had heard Mirontaine bark.

Roncherolle approached the bed softly; Violette was not asleep and the return of health could already be read in her eyes. At nineteen, sickness often disappears as rapidly as it comes; it is simply the storm which disturbs the tranquillity of a beautiful day, but leaves no traces behind.

When she saw in her room a gentleman whom she did not know, the girl opened her eyes in surprise and started to speak, but Roncherolle very soon reassured her, saying:

"Mademoiselle, I am your neighbor from below—indeed, I could not very well be from above; excuse me for intruding upon you thus, but Chicotin asked me to come up yesterday to see you, because he was anxious about your condition; to-day he came to tell me that the draught I ordered had done marvels, that you were almost well. As I did not deem myself capable of executing so rapid a cure, I wished to satisfy myself with my own eyes as to whether he had told me the truth; but if I disturb you, if my presence annoys you, tell me so frankly, and I will go away at once."

Roncherolle's courteous and amiable tone instantly banished the girl's embarrassment, and she replied with a smile:

"Oh, no! it doesn't annoy me, monsieur. It was you who were kind enough to come up to see me yesterday; Chicotin told me, and I should have come to thank you—excuse me—pray take a chair."

"Then it's understood that I don't disturb you? In that case, I will take a seat and talk with you a moment; shall I?"

"Yes, monsieur, you are very kind."

"Let us not stand on ceremony any longer, now that we know each other. All the necessary courtesies have been performed, and I am a neighbor come to chat with a neighbor; and when his neighbor has had chatting enough, she will show her neighbor the door."

"Oh! monsieur——"

"No, never fear, I shall know enough to show myself the door. First of all, I am glad to see that you are really much better; I will wager that two days hence you will not have a sign of your illness."

"Oh! I hope not, monsieur; then I shall be able to go back to my flower stand."

"Yes, but you must not be imprudent, and go out too soon. I am well aware that to keep one's room is not amusing, when one is all alone. Oh! I know all about that, I have had too much experience; but at my age reverie is melancholy, whereas at yours it should be rose-colored."

"Not always, monsieur."

"Have you no parents?"

"No, monsieur, I have none."

"Poor girl! and despair had taken possession of your pretty head, and you proposed to die?"

"What! you know, monsieur?"

"Yes, yes. Chicotin told me that whole story; he is very fond of talking, is that fellow; he told me that your lover, no, I mean the young man who is in love with you, had ceased to speak to you because he thought that you had listened to a young dandy; you see that I am well posted."

"Georget believes me guilty, monsieur. I know that appearances are against me, but I assure you that Monsieur Jéricourt lies; it was he who prepared the trap into which I fell."

"A trap! come, while we are alone, suppose you tell me all about it; I should not be sorry to know the whole story—that is, unless it tires you to talk."

"No, monsieur; besides it will not take long."

Roncherolle drew his chair nearer to the sick girl's bed, so that she might not raise her voice, and Violette began:

"Some time ago, monsieur, I was at my flower booth on Boulevard du Château d'Eau."

"Yes, I know where it is."

"A servant came to order a handsome bouquet, and gave me one hundred sous in advance, saying to me: 'You must carry this bouquet to Madame de Belleval's, Boulevard Beaumarchais, number 88; be sure to take it

up to the lady yourself, because she wants to order others
for a wedding.'—I accepted the order, monsieur; for
you see, a bouquet for a hundred sous is worth the
trouble; we don't sell many at that price on the boulevard.—The servant went away. When I had made a
magnificent bouquet, I asked a neighbor to look after
my booth, and I hurried to the address that was given
me. I arrived there and asked the concierge for Madame
de Belleval. He hesitated for a moment, then said: ' Go
up to the fifth floor, the door to the right.'—Ought I
not to have gone up, monsieur? "

" Why thus far I see no reason why you should have
hesitated."

" I reached the fifth floor, and rang at the right hand
door. A woman answered the bell. I asked for Madame
de Belleval.—' Come in,' she said.—' But I simply have
a bouquet to deliver.'—' Come in all the same,' she said;
' madame wants to speak to you;' and she opened the
door of a small salon where I saw nobody, and left me
there, saying: ' Wait, she will come.'—Should I not have
gone in, monsieur? "

" Why not, my child? There was nothing to arouse
your suspicion so far."

" I waited for a few moments, then a door opened; but
instead of a lady, I saw Monsieur Jéricourt come in; a
man whom I detest, and who had been pestering me for
a long while with his love and his insulting propositions;
he is a swell who thinks that a woman, especially a flower
girl, cannot resist him."

" I know him; go on, go on."

" When I recognized that man, I guessed that I had
fallen into a trap; I tried to go away, but he held me and
began to talk to me of his love; he laughed when I re-
proached him with his treachery, and dared to tell me
that I had no choice, because we were in his rooms and no
one would come to my help. Ah! if you knew, monsieur,
what strength despair and indignation gave me then; I
began to shriek. Monsieur Jéricourt tried to kiss me,
but I clawed his face so that he had no inclination to try
again! He was furious with rage, but he let me go, and
as you can imagine, monsieur, I left the room instantly.
But it seems that there was somebody on his landing when
I went out: that little squint-eyed young man, who lives
in the same house, saw me come out all excited and upset.
It is quite possible that I was; but I was so happy to
escape, so terrified by the risk I had run, that I saw nobody; I was no longer in that man's power, that was
my only thought; and I am sure that I went downstairs
very quickly.—That is the whole truth; that is how I
happened to go to Monsieur Jéricourt's, without a suspicion that that was where I was going; but that is exactly what took place there—I swear it to you, monsieur;
and may the good Lord prevent me from ever leaving
this bed if I have lied in any one detail! "

Roncherolle gazed attentively at the young girl while
she was speaking, and for the first time in his life, perhaps, he felt deeply moved. He pressed Violette's hand,
and said:

" I believe you, my child, I believe you. In fact, there is nothing improbable in your story; it isn't the first time that a pretty girl has been lured into a trap in this way. It is very wrong, but still I could forgive this Jéricourt, if, having failed in his attempt, he had admitted his defeat; but when you were virtuous, when you resisted his attack, to go about proclaiming that he had triumphed over you, that you had yielded to him—why that is going too far, deuce take it! Men ruin enough women who are willing to be ruined; they should not ruin those who object!"

" Oh! how glad I am that you believe me, monsieur!"

" But do you mean to say that when you told all this to your sweetheart, he refused to believe you?"

" He has never given me a chance to justify myself; he ran away from me without deigning to listen to me."

" Be calm, and get well; before long, he will do you justice, and will himself ask your pardon for having suspected you."

" Do you think so, monsieur?"

" I am sure of it."

" You make me very happy, monsieur."

" I no longer believed myself capable of making a young girl happy, and I am exceedingly proud. I am very glad that you have told me this whole story, my little neighbor; and on your side, I hope that you will not regret it."

" How kind you are to take an interest in me, monsieur."

"Now we have talked enough and I must leave you;
rest, sleep, and everything will go well; but above all,
no more flowers in your bedroom!"

"Oh, no! you see that there are none here now, monsieur."

"There is still one—but that one will never do any
harm."

Roncherolle went away, and the girl fell asleep.

XXXIX

PURE LOVE

For several days the Comte de Brévanne walked upon
the boulevard where the pretty flower girl ordinarily
stood, to no purpose. At last, after allowing three days
to elapse without going to Paris, he went thither again,
and as he drew near the Château d'Eau, he saw that Violette was once more in her place.

Violette did not notice the gentleman who approached
her and halted in front of her flowers. But on raising
her eyes and recognizing Georget's protector, the man
who had treated her so harshly and turned her out of his
house, the poor child shuddered and had not courage to
utter a word.

"Yes, it is I, mademoiselle," said the count, imparting
to his voice its mildest intonation; "I frighten you, I

see; you lower your eyes in order not to meet mine. Oh!
do not be afraid; you would not read in them any trace
of anger, but rather an expression of sorrow; for I behaved very badly toward you, poor girl! But at that
time cruel memories led my reason astray; since then I
have realized how unjust, how cruel I was to you, when
you came to ask for aid and protection; and so, on the
day after that scene, I came here to ask your pardon."

"Pardon! pardon!" murmured Violette, not daring
as yet to believe what she had heard, and timidly raising
her eyes to Monsieur de Brévanne's face. "Ah! is it
possible, monsieur? Then you no longer despise me?"

"I have never despised you, my child; I simply vented
upon you a fit of anger which never should have touched
you; for you are not the guilty one.—Once more, are
you willing to forget my injustice? Are you willing to
forgive me?"

"Oh! with all my heart, monsieur; I have never been
angry with you, but it made me very unhappy."

"Have you been sick, that you have not been here sell-
ing your flowers?"

"Yes, monsieur, I have been sick; but only for a week;
it is all over now, and I have forgotten about it."

"But you are still pale and changed."

"It is the result of the fever; but I feel better, and
now, monsieur, that you have told me that you are not
angry with me any more, why, I feel perfectly well; it
seems to me that my strength has come back to me, and
that my health is as it was."

"I am glad to hear that, for your absence from this place worried me a great deal; and if I had known where you lived, I should have gone to inquire for you."

"And—and—is he still with you, monsieur?"

"He? You mean Georget, do you not?"

"Yes, monsieur, Georget."

"To be sure; but he didn't come with me; I left him at Nogent. I must also confess to you, my child, that I didn't tell him that you had been to Nogent; after what happened, I knew that I should simply make him unhappy; and before telling him anything, I wished to see you again."

"You did well, monsieur."

"However, as the winter is approaching, we shall return to Paris in a few days."

"Will he come back with you?"

"Yes, I shall bring him with me; I shall find work for him here; he is an intelligent fellow and he writes well —it would be a pity to have him continue as a messenger."

"And you will return soon, monsieur?"

"Yes, and then I expect to see you again; you will not be afraid to come to my house? you won't bear me a grudge?"

"No, no, monsieur, I shall be at your service."

"I still have a—a certain handkerchief of yours; I am keeping it as a sacred trust; but do not fear, I will return it whenever it is likely to be of any use to you."

"Oh! I don't want it, monsieur. You know better than I if I can—if I ought to hope to find my parents

some day. But no, I probably shall never find them, and
I had better give up thinking about them, hadn't I, monsieur?"

"You must come to see me in Paris; I shall probably
return next week. Georget will let you know."

"Georget! do you think he will speak to me?"

"I think that he will ask nothing better; for he has
been very unhappy about not coming to Paris these last
few days, the poor boy!"

"Oh! how kind you are to tell me that, monsieur!"

And tears of joy glistened in the pretty flower girl's
eyes. The count, with a friendly nod, walked away,
bidding her au revoir, and leaving in the girl's heart so
much joy and happiness that there was no room there
for the memory of her past sorrow.

While these things were taking place in Paris, Chicotin,
seeing that Violette had recovered her health, had started
early in the morning, on foot, for Nogent, in order to
tell Georget all that had happened to the young flower
girl.

Chicotin had found his former comrade walking sadly
back and forth on the lawn in front of the count's house,
gazing with a melancholy air at the Paris road, by which
Monsieur de Brévanne had departed, without bidding him
accompany him, and wondering why he went to Paris so
often.

At sight of his friend, Georget uttered a joyful exclamation and threw himself into Chicotin's arms; whereupon the latter, without stopping to rest or to take breath,

proceeded to tell his comrade all that had happened to Violette,—her journey to Nogent, her despair, her illness, and finally her recovery.

It would be difficult to describe Georget's state during this narrative; listening intently, choking with grief, weeping and uttering cries of joy in turn, he exclaimed:

" She is not guilty! what joy! poor girl, turned away, determined to die! Oh! mon Dieu! I should have died too!"

He hardly gave his friend time to finish his story; he leaped on his neck, embraced him, kissed him again and again, stammering in a voice broken by sobs:

"It was you who saved her; it was due to you that she did not throw herself into the canal, where she would have died; for so late at night no one would have seen her, no one would have taken her out of the water! Ah! I love you almost as much as I do her; I pray for only one thing, and that is, that I may be able to prove my gratitude some day!"

" Well, well! what a silly fellow! here's a lot of talk for the simplest kind of an action: a man sees a girl trying to kill herself, and prevents her—I should like to know if that thing isn't done every day; any boy in the street would do as much."

" So it was really she who came here! My heart guessed it, but that cruel man deceived me; he told me that it wasn't she, because he had made her cry and had turned her out of the house with harsh words! Oh! that was shameful, and I will not stay any longer in a house

where Violette received such an affront. Wait here for
me, Chicotin."

"What are you going to do?"

"Pack up my things, and I'll go away with you; my
mother will come after us."

"Bah! more nonsense! what does this mean? You
mean to leave a man who has never been anything but
kind to you, in such a way as this, without even saying
good-bye to him? A man who, when your mother was
sick and you hadn't a sou, gave you all that you needed
to take care of her; a man who has taken you into his
family, with your mother, and quartered you in this
little château, where you are living like pigs in clover
—you yourself said so? Well! that would be pretty!
and you talk of gratitude, and this is the way you propose to treat your protector!"

"What difference does it make what he has done for
me? He made Violette so unhappy by turning her out
of this house that she wanted to die, and that she would
have died without you!"

"As if he could have guessed that! You must see that
this gentleman must know Violette's parents, and that
they have played some vile trick on him, and that there's
some deviltry in all this that we don't know about."

"I don't care; I propose to go to Paris and ask her
to forgive me for suspecting her."

"So far as that goes, you will do well; but that ain't
any reason for leaving your protector, for behaving mean
to him, and I don't propose——"

"Hush! here he is!"

Monsieur de Brévanne had returned from Paris. He saw the two young men. He observed Georget's excitement and agitation, and, divining a part of the truth, he went at once to his protégé, and asked him, pointing to Chicotin:

"Who is this young man?"

"He is a friend of mine, monsieur, an old comrade; he is Chicotin, whom I've mentioned to you once or twice."

"Ah! yes, I remember. What does he want?"

"He came, monsieur, to tell me that Violette tried to throw herself into the water, when she left this house after you had driven her away; for it was she, monsieur, it was really she who came here, and you told me that it wasn't.—Poor Violette! but for him she would not be alive, and I—my mother would not have any son!"

Georget burst into sobs. Chicotin twisted his face and mouth, and did his utmost not to weep with his friend. Monsieur de Brévanne, who was deeply moved himself, tapped Chicotin on the shoulder, saying to him:

"You are a fine fellow; I shall not forget it."

Chicotin took off his hat and passed the back of his hand over his nose and eyes.

"And you, Georget," continued the count, "you are very angry with me, aren't you? But your young friend Violette has made her peace with me; won't you do as she has done?"

"Violette! monsieur has seen Violette? Is it possible?"

"Yes, my dear boy, and to-day isn't the first time that I have tried to express to her my regret for what had taken place. On the very next day after her unfortunate journey, I went to Paris expressly to see her; but she was not in her place; you must have noticed that I went to Paris several days in succession."

"That is true, monsieur."

"It was always in the hope of meeting Violette; but I did not find her."

"Because she was sick, monsieur," cried Chicotin; "because she was confined to her bed with fever."

"I know it, my boy; she told me all that just now; but she is in her place to-day; and now she is not angry with me any more, and she hopes that you will not be angry with her, Georget; for I told her that you would go to see her; did I do right?"

Georget, who passed as quickly from wrath to affection as from sadness to joy, seized Monsieur de Brévanne's hand and squeezed it violently, crying:

"I was wrong to think that you were unkind, I ought to have known that it was impossible. Oh! let me go at once to see her, monsieur, to ask her pardon for thinking her guilty, to tell her that I have never ceased to love her."

"To-day? Why, it is quite late."

"It is only four o'clock, monsieur, and at six I shall be in Paris; at ten o'clock I will be back again. You will let me go, won't you, monsieur?"

"As I made you unhappy, I must make up for it."

"Ah, monsieur!"

"Go; I will tell your mother that I sent you to Paris on an errand; do not come back until to-morrow morning in order not to run the risk of being on the road so late."

"Oh! thanks, monsieur, thanks a thousand times!—Come, Chicotin, let us go."

"But I haven't had a chance to rest or to eat anything!" muttered the young messenger, making a wry face.

"Come, come; I'll treat you to supper."

"*Fichtre!* the bill of fare will have to be long then."

"Here, my boy," said the count, putting a twenty-franc piece into Chicotin's hand; "here is something for your supper; I propose to treat you, for Georget is quite capable of starting off without any money."

"Thanks, monsieur, we will have a little spree, eh, Georget?—Why, where is he? Out on the road already! Bless my soul! he is capable of making me run all the way to Paris."

Georget was going at the speed of a Basque; Chicotin succeeded in overtaking him, however, and said as he trotted along beside him:

"We'll take a carriage at Vincennes. I have some money, for Monsieur Malberg gave me twenty francs; there's a fine man for you!"

"Why take a carriage? we can go faster on foot."

"Oh, no! not much! and even if we could, is it worth while to use ourselves up and arrive in Paris sick, or to be sick to-morrow? And besides, what hurry is there now? You are sure to find her,—she won't fly away."

"Ah! you are not in love, Chicotin! you don't know what it is to go back to the girl you love; and it seems to me that I have been away from her for years."

"Ah! there's a coucou.—I say, driver, two seats for Paris!"

"On the box, if that suits you?"

"I should say so; we adore the box."

The two friends mounted to the driver's seat. Each moment Georget was tempted to seize the whip and lash the horse, which did not go fast enough to suit him. The driver defended his horse and his whip, and Chicotin's hands were full in trying to keep peace on their seat. At last they arrived in Paris, and Georget said to his friend:

"Go to the wine-shop on the corner of Faubourg du Temple, and wait there for me; then we'll have supper. Au revoir."

And he disappeared like a flash from the eyes of his friend, who said to himself:

"Oh! run as much as you please now; I have no desire to follow you, for I don't propose to ruin my liver."

Georget was not at all anxious that his comrade should go with him to find Violette; when one has been parted for a long while from the girl he loves, when one has been at odds with her, one desires to see her again without witnesses; secrecy, aye, and silence, must preside at that interview, for one speaks with the eyes as much as with the voice, and any witness is a nuisance at such a blissful moment.

Georget drew near the Château d'Eau. It was flower market day, and although the weather was already a little cold, there were still enough people on the boulevard for the young man to approach without being seen by Violette. He spied her at last, but there were two ladies in front of her, selecting bouquets. So that he was fain to be content to look at her, to devour her with his eyes. He drew nearer and nearer, keeping behind her customers. Suddenly, as she raised her eyes, the young flower girl saw Georget standing like a statue and gazing at her as a repentant sinner gazes at a Madonna. Violette blushed and turned pale in quick succession. But her young friend's eyes were so expressive, they implored her forgiveness so eloquently, that the flower girl bestowed her sweetest glance upon him, and being unable as yet to speak to him, began to cover with kisses a small bunch of violets, which she then proceeded to drop on the ground, and which was almost instantly pressed against Georget's lips.

At last the customers went away, and Georget was able to approach.

"How happy I am to see you again, Violette! oh, how long the time has seemed to me while away from you!"

"And to me too, Georget."

"Ah! I suspected you, Violette, I accused you! I know that I was wrong; will you forgive me for thinking you guilty?"

"Yes, I forgive you, for appearances were against me; and even now you have only my word for a proof of my innocence."

"That is enough, and hereafter I want nothing else."

"But I should like right well to force the man who slandered me to tell the truth."

"Let us not talk of that now; I am so happy! I was dying of ennui away from you, dear Violette. If you knew how I love you!"

"Mon Dieu! Georget, I realized that I loved you too, since your desertion caused me so much pain and unhappiness."

"Dear Violette! what joy! you love me, you tell me so! there is no one on earth happier than I am."

"And I am very happy too."

"I am eighteen years old now, Violette, and I can marry you."

"We have time enough, my dear, now that we are sure that we love each other; can we want anything more?"

"We will be married, all the same; you will be my wife, won't you, Violette?"

"What a question! when I refuse to be anybody else's!"

"Ah! it is nice of you to say that!"

"But it is growing dark; it is late, Georget; will you help me to close my booth and carry my flowers away?

As I have been sick and am not very strong yet, I must
not stay out late."

"You are right, you mustn't endanger your health.
Give me all the flowers, all the bunches you have left;
I will carry them, and this tray and the chair."

"Oh, no! I can carry something myself,. Georget."

"Give them all to me, I beg."

"No, monsieur, for then I shall look as if I were lazy."

The two young lovers soon had the booth closed. Then
they walked toward Rue de Crussol, Georget never weary
of gazing at Violette, and she always smiling at Georget.

"So you have changed your lodging, have you?"

"Yes, I live here now, right up at the top; but it is
very pleasant; and then it is a very decent house. I
have a little corner of the courtyard where I keep my
flowers, near a pump; it is always cool there.—Good-
night, Georget."

"What! are we going to part already?"

"You know very well that you can't come up to my
room, Georget, you who are my sweetheart; that wouldn't
be proper."

"Oh! I have no idea of asking you to let me do that,
Violette; but suppose, after you have put your flowers
in the yard, you would take a little walk with me on the
boulevard; we have been together such a short time."

"All right, I will do it; but we mustn't walk long."

"A few minutes, that's all."

Violette went in to arrange her tray and her flowers;
then she returned to Georget, passed her arm through his,

and they walked away, talking together, looking at each other, pressing against each other, happier than the great ones of the earth, happier than the millionaires, happier than all those whom people envy; for true love and youth!—you would seek in vain to find anything superior to these.

Meanwhile the evening advanced, and the two lovers, who had not begun to weary of looking at each other, of squeezing each other's hands and of repeating that they would love each other forever, could not make up their minds to part. When Violette said: "I must go in," Georget replied: "Just a minute more." When he expressed a fear that she was cold, she reassured him by saying that the walk would do her good.

But Chicotin, who was not in love and who was dying of hunger, waited in vain for his friend to join him at the place he had appointed. Weary of waiting, Chicotin went to the flower market, but found no one there. Then he went to Violette's abode, and asked the concierge if the young flower girl had come home; and Madame Lamort informed him that, after putting her flowers in their place, she had gone out on the arm of a very young and comely man, saying that she would soon return.

Chicotin sat down on a carriage stone, muttering:

"For a convalescent, Mamzelle Violette is very imprudent, to walk about so long after dark."

"That's what I told them!" cried the concierge. "But as Mirontaine barked at that moment, I guess they didn't hear me."

Chicotin had been on sentry duty for half an hour, when Monsieur de Roncherolle, on his way to his room, spied him and said:

"What are you doing here, my boy?"

"I am waiting for my friend Georget, who is walking with Mamzelle Violette, bourgeois."

"Ah! so this Georget is——".

"The fellow who loves her so dearly, who suspected her of having gone wrong, and who came to-day to beg her pardon, because I went to Monsieur Malberg, your friend's, at Nogent, where he lives——"

"To Monsieur Malberg's; you mean the friend who came to see me on Rue de Bretagne?"

"Yes, bourgeois."

"And who was the cause of my moving!—Look you, Chicotin, if you take it into your head to mention me to your friend again, and to tell him that I live in this house, I warn you that I will pull your ears so that you can cover your nose with them!"

"Never fear, bourgeois; I won't mention you; I have no desire to force you to move again."

"You will do well."

"Ah! here are the lovers coming back at last!"

"Then I will go up to my room."

"And I am going to supper! I am not sorry for that."

XL

MORE BOUQUETS

Six days after that evening, Monsieur de Brévanne returned to his rooms in Paris, bringing Georget and Pongo. Worthy Mère Brunoy, who enjoyed the country immensely and who was beginning to understand that her son was becoming reasonable enough to be able to do without her, had asked permission to remain at Nogent, where Georget had promised to go to see her twice a week.

On the day following his return to Paris, Monsieur de Brévanne went to see Violette and said to her:

"My dear child, I am going to give you an errand to do; it is not a dangerous one, for it is a bona fide lady to whom I am sending you."

"Oh! monsieur, when it's you who send me, I will go wherever you please."

"Well, it is another bouquet for you to carry; you will make a very fine one, and go to Madame de Grangeville's, Rue Fontaine-Saint-Georges, number 19."

"Very well, monsieur."

"That is not all; you will take the bouquet up yourself, and ask to be allowed to hand it to the lady in person—in person, you understand; I shall be very glad

to have her see you. It is probable that she will ask
you from whom you come, and you will tell her that you
do not know, that it was a gentleman who sent you on
the errand, with many compliments from him. If she
asks you to describe him, be very careful not to draw
my portrait— wait a moment,"—and the count, trying to
recall the features of Monsieur de Merval, continued:
" You will tell her that it was a gentleman, stylishly
dressed, of distinguished bearing, and medium height;
who is no longer young, but who has almost the look of a
young man; of light complexion, with rather a red face.
—Can you remember all that, Violette? "

" I have not lost a word, monsieur."

" I am teaching you to lie, but under these circumstances I assure you that it is excusable. Try to talk a
little with the lady, but be very careful never to mention
my name in the conversation, and not to say that you
have been at Nogent."

" Very good, monsieur."

" If this lady should ask you any questions about
yourself, about your family, say simply that you are
an abandoned child, that you have never known your
parents."

" When I say that, I shall not lie, monsieur."

" No; but say nothing more, do not mention the embroidered handkerchief, and above all things, do not
mention the name of Evelina de Paulausky. Be sure, my
poor girl, that I give you all these instructions in your
own interest."

"Oh! I have no doubt of that, monsieur; but,—forgive me for this question—did this lady ever know my mother?"

"It may be that through her we may succeed in finding her; but to obtain that result, it is necessary that she should know nothing at first of any of the peculiar facts concerning you; that will seem to you most extraordinary, no doubt, my child; but have confidence in me, and if you still have a mother, I will restore her to you, yes, I will restore her to you."

"Then you are not sure that she is still alive, monsieur?"

The count was silent for a moment, then replied:

"No, no; but go and deliver this bouquet, Violette, and forget nothing of what I have enjoined upon you. On your way back from Madame de Grangeville, come to my rooms, and tell me the result of your errand."

The count walked away. The young flower girl hastily made a bouquet of the freshest and prettiest flowers in her stock. Then she set out for Rue Fontaine-Saint-Georges, greatly surprised at the emotion which she felt at having so simple an errand to do. But the injunctions of Georget's protector led her to think that the person to whom she was going knew the secret of her birth, and she said to herself that it was that idea that made her heart beat so fast.

"Madame," said Mademoiselle Lizida, opening the door of the small salon where her mistress was sitting, "there is someone here with a bouquet for you."

"A bouquet! somebody has sent me a bouquet?"

"Yes, madame."

"Well, if it's that Savoyard again, from Monsieur de Roncherolle, I don't propose to receive him; send him away, him and his bouquet; I don't propose to have any further relations with his master. Bah! that man disgusts me!"

"Oh! it isn't the messenger this time, madame; it's a very pretty young girl, really very pretty, and the bouquet is magnificent. I am very sure that it comes from someone else."

"Do you think so? that makes a difference; show the girl in."

Violette was ushered into Madame de Grangeville's presence; the flower girl was agitated, trembling, and her cheeks were a brilliant scarlet; but that emotion simply added to her beauty, and the baroness at sight of her, exclaimed:

"Why, the girl is very pretty, really! very pretty, indeed!"

Violette made a curtsy and offered her bouquet.

"You have brought me a bouquet, mademoiselle?"

"Yes, madame."

"It is very handsome, very tasteful.—But from whom do you come? for I must know to whom I am indebted for this attention."

"I do not know, madame."

"You don't know? Ah! you mean that you were told to keep it secret. But, you know, between women such

Copyright 1904 by G Barrie & Sons

G FRAIPONT.

secrets should be transparent. Come, my girl—why, she is really very pretty indeed!—who sends you? For of course you did not come here of your own motion."

"Madame, it was a gentleman who came to me at my place, at my booth."

"Ah! so you are——"

"A flower girl, madame."

"And where is your booth? on Rue de la Paix?"

"No, madame, on Boulevard Saint-Martin, near the Château d'Eau; I sell out of doors."

"Poor girl! an open air flower girl! what a pity, with that pretty face!—But to return to our subject: a gentleman came to you and told you to bring this bouquet?"

"Yes, madame."

"And he gave you no other message for me?"

"No, madame—that is to say, he said: 'You will also offer the lady many compliments from me!'"

"From him? What sort of looking man was he? Did he walk with difficulty, leaning on a cane?"

"No, madame, this gentleman had no cane, and he walked very well."

"So much the better! so much the better! you set my mind at rest.—About how old was this stranger?"

"Why, he is no longer young, madame; and still he has the appearance and manners of a young man."

"Ah! very good; I am on the track; he is a very stylish, well-dressed man, is he not?"

"Yes, madame, he was very well-dressed; and his manner was very distinguished."

" What is the color of his hair ? "

" He is light-haired, with a rather red face."

" Enough! enough! I know perfectly now who it is."

And Madame de Grangeville, leaning toward her maid, who was behind her chair, said in an undertone:

" It is he again, I was sure of it; it is Monsieur de Merval.—Well, what are you looking at so attentively, Lizida ? "

" I was looking at this girl, madame, and the more I look at her—why, it is perfectly amazing! is it possible that you haven't noticed it, madame ? "

" Noticed what, pray ? "

" This pretty flower girl—for she is pretty, is she not, madame ? "

" Yes, very pretty indeed; well ? "

" Why, madame, she looks like you, yes, she looks very much like you! "

" Do you think so?—Yes, there is in fact something in her features, in her mouth—but I used to be prettier than she is! "

Violette blushed, and was sorely embarrassed when she saw that the mistress and the maid were staring at her. As they said nothing more to her, she curtsied again and murmured:

" Has madame any further orders for me? "

" No, mademoiselle.—By the way, I will ask you, if you see this gentleman again, to thank him a thousand times for me, and to tell him, that, in spite of the mystery in which he envelops himself, I recognize him none the less, and I should be very glad to see him, in order to express in person all my gratitude; can you remember all that, my girl?"

"Oh! yes, madame, I have a good memory; I shan't forget anything, I promise you."

"Very good.—It is certain that there is a something about you—how old are you?"

"Nineteen, madame."

"Nineteen!"

Madame de Grangeville seemed struck by that answer; she reflected a moment, then answered:

"What! you are nineteen years old? You don't look it. Have you many brothers and sisters?"

"No, madame, I am alone."

"Aha! and your mother sells flowers as you do, no doubt?"

"My mother—I don't know her, madame; I am a— an abandoned child."

Madame de Grangeville could not control an impulsive movement; but she soon recovered herself, saying:

"How foolish I am! There are very many things in the world which resemble one another in some details. The most amusing part of this is that this girl looks so much like me; it is a mere freak of chance, for the other, if she's alive, must be in the depths of Picardie."

Then, turning toward the girl, the baroness continued, aloud:

"Well, my child, you may go.—But, perhaps you have not been paid, and you are waiting——"

"Yes, I am paid, madame; I was not waiting for anything but to be dismissed."

"She talks very well.—Go then, and do not forget what I told you to say to Monsieur de Merval."

"Monsieur de——?"

"How thoughtless I am, to mention his name! I meant to say, the gentleman who sent you to bring this bouquet to me."

"I shall not forget anything, madame."

Violette took her leave, deeply moved by the interview she had had with the lady, and wondering what there was in that commonplace conversation to cause her such emotion. She went at once to the count's and found him impatiently awaiting her; he made her repeat the conversation she had had with Madame de Grangeville, to the slightest detail.

"What do you think of that lady?" enquired Monsieur de Brévanne, when Violette had told him everything.

"I think that she is very good-looking, that is to say, she must have been good-looking; her features are worn now—she is not young, is she, monsieur?"

"No, certainly not. Was she pleasant and affable with you?"

"Yes, monsieur, she was very polite; but her manner was rather haughty."

"Very well, my child, go back to your flowers; next week you shall carry another bouquet to Madame de Grangeville."

"Very good, monsieur; and must I let her think that that one too comes from a Monsieur de Merval? For she is fully persuaded that it was a gentleman of that name who sent me to her."

"You must be very careful not to undeceive her."

On leaving the count, the young flower girl met Georget, whom she told what she had been doing, and who walked with her to her booth, saying:

"We have come back to Paris. Monsieur Malberg gives me writing and figuring to do and sends me on errands; but that won't prevent me from seeing you every day. I am so happy! every morning I will come to the boulevard to bid you good-morning, and in the evening I will come to help you carry home your flowers."

"I agree to that, Georget, but only on condition that it doesn't interfere with your work. I haven't told you, but I believe that Monsieur Malberg will help me find my family."

"Your family! what need of them have you now? Don't I fill the place of your family?"

"But, Georget, a person is always very glad to have a family, and if I still had a mother——"

"Your mother! as she abandoned you, it must have been that she didn't love you."

"Who can tell? Perhaps she was compelled to."

"And if your family should prove to be rich, they wouldn't be willing that I should be your husband perhaps. Look you, Violette, I prefer that you shouldn't find anybody."

" What a child you are, Georget ! "

" There is someone that I would like to find, myself !
But I would treat him as he deserves to be treated ! "

" Whom are you talking about, Georget ? "

" That Monsieur Jéricourt, who laid that trap for you,
and then went about saying——"

" I beg you, Georget, let us say no more about that.
You are convinced that I am not guilty, aren't you ? "

" Oh ! can you ask me that, Violette ? "

" Well, my dear, don't think any more about that man ;
I don't want you to find him, do you understand ? And
if anything should happen to you, think of your mother,
and of me. Would you like to kill us with grief ? Besides, I never see him now, he never passes my booth."

" And he does well ! for if I should see him pass—
But I don't know where he keeps himself now ; no one
ever sees him anywhere ; Chicotin isn't any luckier than
I am. I went to his lodgings, but he had moved ; no one
knows where he lives now ; he must have left the quarter."

" I beg of you, Georget, do not look for that man any
more ; if you do, you will make me very unhappy. Do
you think that I haven't had sorrow enough ? "

" I am done, mamzelle ; I will obey you. But you see,
I am past eighteen now, I am no longer a child, and I
don't propose that anyone shall say anything about you ! "

A month passed, during which Violette went every
week to take a bouquet to Madame de Grangeville, who
was still persuaded that it was Monsieur de Merval to
whom she owed that attention. When the young flower

girl returned from Rue Fontaine-Saint-Georges, Monsieur de Brévanne inquired particularly what had taken place between her and Madame de Grangeville; he insisted that the young girl should repeat the most trivial words of their conversation. He did not understand how the baroness could fail to show more interest in Violette, more curiosity to know something about her; that indifference surprised him, for it seemed to him that a secret voice must have spoken to the baroness's heart, and led her to think that the girl was her child.

One morning, Monsieur de Brévanne betook himself to Boulevard du Château d'Eau, with the purpose of sending Violette to Madame de Grangeville again; but the flower girl was not in her place. Fearing that she might be sick, the count was about to return home, in order to send Georget to inquire for Violette, when, as he turned, he saw her approaching with her flowers.

"You thought that I was lazy, did you not, monsieur?" said Violette as she curtsied to the count, "but don't scold me, it isn't that."

"In the first place, my child, I never think anything bad of you; but I was afraid that you might not be feeling well."

"Oh, no! monsieur, it isn't I who am sick; it's a poor gentleman—if you only knew how he suffers! it makes one's heart ache!"

"Is it some one whom you know?"

"It is a neighbor of mine, a gentleman who lives in the same house, just below me, and who, when I was sick

some time ago, was kind enough to come up to see me, to
take an interest in me, and to order a medicine which
cured me; and then he came sometimes to sit with me;
so that it is quite natural now that I should try to be of
some use to him, is it not, monsieur?"

"Certainly, and no one could blame you for it, my
child."

"Besides that, I have an idea that this gentleman—oh!
he won't admit it, but I am inclined to think that he is
short of money, and that he can't supply himself with all
that he needs to cure himself."

"Do you think so? But, if he is a worthy man, if he
deserves, as you say, to be aided, we will come to his
assistance."

"Oh! that won't be easy, I tell you, monsieur; for,
you see, he is very, very proud, and won't allow anyone
to lend him money. I was unfortunate enough last night
to propose to go and order a prescription which the
doctor had left for him. He said to me: 'How are you
going to pay for it? I haven't given you any money.'
I answered: 'Dear me! that doesn't make any difference;
I have some money, and you can pay me back.'—At that,
he shouted at me almost angrily: 'I don't propose to
have anyone lend me money! I haven't asked you for it,
I don't need any medicine, and I won't have it, I won't
have anything!'—And it isn't possible to make him listen
to reason. Aside from that, he is very good-natured,
and whenever his pain grows a little less, he always has
something amusing to say. The fact is, that he has a

very *comme il faut* manner, like you, monsieur; and perhaps he was once rich like you."

" What is the matter with him?"

" Gout, so he says."

" Gout?—and his name—do you know his name?"

" Yes, his name is Monsieur de Roncherolle."

"'Roncherolle!"

The count repeated the name with such evident surprise and agitation that the girl was terrified.

" What is the matter, monsieur?" she stammered; " does that name also recall painful memories? Do you know my unfortunate neighbor?"

" Yes, yes, my child, I do know him; but be very careful not to speak to him of me, not to mention my name before him, for you would simply aggravate his trouble."

" Very well, monsieur, I will be careful.—But, monsieur, does it make you angry that I go to take care of my neighbor when I have time?"

" No, Violette, no, no! on the contrary, devote yourself to this Monsieur de Roncherolle; far from blaming you for it, I urge you to do it; it is your duty, for it is always a duty to help one's neighbor. But listen to me: if, while talking, this gentleman should question you about your family,—I mean, concerning what you know as to the manner in which you were given in charge to your nurse,—don't tell him any more than you have told Madame de Grangeville."

" I will remember, monsieur."

" All this must seem very strange to you; but pray believe that it is for your own welfare that I advise you to act thus."

" Oh! you tell me to do it, monsieur, and that is enough for me; have I not placed all my confidence in you? "

" I will reward you for it, my child. Au revoir."

" Are you going, monsieur? have you no orders for me? don't you want me to carry a bouquet to Madame de Grangeville to-day? "

" No, no; it is better that you should make haste to sell your flowers and return to do what you can for Monsieur de Roncherolle. Madame de Grangeville can do without flowers, but the man who is suffering cannot do without help."

The count left the young flower girl and returned home deep in thought, saying to himself:

" I see the finger of Providence in all this. Now this girl passes a part of each day with her father—and her mother, and she does not know them! Ought I to make them known to her? Are they worthy of her affection, of her love?—Guide me, oh God, and show me where my duty lies."

XLI

A NEW WAY OF OBTAINING REVENGE

The weather was cold and dull, and a fall of snow ending in rain added to the discomfort of a penetrating dampness. But the fireplace of the small room in which Roncherolle lay contained only two small sticks, which had been laid near together, but which imparted no heat to the room.

Roncherolle was suffering horribly with his gout, and as he was alone, he did not hesitate to complain in very energetic fashion; despite his resolutions to be philosophical, pain sometimes won the victory over his courage; but when Violette was with him he did his utmost to conceal his suffering.

The young girl came in; she held in one hand a teapot, in the other a cup and a sugar-bowl full of sugar; she approached the invalid and placed all those objects on the table beside his bed.

" Here I am, monsieur; I'm a little late this morning, perhaps, but I wanted to make this tea that was ordered for you, before I came down; I have brought it with me; it's scalding hot, and you must drink it."

Roncherolle dissembled his agony and tried to smile at Violette, as he said to her:

"How good you are, my child! how kind to a person whom you hardly know, and who has no claim upon your interest!"

"No claim! well, upon my word! when I was sick, didn't you come to see me? And you didn't know me at all! I should be very ungrateful if I did not do for you what you did for me."

"But such a difference; in the first place, you were hardly sick at all; and then it is always a pleasure to make oneself useful to a young lady; whereas a sick old man is not an agreeable object."

"Oh, yes! you are very agreeable, when you are not in too much pain; you always have stories and adventures to tell us.—But how are you feeling this morning?"

"Still about the same; a little better, perhaps."

"No, I see by your face that you suffered terribly during the night, that you are suffering still!"

"No; when you are here, I suffer less."

"Very well; then you should let me pass the night with you, as I wanted to."

"God forbid that you should go without sleep on my account, and be sick again perhaps. I won't have it; and besides, my dear neighbor, there's nothing to be done for the disease that I have—one simply must know how to suffer."

"I don't believe that myself; there must be remedies for everything. Drink this now. Here, sweeten it to suit yourself."

"This is strange; this sugar-bowl is full, and yet I remember that there were only a few pieces in it yesterday."

Violette turned her face away as she replied:

"Oh! you were—you had some more—in a paper, and I put it with the other."

Roncherolle looked at the girl, but she was busily engaged in putting the room in order.—Chicotin arrived at that moment, with a red nose, and beating his hands together.

"Good-morning, bourgeois and the company," he cried. "How does it go this morning, bourgeois?"

"Not very well, my boy."

"Mère Lamort told me to tell you that she couldn't come up this morning; Mirontaine has swallowed a bone that stuck in his throat, so that he ain't able to bark and watch the door."

"Oh! bless my soul! we don't need the concierge," said Violette; "am I not here?"

"But you have your business that demands your attention, my child," said Roncherolle, "and I don't propose that you shall neglect your business for me; in fact, it's already late, I think, and you should be at your stand."

"No, monsieur, it isn't late; and anyway this isn't a market day, and in such weather as this, I am in no hurry; I shouldn't sell anything, for there won't be anyone out of doors."

"It's beastly weather, that's true enough!" cried Chicotin; "and cold! why, my nose and fingers are frozen stiff. But it ain't very warm in your room either, bourgeois; *bigre!* it's just the same as being on the boulevard."

"Well, stir up the fire, put on some wood."

"I ask nothing better."

Chicotin looked in all directions, then went into the outer room, and returned in a moment, saying:

"There's one little difficulty, bourgeois, and that is that I don't find any wood; the wood pile seems to have gone up in smoke."

"Already! the devil! the wood seems to go faster than the sugar!"

"Oh! that's easy to understand—it's dearer, because —look you, bourgeois, here's a comparison: for fifteen sous, you get three or four sticks of wood; they're bigger than a pound of sugar, to be sure, but they're very soon burned up; in one day they're all gone; whereas, with a pound of sugar, you've got something to lap and sip for a long while!"

"I'll do without fire," said Roncherolle. "Lying in bed, I don't need it, and my little neighbor is going away."

"What a bungling fellow you are, Chicotin!" said Violette to the young messenger, in an undertone; "you shouldn't have said anything, but when you saw that there wasn't any wood in the other room, you should have gone up to my room; you would have found some there. You know that Monsieur de Roncherolle isn't willing that anybody should lend him anything, so we must help him without letting him suspect it; and I don't propose that he shall stay without a fire."

"That is true, I am an idiot!" muttered Chicotin, shaking his head; "but bless my soul! I couldn't guess all that. Never mind, don't worry, I'll fix it all right; I'll find some way to make a fire." .

"Monsieur," said the girl, returning to the invalid, "if I remember right, the doctor who came to see you yesterday prescribed medicine for your gout."

"Doctors don't know of any remedy for this disease, my neighbor; several of them have told me this themselves when talking with me."

"Nonsense! I have been told of several people who were entirely cured; and I remember now—it was syrup of *Boubée* that he told you to take."

"That is quite possible."

"I beg you, monsieur, take some of it; even if it should do nothing but lessen the pain, would that not be a great gain?"

"As you insist upon it, I will take some."

"If you are willing, monsieur, I won't stay long in my booth to-day, and I will bring you some in a little while when I come home."

"No, no, my little neighbor, I won't have it; for you never tell me the price of things; you manage so that they cost me almost nothing. But I don't propose to have that, and I shall be angry if you go on acting in that way; I shall be obliged to deprive myself of the pleasure of seeing you."

"Oh! it wouldn't do any good for you to forbid me to come, monsieur; I should come all the same!"

Violette said this with such heartfelt earnestness that Roncherolle felt the tears gather in his eyes. He pressed the girl's hand and replied in a cheerful tone:

"I will obey you, neighbor; come, Chicotin, my groom, come here."

"Here I am, bourgeois."

"Go to the druggist's on the corner of the boulevard, and ask for some syrup of Boubée. Will you remember that name?"

"I should say so; it isn't hard to remember. Syrup of Poupée."

"Boubée, you idiot! not Poupée."

"Oh! very good."

"Wait; I prefer to write it for you."

"On the whole, that will be better; my tongue might slip again."

"Here you are; and take that two-franc piece there —upon my table; I am inclined to believe that that will be enough."

"Let us hope so! a paltry syrup—that can't cost so much as that; for two francs you could get a lot of molasses.—I will go right away, bourgeois."

"Aren't you going to your stand, my little neighbor?" Roncherolle asked Violette, who was stooping in front of the fire, trying to make the two sticks burn by putting under them all the old papers that were lying about the room.

"In a minute, neighbor; I will wait until Chicotin comes back."

" And your love-affairs, my child, how do they come
on? You are fully reconciled with your young lover now,
I hope?"

" Yes, monsieur. Oh! Georget loves me dearly; he
comes to see me every day at my booth, and I am very
happy, except when he frightens me."

" What's that? your lover frightens you?"

" You will understand, monsieur; Georget has never
forgotten the abominable remarks that that Monsieur
Jéricourt made about me, and the trap he led me into;
but, monsieur, you don't know—Georget says that he will
kill Monsieur Jéricourt."

" He is right; he is a fine fellow; in his place, I
would do the same."

" But I don't want him to fight; for, after all, monsieur, the man who is in the right doesn't always win;
and if Georget were killed, I should be very unhappy."

" You are right; that boy must not take the risk; he
is so young—eighteen, did you tell me?"

" Yes, monsieur."

" Then he probably doesn't know anything about the
sword or the pistol?"

" Nothing at all; he would be killed instantly."

" Patience, my little neighbor. Corbleu! if only I
could get well!—But I hear Chicotin, I believe."

The young messenger returned with a sheepish expression, holding the two-franc piece in his hand.

" Well, where is the syrup, Chicotin?" asked Roncherolle.

" The syrup is at the druggist's, monsieur."

" What do you mean by that?"

" I mean that it's an outrage! Just fancy that a little bottle no bigger than my wrist costs twelve francs!"

" Twelve francs?"

" Yes, monsieur, syrup of Poupée twelve francs, no less; it wasn't any use for me to say: ' Put me up forty sous' worth in a little pomade box'; he laughed in my face and told me they didn't sell it at retail; he showed me a bottle, all sealed, with the price on it. Then I said: ' If the gout can only be cured at that price, only rich people can be cured!' —' Only rich people have the gout,' said the clerk. I say, bourgeois, that's nonsense, ain't it? For it seems to me that you're none too well fixed."

Violette nudged Chicotin, saying in an undertone:

" You ought to have said that the syrup wasn't ready, and I would have gone out and bought it and paid for it without letting Monsieur de Roncherolle know the price."

" He would have found it out all the same, mamzelle, for the price is pasted on the bottle; it wouldn't have been possible to deceive him, and how he would have sworn then!"

Roncherolle had dropped his head on the pillow, and said nothing more. Chicotin handed him the two-franc piece, saying:

" Shall I buy anything else with this, bourgeois?"

" You may buy some wood, my boy, and make a fire; but not until evening; for my little neighbor comes to sit with me in the evening, and I don't want her to freeze in my room.—Now leave me, my children; I don't want anything more, and I am going to try to sleep."

Violette pressed the invalid's hand and went out, with a feeling of oppression at her heart; Chicotin followed her, muttering:

"Poor dear man, not to be able to buy what might cure him; it ain't very gay here; but never mind, I will come back soon and see if he wants something else that don't cost so much."

"And you won't spend his two francs, will you, Chicotin? you must get some wood in my room."

"Yes, mamzelle, but what shall I do with his money? I can't give it back to him."

"Keep it; it will serve to buy something else which may be dearer still; and you mustn't tell him, as you did to-day. To think of his being without a fire, in such cold weather, and when he is suffering so! for to-day I could see on his face the efforts he made to conceal his suffering; why, it makes me want to cry!"

"After all, Mamzelle Violette, you mustn't feel so bad for somebody who ain't anything to you."

"Oh! he is so wretched, without relations, or friends, sick and poor; and then there are people for whom you feel affection right away; and Georget won't be jealous of him; I feel that I have a sincere affection for him."

"I am going to see if Mirontaine is cured, and if Madame Lamort can go up."

Violette had been at her stand for some time, when Monsieur de Brévanne came there and inquired about her neighbor. The girl gave him an exact description of his plight; she concealed nothing from him, neither his suffering, nor the privations which he was obliged to undergo, nor the pride which made him refuse any assistance in the form of money.

"He has no fire now," said Violette, her eyes wet with tears; "and he isn't willing that we should make him one before evening, because I go to sit with him in the evening, poor man! and he did not have the money to buy something that might perhaps have cured him.— Ah! he is very unfortunate!"

The count listened attentively to the girl's story; Roncherolle's position touched him more than he chose to show. He stood for some time buried in thought, then he said to Violette:

"I would like to judge for myself of this gentleman's plight, of his situation, but I should not want him to see me."

"That is very easy, monsieur; in the first place, Monsieur de Roncherolle never leaves his bed, and a person can stand in the outer room and look into the other without his seeing him; in the second place, he often sleeps, and I am always careful not to wake him."

"Well, I will go this evening, I will go to see you, with Georget."

"Oh! how kind it is of you, monsieur! I am very sure that you will have compassion on my poor neighbor."

"On your account—it is possible.—But not a word concerning me, my child!"

"Oh! I am dumb, monsieur; but I am very glad that you are coming to see my neighbor."

About eight o'clock in the evening, Violette was installed in Roncherolle's room; he had been dozing for some time, and when he woke, his eyes met those of the young girl, who, as she mended her neighbor's linen, glanced at him often to see if he were asleep.

"Really, my dear child," said Roncherolle, "your kindness to me fills me with gratitude, and reconciles me to your sex; for, if I must admit it, I had but a very slight esteem for women."

"Why so, monsieur? have they injured you?"

"Not exactly; but they are responsible for my having injured others, and that amounts to the same thing."

"Why no, monsieur, if they didn't advise you to do it."

"They do not need to advise us to make fools of ourselves; they lead us into it easily enough without that."

"I don't understand, monsieur."

"So much the better for you, my child.—But what are you doing there? God forgive me, I believe that you are patching my rags!"

"Well! I had nothing to do, and I like to be busy; I thought that it wouldn't offend you if I should take a few stitches in your linen."

"Offend me! ah! my dear girl, you are too kind to me; one does not take offence with those who are so kind to them. Ah me! when I think——"

Here Roncherolle paused and heaved a profound sigh. Violette looked up at him and said:

"What are you thinking about, monsieur, that makes you sigh so? You mustn't think of melancholy things when you are sick."

"I am thinking, my dear child, that I might have with me—my own daughter,—who, however, I am sure, would take no better care of me than you do."

"Your daughter! what, monsieur, you have a daughter, and she is not with you when you are ill and suffering!"

"If she is not with me, it is not her fault,—it is mine."

"Ah! then it is you who have sent her away, and she is not in Paris, of course?"

"No, she is not in Paris."

"Why don't you write for her to come, to join you?"

"I don't want to disturb her."

"How old is your daughter?"

"Nineteen."

"Why, that is just my age!"

"Ah! you are nineteen? And what about your parents? I never see them with you. But I remember now, that you told me that you had lost them."

"I never knew my parents, monsieur; I am an abandoned child!"

"Abandoned! is it possible? what a strange coincidence!—Were you abandoned in Paris?"

Violette, remembering the count's injunction, replied hesitatingly:

"Why—I don't know, monsieur; I—I think so."

"Poor child, what a pity! her parents do not realize what a treasure they cast away."

Roncherolle buried his face in his pillow, murmuring:

"But my child—I do not know her; perhaps she too is lovely and good! ah! if I could only find her! But no! why should I wish to? to force her to share my destitution?—No, it is better as it is."

The invalid dropped asleep. Violette was anxiously awaiting that moment, for she had heard noises in the outer room for several moments, and she guessed who it might be. As soon as she was certain that Roncherolle was asleep, she arose and softly opened the door of the other room, where she found Monsieur de Brévanne and Georget.

"My neighbor is asleep; you may come in, monsieur," said Violette to the count.

"You are quite sure that he is asleep, my child?"

"Yes, monsieur. You can tell by listening to him, his breathing is so difficult. Poor man! it seems that he has suffered terribly all day, and he is taking advantage of a little respite from pain, to rest."

"But you were talking just now."

"Yes, monsieur.—Oh! if you knew—he has a daughter, the poor man, and he said that he bitterly regretted not having her with him."

"Oho! he spoke to you of his daughter, did he?"

"Yes, monsieur; can you imagine that she does not come to take care of him, her father, when he is sick?"

"Did he tell you why she was not with him?"

" No, monsieur; he simply said that it was his fault.
—But come in, monsieur; he is sound asleep."

" Yes, I will come in. Stay here, my child, and talk
with Georget; but don't talk too loud."

" No, there's no danger of that, monsieur," said Georget; "we understand each other perfectly well simply
by looking at each other."

The count entered the room occupied by Roncherolle.
A single tallow candle, which was badly in need of snuff-
ing, lighted that room with a dim, uncertain light; it
enabled the visitor, however, to distinguish a cheap wall
paper, torn or lacking altogether in several places; a
window with large cracks, and without curtains, in which
one pane was broken, its place being ill supplied by paper;
two or three pieces of cheap black walnut furniture; a
painted cot, on which was a coarse flock bed and a very
thin mattress; on the mantel, a small mirror in a wooden
frame, and on the hearth two tiny bits of wood, which
were hardly burning.

Everything in that abode indicated poverty and privation; and the cold that one felt there, the wind that one
could hear whistling in all directions, heightened the
melancholy impression which one was certain to feel at
finding an invalid in such a place.

Monsieur de Brévanne noticed and scrutinized everything; then he walked to the bed and gazed at Roncherolle, whose features were more than ever changed by
suffering and want, and who, even in his sleep, seemed
to be struggling with pain.

" The wretched man!" said the count to himself; "is this what the future seemed to promise him? Endowed with every advantage, possessor of a handsome fortune, this is what his passions have brought him to!—It is all over; I can think no more of the vengeance which I was determined to wreak upon him; heaven has undertaken that duty; and besides, I should not have the courage to deprive Violette of her father; I do not know whether men will blame me, but something tells me that the time has come to forgive."

Roncherolle moved in his sleep, and the count instantly left the room and joined the two young sweethearts, who had not found the time long.

" Well, monsieur, you have seen him," said Violette; " is he really the man whom you used to know?"

" Yes, my child; but not a word about my visit!"

" Oh! have no fear, monsieur."

" Come, Georget, let us go."

Georget considered that he had had very little time to talk to Violette; but he dared not make any remark, and took his leave with the count, after exchanging a loving pressure of the hand with his sweetheart.

The next morning, about nine o'clock, Violette was in her neighbor's room once more; he was feeling a little better, and was telling her about a strange dream he had had, when Chicotin arrived, bringing with him a letter, which he handed to Roncherolle.

" For you, bourgeois; it just came, so your concierge told me."

"Who can have written me? I don't know this writing," said Roncherolle, as he broke the seal. But in an instant, he uttered a cry of surprise.

"My children, you could never guess what this letter contains; listen.

"'Monsieur:

"'One of your debtors, Monsieur de Juvigny, has instructed me to send you a thousand francs on account of what he owes you.'

"Signed—the devil take me if I can read it—Dubois or Dubosc.—But the thousand-franc note is inside all right; here it is!"

"Ah! what good luck, monsieur! how happy it makes me for you!" said Violette.

"Name of an—excuse me, bourgeois, but I am so glad that I brought that letter for you!"

"Thanks, my friends, thanks, I am trying to remember—Yes, Juvigny did owe me money—I can't remember just how much; but when I inquired about him a few months ago, I was told that he was travelling."

"He must have sent word to this person to send you this sum, monsieur."

"Faith! I hardly expected this restitution. The money arrives most opportunely, but I can't get over my surprise!"

"You see, monsieur, that I told you that your dream meant good luck."

"You can buy all the syrup of Poupée that you want now, bourgeois."

"Yes, my boy, and my little neighbor will be kind enough to do that for me, and change this note. Here, my dear, is the note, here's the thousand francs which seems to have fallen from heaven!"

"Ah! I have a strong suspicion where it fell from, myself!" thought Violette as she left the room.

XLII

THE PIE

Ten days after the receipt of the letter containing the thousand francs, Roncherolle was walking on the boulevard, alert and active, feeling not a trace of his gout, and wrapped in a warm, stylish overcoat, with a new hat on his head, patent leather shoes on his feet, in a word, dressed with a care and elegance which changed him completely and made him look almost like a young man.

In front of the Gymnase Theatre, Roncherolle felt a hand on his arm, and he turned and recognized his former neighbor, young Alfred de Saint-Arthur.

"Ah! good-morning, my dear monsieur, delighted to meet you!"

" Good-morning, my dear Monsieur de Roncherolle. I can no longer say my neighbor, for you are not my neighbor now. You went off like a bomb without telling me, without leaving me your address; that was very unkind. That idiot of a Beauvinet,—you know, the young man at the hotel,—insisted upon it that you lived at Passage I-don't-know-where. Ah! that was a good one! that was very good!"

" You didn't try to find me at that place?"

" Oh, no! I wasn't taken in by that blockhead of a Beauvinet. I said to myself: ' My neighbor must have had reasons for moving and not leaving his address; such things happen every day, and indeed I think that it may happen to me very soon.'—But I regretted you all the same; on my word of honor I regretted you."

" That is too kind of you."

" But there was someone who regretted you much more than I did. Can't you guess?"

" Faith, no."

" It was Zizi—you know—Zizi Dutaillis."

" Oh, yes! I remember perfectly—a very agreeable little woman."

" Well, you made a conquest of her. Every day she said to me: ' Do find Monsieur de Roncherolle; invite me to dine again with Monsieur de Roncherolle; I want him to teach me other ways of—you know what.' —In fact, I never see her that she doesn't talk about you, and if you were younger and—and—and fresher, I should be jealous of you."

" Thanks, thanks, a thousand times ! "

" By the way, allow me to congratulate you; you walk very well; have you got rid of your gout? "

" For the time; it has held me pretty tight this fall."

" And you have a bearing, a style—that coat you have on is very well-made, very well-cut, and of handsome cloth; is it wadded? "

" As you say."

" On my word of honor ! I don't say it to flatter you, but in that overcoat you look ten years younger ! "

" In that case I am very sorry that I have only one."

" By the way, let me tell you that I have profited by your lessons—you know, the way to drink champagne, —two glasses, one on top of the other, in a plate."

" Yes; well? "

" I have succeeded, I can do it; to be sure, I broke a dozen glasses, but I succeeded; your pupil does you credit."

" I never doubted your ability—to drink champagne."

" And that isn't all: you know my parrot, that I was teaching—the one that led to our becoming acquainted? "

" Yes, I remember him; is he dead? "

" No indeed; he is as well as you or I. But the delightful part of it is that I have succeeded again."

" Really, you have made great progress since we last met."

" My parrot says now what I wanted him to."

" That was ' Good-morning, Monsieur Brillant,' I believe? "

"No, deuce take it! he said that too much! He says
—and only since yesterday, so you see that it isn't an
old story—he says: 'Dutaillis is lovely! applaud, clap
Zizi!'"

"Ah! if he says all that, it's very fine; your friend
must be enchanted."

"I haven't given him to her yet, because it was only
yesterday that he said the whole sentence; and you understand that, before giving him to Zizi, I wanted to be
certain that he wouldn't make a mistake, that he wouldn't
make a slip of the tongue."

"That was decidedly prudent on your part."

"By the way, an idea, a splendid idea has just occurred
to me!"

"The deuce! try to hold on to it."

"You must be kind enough to dine with Zizi and me.
In the first place, you owe us more lessons in champagne
drinking."

"Really, you are very tempting, but——"

"Listen: during the dinner, I will have my parrot
brought in, in—no matter what, I will find something—
and he will deliver his compliment to my wife; you know
we say 'my wife' now in speaking of a mistress, and
she says 'my husband.'"

"I didn't know that, and I confess that I should prefer
anything else."

"And what do you say to my idea about the bird?
Fancy Zizi's surprise when she hears a compliment, and
doesn't know where it comes from!"

" Why yes, that may well be amusing."

" Then it is agreed; we will dine together the day after to-morrow. Yes, two days more, and then I shall be very sure that my parrot won't make a mistake. Just we three will dine together, to laugh as loud as we please, and talk nonsense; and at Bonvalet's as before. You agree, do you not, my dear neighbor? I say ' my dear neighbor ' from habit."

" Excuse me, my dear Saint-Arthur, your invitation is certainly very kind, but——"

" Oh! no buts! Zizi will be so pleased to dine with you again! you can't refuse."

" I accept, but on one condition."

" Well, what is it? Speak; I agree to it in advance."

" Well, it is that your friend, Monsieur Jéricourt, shall also be of the party as before."

" The deuce! you surprise me! you want Jéricourt to be one of us? Why, I thought that you didn't like him."

" I say again, if you wish to have me, have that gentleman too; I have a special reason for wishing to meet him."

" That makes a difference; in that case, I will invite him; he shall be one of us. I have not seen so much of him lately. He lives in the Chaussée d'Antin. He puts on a lot of airs because he has had a play accepted at the Odéon.—But no matter, he will come."

" Don't mention me to him; I fancy that that would make him disinclined to come."

" I will mention nothing but the bird to him."

"What I ask you will not annoy mademoiselle, I hope?"

"Annoy her? why, pray? She will worry Jéricourt, and we will laugh at him.—I may rely upon you now, may I not?"

"Absolutely."

"Until the day after to-morrow then, at half-past five, at Bonvalet's."

"I shall not fail you."

Saint-Arthur shook Roncherolle's hand and left him; Roncherolle continued his walk, but more slowly, like a person too much engrossed to notice what is going on about him.

On the second day thereafter, about five o'clock in the afternoon, Roncherolle, who had taken much pains with his toilet, walked toward the booth of the pretty flower girl of the Château d'Eau.

Violette greeted her neighbor with a pleasant smile, saying:

"Ah! what a pleasure it is to see you like this, monsieur! how well you look! no one would ever suspect that you had been so sick."

"If I have recovered my health, it is due to you, my dear child, due to your nursing, to your pleasant company."

"Oh! monsieur, you forget that syrup which did you so much good, which cured you."

"Perhaps the syrup may have had something to do with it, but you had much more."

"Are you going to walk, monsieur? It is cold, but fine."

"I am going to dine out, my little neighbor; a feast at Monsieur Bonvalet's, nothing less."

"Oh! do be prudent then, monsieur; they say, you know, that with gout you mustn't drink champagne."

"But I no longer have the gout."

"True, but suppose that should bring it back again?"

"We mustn't anticipate misfortunes so far ahead. However, I will be prudent, and in order that I may not forget your advice, I will ask you for a small bunch of violets."

"With pleasure, monsieur.—See, is this one big enough?"

"Quite big enough; be kind enough to fasten it tight into my buttonhole."

"Gladly; there, now it is done, and I promise you that it won't come out.—That is very nice! you look as if you were my true knight now."

"And so I am, my child," replied Roncherolle, emphasizing his words, "and I hope to perform the duties of the post."

"Why, how solemnly you say that!"

"Au revoir, my dear neighbor, au revoir!"

The young flower girl looked after Roncherolle, overcome by an emotion which she could not understand, and still murmuring:

"How he said that! I will bet that he has some purpose in wearing that bouquet in his buttonhole."

Meanwhile, Roncherolle, who did not propose to keep the others waiting, soon arrived at Bonvalet's, where he found the young actress and Saint-Arthur. Mademoiselle Zizi expressed all the pleasure that she felt at renewing her acquaintance with the professor of champagne, and said to him, scrutinizing him from head to foot:

"Why, how fine we are! how coquettish we are! we walk almost without limping, and we have such a *chicarde* air!—you look after yourself, you do, whereas Alfred takes no care of himself at all."

"What's that? I take no care of myself?"

"No, monsieur; your cravats have been wretchedly tied lately, and your trousers don't fit as tight as they used to."

"They are not worn tight now."

"If I want you to wear tight ones, why it seems to me that you ought to adopt my taste.—Ah! what a pretty bunch of violets you have there, old fellow! where did you get that, you old Cupid? From some charmer, I will wager!"

"It is true that I got them from a charming young girl."

"Aha! give us the story; tell us all about it."

"I will tell you about it, but not now; at dessert, with your permission; it will have all the more charm."

"All right, at dessert it is. By the way, so you wanted to dine with Jéricourt, did you? When Alfred told me that, I confess that I was mightily surprised, you agreed so badly the other time. I said to myself: 'There's something underneath this; Monsieur de Roncherolle has invented some practical joke, some farce that he proposes to play on him;' am I right?"

"I don't say no; but don't ask any more questions; I am keeping that also in reserve for the dessert."

"Well, well! it seems that we shall laugh at dessert."

"Yes, yes," said Saint-Arthur with a meaning glance at Roncherolle. "Oh yes! our dinner will be most amusing, and we shall laugh, I trust, at dessert. We shall have some surprises, some unexpected incidents."

"What on earth is that idiot talking about? He assumes a mysterious air. Frefred, I have an idea that you have some gallant attention in store for me—is it true, my adored one?"

"I can't tell you anything; you will see!"

This conversation was interrupted by Jéricourt's arrival. That gentleman seemed surprised at sight of Roncherolle; however, he manifested no annoyance, and saluted the party with a smile.

"Aha! Jéricourt doesn't keep us waiting to-day; that is magnificent!" cried Zizi; "but something extraordinary must have happened to him."

"Nothing has happened to me but the desire to be in your company as soon as possible, fair lady."

"Well! what did I say? that is extraordinary enough!"

While the literary man addressed a few words to the young actress, Saint-Arthur approached Roncherolle and whispered in his ear:

"I have thought of a delightful way to have my bird come in and speak, without being seen."

"Indeed! what is it?"

"A pie—you know, like those they have on the stage; it will be brought in and put on the table, and the parrot will be inside."

"That may be amusing, in truth; but on the stage pasteboard pies may create an illusion; here, on the contrary, seen at such close quarters, I am afraid that it will miss its effect."

"Oh! I anticipated that, and so it will have a genuine pie crust. I gave my orders to Beauvinet, and he is to take the bird to an excellent pastry cook, who is to cover it with the crust; then Beauvinet will bring us the pie."

"That makes a difference; in that case, the illusion will be perfect."

"Isn't it an ingenious plan?"

"But aren't you afraid that your parrot will stifle in the pie?"

"Why so? They are shut up in cages."

"True, but I should say that they have more air there."

"Bah! just for a short time. Besides, I told Beauvinet to tell them to make some little holes on top, so that he may have light, and that we may hear him plainly."

"In that case, everything will be all right."

They took their places at the table. Jéricourt treated Roncherolle with the utmost ceremony; but from time to time, he cast his eyes upon the bunch of violets which the latter wore in his buttonhole, and then a mocking smile played about his lips; but Roncherolle apparently did not notice it.

"The champagne lessons will come with the dessert," said Saint-Arthur, "because they always disarrange the table a bit. We spill the champagne over ourselves, so it is better to wait."

"It is all one to me," said Zizi; "I am quite willing to wait now, for I have fallen violently in love with madeira."

"And monsieur is arranging some lessons even more unique than the last, no doubt?" said Jéricourt, addressing Roncherolle.

"Yes, monsieur; in fact, I am preparing a lesson for you, which, I fancy, you hardly expect."

Meanwhile, after the first course, Saint-Arthur betrayed the liveliest impatience, and kept ringing for the waiter and asking him:

"Has no one come to see me? Isn't there any messenger outside for me?"

"No, monsieur, no one has come."

"The deuce! he is very late!"

"What! are you expecting other guests?" said Jéricourt.

"Yes,—that is to say, I am expecting something for the dinner."

"A surprise he has arranged for me," said Zizi; "I haven't any idea what it is, but I like to think that it will be superb!"

At last the waiter announced:

"Monsieur, there's a man here with a pie."

"Ah! very good! bravo! show him in."

"What! is your surprise a pie?" cried the young woman; "why, that is perfectly ridiculous. I don't like pie at dinner!"

"This one, my dear love, is not like most pies.—Come, Beauvinet, come in!"

The old young man from the lodging house appeared, bringing a very handsome pie, which he held as if it were the keys of a conquered town; he placed it on the table, looked about at everybody with a self-satisfied expression; then pulled his wig over his left ear.

Everybody looked at the pie, which had an inviting aspect. Saint-Arthur seemed overjoyed; he jumped up and down on his chair, exclaiming:

"Ah! I should say that that is the thing!"

"It is a very handsome pie," said Jéricourt. "Where did it come from? Strasbourg?"

"Oh, no! not from so far away."

"Come, Frefred," said Zizi, "if the pie is so delicious, cut into it and let us taste it."

"One moment, my dear love, one moment; it isn't to be cut into like that; I request silence for a moment, and attention."

And the young host, putting his face down to the pie, said in an undertone:

"Dutaillis is lovely.—Come, Coco, come, come!"

"What's this? Alfred is talking to the pie now!" cried Zizi, opening her eyes to their fullest extent.

"Hush, my dear love! hush I say!—Come, Coco—Dutaillis is—go on."

But in vain did they listen and wait; the pie maintained the most profound silence.

"Are you playing proverbs with the pie, my Bibi?"

"Yes, I am playing—that is to say, the pie is going to speak."

"The pie going to speak! ah! I would like right well to hear it, on my word!"

"Just a little patience. I can't understand what the matter is with him; he must have gone to sleep in there.—Coco, Coco—Dutaillis is lovely.—Ah! you won't speak, won't you? I will wake you up."

And Saint-Arthur, taking the huge pie in both hands, began to shake it with all his strength; then he replaced it on the table, saying:

"Will you speak now, you beast?"

While they waited again in silence, Monsieur Beauvinet ventured to blow his nose, which drew down upon his head a stern reprimand from his tenant.

"But whom are you calling a beast, and what is it that's in the pie?" asked Mademoiselle Zizi, beginning to get tired of keeping still for nothing.

"Well, my dear love, it is a parrot, a magnificent parrot, which I have taught to say: ' Dutaillis is lovely! applaud, clap Zizi!'"

"Ah! the poor creature! is it possible? Why, he must be stifled in there; that's why he doesn't speak.—Monsieur de Roncherolle, take the crust off at once."

"Are all the windows closed?" asked Saint-Arthur; "we must look out that he doesn't fly away.—See to it, Beauvinet."

Beauvinet made a strange grimace, but did not stir.

"I have a shrewd idea that he won't fly away;" said Roncherolle, as he ran his knife around the crust of the pie.

"Look out, be careful, don't stick the knife in, or you will cut the bird."

"There's no danger."

At last the upper crust was taken off, and nothing came out of the pie. They all put their heads forward to look inside; but instead of a living bird, they saw only what is always found in a chicken pie: jelly, and the stuffing around the principal piece, on top of which there was a slice of pork.

Saint-Arthur was stupefied; his guests with difficulty restrained their desire to laugh.

"What does this mean, Beauvinet? where is my bird, my parrot? what have you done with him?"

"Your bird is there, monsieur; I did what you told me to: I carried him to the pastry cook, and told him to put him into the pie."

"Ah! you villain! you miserable wretch! how could you fail to understand me? I told you that I only wanted the crust put around him."

"Well, there is nothing but crust around him."

"And I added: 'You must have holes made in the top to give him air, so that we may hear him plainly.'"

" I understood: ' So that we may smell him plainly ; ' *
and the pastry cook said: ' I never make holes in my
pies ; your parrot will be a little tough, but I'll just lard
him and stuff him, so that no one will ever know what
it is.' "

At that point, roars of laughter from Zizi, Roncherolle
and Jéricourt made it impossible to hear the groans and
lamentations of Alfred, who, in a fit of desperation, attempted to throw the pie at Beauvinet's head ; but he
was prevented, and Roncherolle said to him :

" As the harm is done, we must make the best of it ;
as I presume that no one here has ever eaten parrot pie,
I suggest that we taste it."

" Yes, let us taste it," said Zizi. " I will tell this story
at the theatre, and my comrades will have a good laugh
at it."

" It doesn't make me laugh ! the result of such long-
continued toil ; and just at the moment when I had
finished his education, and when he began to talk so
famously ! "

" Will you have a little piece, Saint-Arthur ? "

" I? never ! but yes—just a taste.—That rascally
pastry cook ! he was quite right to say that no one would
know what it was ; but he will have to give me back the
feathers, at least."

" Pouah ! how nasty it is ! " said Zizi, pushing her
plate away. " So tough that you can't chew it."

---

* I said : ' pour qu'on l'entende bien.'
I understood: ' pour qu'on le sente bien.'

"And a certain flavor which is not exactly agreeable," said Jéricourt. "The pastry cook did not disguise it quite enough."

"Here, take all this away," said Roncherolle, handing the plate with the pie to Beauvinet; "and for your punishment, eat it!"

"Yes, clear out with it, you stupid beast!" cried Saint-Arthur. "Off with you, and if I wasn't holding myself back—What an ass he is! I am sure that if one should tell him to take a dog to the pastry-cook he would have it made into a pie."

Beauvinet took the pie under his arm, and angrily pulled his wig over his right ear, grumbling: "They don't know what they want; I do what they tell me to, and they ain't satisfied! Let them make their pies themselves after this."

XLIII

A DUEL

The adventure of the pie amused the guests mightily; Saint-Arthur alone did not share his friends' gayety; at every mouthful that he swallowed, he muttered:

"My poor parrot! my poor Coco! how prettily he said: 'Dutaillis is lovely!'—What a misfortune!—'Applaud, clap Zizi!'—I shall never be consoled."

"You are going to begin by being consoled right away," said the young actress; "and don't bore us any longer with your complaints. Don't you see that the story of your pie is a hundred times better and funnier than your bird would have been? But here comes the dessert. I want some champagne now, and I want my good friend Roncherolle to keep his promise to us."

"Monsieur is going to begin his exercises!" said Jéricourt ironically. "Let us see if it is the same thing as at Nicolet's: worse and worse and more of it."

"We will do our utmost to satisfy monsieur," replied Roncherolle, emptying a glass of champagne.

"But first of all," said Zizi, "as I am rather inquisitive, I want to hear the story of that little bunch of violets that you promised me."

"Ah! so he has stories too!" muttered the literary man; "sapristi! we are going to have a deal of entertainment!"

"Perhaps you will have much more than you expect, monsieur," replied Roncherolle, with a meaning glance at Jéricourt. "But I begin—this little bunch of violets I got from a flower girl,—nothing more commonplace than that, eh? But what is less commonplace is that this young flower girl, who is remarkably pretty, is as virtuous and respectable as she is pretty. Now, this is what happened to her last summer: a young man of the world, a dandy, who, I believe, claims to be a literary man, saw the charming flower girl and found her to his liking; he made such speeches to her as all young men make to

pretty girls—thus far there was nothing that was not
perfectly natural."

"I say!" cried Saint-Arthur; "why, that's like Jéricourt and——"

"Pray let monsieur finish!" said Jéricourt, who had
become very attentive within a few seconds.

"But, as I was saying, the pretty flower girl, who is
virtuous and who, moreover, is in love with a handsome
young fellow, did not listen to our dandy's suggestions,
but received them very coldly. What does he do to
triumph over the girl? He sends a man to order and pay
for a very handsome bouquet, with a request to the flower
girl to carry it herself to a lady whose address he gives
her, informing her that that lady will have other orders
for her. The girl falls into the snare—for you will guess
that she was sent to the gallant himself, who had told
his concierge to allow the flower girl to go up to his
room."

"Why, this is strange, it resembles——"

"Hold your tongue, Frefred! this story interests me
immensely."

Jéricourt did not utter a word, but he had become very
pale. Roncherolle continued his narrative, with his eyes
still fastened upon him.

"Behold then our flower girl in the young man's room,
which she had entered without suspicion, for a woman
had opened the door. But soon he who has been per-
secuting her with his addresses appears; he is alone with
her, he no longer conceals his purpose to triumph over

her resistance; the girl sees her danger, summons all
her courage, and resists so effectively that the enterpris-
ing gentleman receives upon his face the marks of that
stout defence—indeed, they have not altogether disappeared yet; he is obliged to let a woman who defends
herself so well go her way. You will assume that that
was the end of it all; and indeed, it should have been;
but no, because that girl was virtuous, because she did
not choose to cease to be virtuous, because she had given
her heart to another, the gentleman in question deemed
it becoming to proclaim everywhere that the pretty flower
girl had been his mistress, that she had come to his room
of her own free will,—in short, that she was an abandoned
girl; he dishonored her in the eyes of all those who loved
her. I say that that is dastardly, infamous! and do not
you think that so much lying and slander deserve to be
punished?"

Zizi said nothing because she had guessed the truth;
Jéricourt bit his lips and also held his peace; but Frefred
exclaimed:

"This is strange—your story—one would say—where
does your pretty flower girl stand?"

"Near here, on Boulevard du Château d'Eau; you
know her perfectly well."

"What! is it Violette?"

"It is Violette."

"Why, in that case, the young man who pretends to
have had her favors—is——"

"Just so; it is monsieur."

Thereupon Jéricourt felt called upon to draw himself up and assume an impertinent tone.

"Monsieur," said he to Roncherolle, "I do not understand all the absurd stories and fairy-tales which you have been telling us, and which have neither head nor tail; but what seems even more inconceivable is that a man of your age should pose as the knight of flower girls!"

"A man of my age, monsieur, knows the world well enough to distinguish the false from the true; and when one can avenge a woman who has been shamelessly defamed by a conceited coxcomb, age makes no difference, monsieur, as I hope to prove to your satisfaction."

"Really, I am very condescending to answer you!" retorted Jéricourt, throwing himself back and swinging his legs. "Be off with you, monsieur; leave me in peace."

"I will be off, monsieur, but with you, I hope."

"Oh! that would be amusing! Faith, my dear monsieur, lose your temper if you choose, but I will not fight for a flower girl."

"Well! will you fight for this, monsieur?"

As he spoke, Roncherolle, who had left his seat and walked toward Jéricourt, struck him across the face with his glove.

The young man leaped from his chair, his face became livid, and he seemed to contemplate rushing upon Roncherolle; but the latter maintained such a calm and impassive attitude, while holding the prongs of a fork toward his adversary to keep him at a respectful distance, that Jéricourt contented himself with saying in a voice choked with wrath:

"That insult will cost you dear, monsieur!"

"I shall be enchanted to find out whether that is so, monsieur; and I propose that we finish this matter not later than to-morrow morning."

"Yes, monsieur; to-morrow, at nine o'clock in the morning, I will be in the woods, near Porte Saint-Mandé."

"I will be there at that time."

"Saint-Arthur, you witnessed the insult, you must be my second."

"I, your second; why, I don't know if——"

"Be kind enough to have two seconds," said Roncherolle, "for I shall bring two."

"Until to-morrow, monsieur; Saint-Arthur, be at my rooms before eight o'clock."

Jéricourt seized his hat and rushed from the room like a madman, without saluting anybody.

The young actress did not think of laughing, she was deeply impressed by all that had happened. As for Alfred, he turned white, red and yellow by turns, and seemed to be inclined to weep.

"My dear friends," said Roncherolle, resuming his seat at the table, "I am truly sorry to have disturbed the end of your dinner thus. But what would you have? I have been waiting for a long time for an opportunity to settle affairs with this fellow Jéricourt."

"Then you are certain that the pretty flower girl has been slandered?" said Zizi.

" Perfectly sure. However, this duel will be the judgment of God. Let us drink to the triumph of the truth."

" I am not thirsty any more," faltered Saint-Arthur. " Here I am forced to be a second in a duel! I don't like that at all, for—are your seconds quick-tempered? "

" Not the least in the world; I shall bring two mere boys; you have nothing to fear; your part will be absolutely passive; you will be there only to look on, for there is no possible adjustment of the affair with my adversary."

" Ah! if it's only a matter of looking on, that's different; rely on me."

" Oh! how I wish it were to-morrow noon! " said Zizi. " But now good-night, let us separate; I am no longer in the mood for talking nonsense. I am only a good-for-nothing, Monsieur de Roncherolle, but all the same I will pray to God for you; and who knows? perhaps He will listen to me."

On leaving the restaurant, Roncherolle walked back and forth in front of the theatres on Boulevard du Temple; he knew that Chicotin was particularly devoted to that place, where he often succeeded in obtaining an admission ticket, which he did not sell, but with which he went into the theatre. And in fact Roncherolle had not been walking there ten minutes when he spied the person for whom he was looking.

" Hello! is that you, bourgeois? " cried the young messenger. " Have you been to the play? If you are not going back, make me a present of your check."

Copyright 1906 by G. Barrie & Sons

"No, my boy, I haven't been to the play; but listen carefully to what I am going to say to you, for it is very serious, very important; I need you to-morrow, you must be at my room at eight o'clock at the latest."

"That is easy enough, I will be there. Is that all?"

"No, I also want your friend Georget, Violette's young sweetheart, to come with you; I need him too."

"Is that so? What for, bourgeois?"

"I will tell you both to-morrow, not before; meanwhile, let your friend understand that his future happiness and Violette's are concerned."

"Oh! in that case, never fear; he won't fail to come!"

"But don't mention this to anybody, not even to Violette; it is a secret."

"We won't say a word."

"Are you sure of seeing Georget this evening?"

"Pardi! when he doesn't go to walk with Violette, he is at home; at any rate, he must go home, and I will wait for him."

"Very well, is he still with Monsieur Malberg?"

"Yes, but he sleeps in his own lodgings."

"Don't let him say a word of this to—to Monsieur Malberg."

"Never you fear; indeed, he probably won't see him until after he sees you."

"Until to-morrow then, and both of you."

"We will be there, monsieur."

"By the way, bring a cab with you; don't forget."

"A cab, all right, monsieur."

The next morning at half-past seven, Roncherolle was up and dressed and was cleaning a pair of pistols, which, despite his destitution, he had always kept. At a few minutes before eight, the door was opened softly and Chicotin appeared, accompanied by Georget. The latter, instead of a blouse, wore a short coat buttoned to his chin, and on his head a blue cloth cap of stylish shape; he held himself very erect, and his new costume heightened the attractiveness of his face and the grace of his figure.

Roncherolle could not help admiring the fine appearance of the young man, and he offered him his hand, which Georget took with an air of respect.

"Here we are, bourgeois," said Chicotin; "I hope we haven't kept you waiting; I bring Georget, as you see, and the cab is downstairs."

"That is very good, my boy. Monsieur Georget, I thank you for coming here at my invitation; when you know what is on foot, I am sure that you will not be sorry."

"I am very happy, monsieur, if I can be of use to you in any way; I know you already through Violette, whom you were kind enough to visit when she was sick; and Chicotin told me——"

"I told him that this morning's business had something to do with her; but monsieur will explain the whole thing to us, and tell us why——"

"You are in a great hurry; the most important thing now is to start; and especially to avoid meeting my little neighbor on the stairs, for she would ask questions which we could not very well answer at this moment."

"Oh! it's only eight o'clock; it's cold too, and Violette doesn't go out so early in such weather."

"Very well, let us start, young men."

Roncherolle took his box of pistols, which seemed to puzzle Chicotin greatly. Georget went out first, walked to the stairs cautiously, then motioned to them that they might go down. All three were soon at the door, which was kept by Mirontaine only; he barked when anybody came in, but never when they went out.

Monsieur de Roncherolle entered the cab, told Georget and Chicotin to enter with him, although the latter declared that he would be quite as comfortable behind, and bade the coachman take them to the Porte Saint-Mandé, by the Vincennes road.

"Oho! we are going to the country," cried Chicotin; "we shan't find much shade there!"

"I can tell you now, messieurs, why I have brought you with me," said Roncherolle. "It is for the purpose of being my seconds; for I have a duel on hand, I am going to fight a duel with pistols this morning."

"You are going to fight?" cried Georget, deeply moved.

"Yes, my friend; if I had told you that beforehand, would you have refused to come with me?"

"Oh, no! on the contrary, I would have begged you to take me."

"I was sure of it beforehand, young man."

"And I too, bourgeois; I like fights! they just suit me! But what are we two going to fight with? We haven't any weapons; are we to fight with fists? I like that too."

"No, not with fists or anything else; you are my seconds, and you will not be called upon to fight at all."

"So much the worse! of what use shall we be then?"

"To affirm the innocence of a young girl whom I hope to avenge. I am going to fight with Monsieur Jéricourt."

"With Monsieur Jéricourt?" cried Georget; "with that man who laid the trap for Violette and then slandered her so abominably?"

"Just so; do you consider that I am doing wrong?"

"Oh, monsieur! what good fortune! that Jéricourt! I have been looking for him everywhere, and haven't found him. But you are not the one who's going to fight with him, monsieur; I am; for I am the man whom he insulted most cruelly; I am the man whom he injured most; I am to be the husband of the woman whom he tried to dishonor. You must see, monsieur, that I am the one who must fight with him."

"My dear Georget, I was very sure that you would say all that; I expected it; but be calm and listen to me. I was in this gentleman's company yesterday; I have long been looking for an opportunity. I told him what I thought of his conduct toward Violette. I demanded satisfaction for his slanders, but he refused; then I struck him in the face. The duel was instantly arranged for this morning. Now, this gentleman has the right to demand satisfaction for the outrage inflicted upon his face; if I did not fight, if I allowed you to fight in my place, I should act like a coward; and as I have never had that reputation, you will permit me not to earn it now. All that I can do, my dear Monsieur Georget, is, if I fall, to allow you to take my place and to renew the combat with this gentleman. Now it is all understood and arranged. Not a word more on that subject, for it would be useless.—But we have arrived."

The carriage stopped on the outskirts of the wood; Roncherolle alighted with the two young men, Chicotin carrying the box of pistols. They looked about in all directions but saw nobody.

"Is it possible that he will not come?" murmured Georget, stamping the ground impatiently.

"Is he going to squeal?" said Chicotin.

"There is no time wasted yet, messieurs, and his seconds may have kept him waiting.—But look, I see a carriage in the distance.—I'll wager that they're the people we expect."

The carriage reached the wood and they saw Jéricourt, Saint-Arthur and little Astianax at once alight from it.

"*Saperlotte!* the seconds are not big fellows," cried Chicotin; "I know 'em; both of 'em together wouldn't make one decent man. I could eat half a dozen of them without difficulty!"

Roncherolle imposed silence upon Chicotin with a glance. Jéricourt came forward with his two friends;

Saint-Arthur acted as if he had a pain in his stomach, and little Astianax looked in both directions at once.

"What does this mean?" cried Jéricourt, as he scrutinized Chicotin, while Georget glared at him with flaming eyes; "what! Monsieur de Roncherolle chooses a messenger for his second? Really, I should have supposed that he could find some one better than that.— You see, messieurs, the honor that he does you, and with whom you are brought into relations!"

"What's that? what's that?" cried Chicotin, turning up his sleeves; "do I hear anybody sneering at me? Ah! as I live! I'll smash the principal and his seconds in a second."

"Be quiet," said Roncherolle sternly. Then, walking toward his adversary's two seconds, he said to them:

"I have brought this young man, messieurs, Monsieur Georget, because he is the fiancé, the future husband of the young girl whom monsieur attempted to ruin. No one has a better right to be here than he, for the honor of the woman whom he is to marry is the motive of this duel. As for my other second, this honest fellow here, he is only a messenger, it is true, but it was he who saved the young flower girl when, driven to desperation by contemptuous treatment and humiliation, and by the thought of passing for what she was not, she was on the point of jumping into the canal and seeking an end to her suffering there. Do you not think, messieurs, that this honest fellow who brought back hope to Violette's heart, also has a right to be present at a battle which is to rehabilitate her honor? Come, messieurs, which of you will undertake to maintain the contrary, and will blush to have to deal with such seconds? Neither of you, I am sure!"

Saint-Arthur and Astianax contented themselves with bowing low to Roncherolle, who continued:

"Very good, everything is arranged; now, my adversary has the choice of weapons."

"He chooses pistols," said Astianax.

"Pistols it is; I have brought some."

"So have we."

"We will take yours, if you choose; it makes no difference to me. My adversary has the right to fire first also, I recognize that; you see that we shall have no difficulty. Let us go a little way into the woods, and have done with it."

The whole party walked into the woods and stopped in a solitary place, where there was a clearing suitable for the duel. Astianax, having spoken to Jéricourt, returned to Roncherolle and said:

"Is fifteen paces satisfactory to you, monsieur?"

"Ordinarily, the seconds would decide such matters among themselves; but no matter, that is satisfactory to me; mark off the distance and I will take my place."

Astianax counted the paces, while Saint-Arthur leaned against a tree at a distance; as for Georget and Chicotin, Roncherolle was obliged to hold them back by his glance.

Young Astianax, having finished measuring the distance, handed to each combatant a pistol, which he took from the box he had brought; then he stood aside, saying:

"They are loaded; I believe there is nothing more for me to do now."

"It is for you to begin, monsieur," said Roncherolle, bowing to Jéricourt.

Jéricourt took a long aim, then fired; the ball from his pistol grazed his adversary's right side and made him turn slightly; Georget started to run to him, but Roncherolle motioned to him not to stir and speedily resumed his position, saying:

"That was not bad, but it was not quite the thing."

He fired almost instantly, and Jéricourt, wounded in the breast, fell to the ground.

The four seconds rushed at once to the assistance of the wounded man, who was already discharging blood through his mouth; and when he saw Georget, he said to him in a faint voice:

"I lied—she is innocent—tell her that I confess, that——"

The unhappy wretch closed his eyes and could say no more; Chicotin took him in his arms and carried him to the carriage which had brought him, which Astianax also entered. As for Saint-Arthur, he had disappeared and they were unable to find him.

Georget ran back to Roncherolle, crying:

"He confessed, monsieur; he confessed; he admitted that he had slandered Violette! all those gentlemen heard him as well as I!"

" That is well, my young friend; that is what I wanted. Now you must give me your arm to help me to walk back to the carriage."

" Oh! are you wounded too, monsieur? "

" A scratch, a mere scratch, but it troubles me when walking. I will lean on you."

" Oh! as hard as you please, monsieur. What a debt of gratitude I owe you! And Violette, when she knows it——"

" I knew perfectly well that she deserved to be defended; but I am very glad to have spared you that trouble; and then, you see, I have done a lot of foolish things in my life, and I am not sorry to do some good now and then."

Chicotin reached the carriage just as Monsieur de Roncherolle and Georget entered it. The young messenger's face was all awry, and he faltered:

" All the same, it gives a man a shock—a young man, who was so well a minute ago——"

" Well? Monsieur Jéricourt, how is he? " asked Roncherolle.

" He is stone dead! "

XLIV

THE EMBROIDERED HANDKERCHIEF

While the duel which concerned the pretty flower girl was in progress, the girl herself was greatly surprised to see Pongo appear at her door about nine o'clock.

"Master," he said, "he want mamzelle to come and see him after her dress herself all fine; yes, dress herself all fine, and bring a big bouquet."

Violette hastened to answer that she would obey Monsieur Malberg's orders; but as she donned her best dress and her prettiest cap, she said to herself:

"Probably Monsieur Malberg wants to send me somewhere, for he would not tell me to dress in my best just to go to his house. Besides, the bouquet that he wants —no doubt I shall have to go to Madame de Grangeville's.—So much the better! I like that lady very much, and it's a long time since I carried her a bouquet."

When he saw Violette enter his room, so fresh and pretty and graceful, and wearing a dress, which, although appropriate to her rank in life, gave an added charm to her person, none the less, the count could not help sighing, as he said to himself:

"I should have been very happy if I could have called her my daughter."

" Here I am, monsieur, I have obeyed your orders," said Violette; " I have done what your servant told me to do; do I look well, monsieur? "

" Yes, my child, yes, very well; and I have no doubt that Madame de Grangeville will find you charming thus."

" Am I going to that lady's house? I suspected it, monsieur."

" So much the better!—Listen to me, Violette; I must tell you now that this lady to whom I am sending you knew your mother and the secret of your birth; if your mother is still alive, if she is disposed to recognize you as her daughter, this lady will tell you so."

" Is it possible, monsieur? "

" Yes, and for that purpose, you are going to-day to tell her all that you know about your birth, giving her to understand that you have known it only a short time; and then you will finish your story by showing her this handkerchief, which I give back to you to-day, so that it may help you to find your parents."

" Ah! I am all of a tremble, monsieur; the thought that perhaps I am going to find my mother—why haven't you let me say all this to that lady before? "

" Because, my child, before confiding such an important matter to her, I wanted her to have time to appreciate you, so that you might not be a stranger to her."

" And suppose this lady, after listening to me, after seeing this handkerchief, should not mention my mother to me? "

"In that case, my poor girl, it would mean that you no longer have a mother, that all hope of finding her is vanished. But such a supposition does not seem possible to me; no, she cannot spurn you again; and those who brought you into this world will be only too happy to lavish their caresses upon you."

"Shall I tell this lady it's you who send me this time?"

"Not by any means; let her still think that it is Monsieur de Merval.—Go, Violette; and if it is possible, come back here and tell me the result of your visit to—to Madame de Grangeville."

"If it is possible! who could prevent me from coming back to you, monsieur?—I will go at once, and you will see me again soon."

The young girl took her bouquet and started for the abode of the lady who, as she had been told, might restore her mother to her; a thousand confused thoughts, a thousand hopes surged through Violette's mind, and she reached the house intensely excited and trembling from head to foot, and asked Mademoiselle Lizida if she could see her mistress.

"I think so," said the lady's maid; "madame was at a ball last night, but she did not return very late; it is twelve o'clock, and she has just risen; I will announce you and your bouquet."

After a few moments, Violette was ushered into the presence of Madame de Grangeville, who was seated before her mirror, completing her morning toilet, and who smiled at the young girl, saying to her:

"Ah! here is my pretty little flower girl. It is a long while since you came last, little one; I am neglected nowadays; Monsieur de Merval is less attentive to me."

"I don't know, madame——"

"Let me see your bouquet; it is very pretty, but I saw finer ones at the ball last night. Sit down, my girl, and let us talk a bit. Why! how you are dressed up to-day! where are you going this morning, pray?"

"I am going nowhere but here, madame."

"Oho! then it was for me that you made this toilet. You look very well; and I—this cap—do you think that it is becoming to me? I look a little tired, do I not? They absolutely insisted upon making me dance last night.—But what ails you, my child? One would say that you were not listening to me; you seem distraught."

"Ah! madame, it is because——"

"Because what? finish your sentence."

"Since I had the honor to see you last, I have learned something about——"

"About what?"

"About my birth, about my family."

"Your family; you told me that you were an abandoned child."

"True, madame; but someone who knew my nurse has told me several things which may help me, they say, to find my parents."

"Really—I think I will put on a blue ribbon instead of a pink one, it will look better.—Were you not left at the Foundling Hospital in Paris?"

" No, madame, I was born in Paris, but I was given in charge of a nurse, who came from Picardie, and who went back to her province at once."

Madame de Grangeville ceased to toy with her cap and said to Mademoiselle Lizida, who was putting the room in order:

" Leave us, go.—You were saying that your nurse lived in Picardie?"

" Yes, madame."

" What was her name?"

" Marguerite Thomasseau."

" Marguerite—are you sure that her name was Marguerite?"

" Yes, madame."

" And—and you—what name did your parents give you?"

" The gentleman who placed me in my nurse's hands— she did not know whether he was my father, but she presumed that he was—told her that my name was Evelina de Paulausky."

Madame de Grangeville moved suddenly on her chair; but instead of approaching Violette, she drew away from her; one would have thought that she was afraid of the girl. The latter waited anxiously to hear what the lady was going to say to her; but several moments, which seemed very long, passed, and not a word fell from the lips of Madame de Grangeville, whose head had fallen on her breast, and who seemed to be absorbed in her reflections.

Violette decided to continue.

"That is not all, madame," she said; "it seems that when he placed me in charge of my nurse, instead of giving her a *layette,* he gave her some men's clothes, among which there was a handkerchief belonging to my mother.

"Aha! did he say that?"

"Yes, the gentleman said so when he gave it to my nurse; and she always kept it, hoping that it might enable me some day to make myself known to her who brought me into the world."

"Well! and that handkerchief——"

"It was given to me to-day; here it is—would you like to look at it, madame?"

With a trembling hand Violette held out the handkerchief to the woman whom a secret voice told her was her mother. Madame de Grangeville took it without turning her head, and examined it a moment; only a glance was necessary for her to recognize it; but she had already ceased to doubt that Violette was her daughter, and although she had been reflecting in silence for some moments, it was only to consider whether she should confess to the young flower girl that she was her mother. After some moments' reflection, she said to herself that there was no reason why she should recognize as her daughter a little flower girl, whose presence in her house would constantly embarrass her and incommode her, and would necessarily let everyone know that she was over thirty-five years old.

Violette, who was waiting, hoping, hardly breathing while Madame de Grangeville held the handkerchief in her hands, said to her at last:

"Well, madame—that handkerchief——"

"It is very handsome, mademoiselle, and beautifully embroidered."

As she spoke, the lady handed the handkerchief back to her; the girl could not make up her mind to take it, but said in a faltering tone:

"Has madame—nothing else—to say to me?"

"Why, mademoiselle, what do you suppose that I can have to say to you?"

"I beg pardon; but I was led to hope—that madame—that madame knew—my mother, and that——"

"Somebody has been telling you things that are utterly absurd, mademoiselle," replied Madame de Grangeville, in a very cold tone; "and you may say to those who told you that, that they have been dreaming, nothing more.—Here, take your handkerchief, I have no use for it.—Lizida! Lizida! come and dress me; I am going out."

Violette understood that she had her dismissal; she rose with a heavy heart, carefully replaced the handkerchief in her breast; and as she bowed to Madame de Grangeville, she said to her in a voice choked by sobs:

"Adieu, madame; forgive me for weeping before you, but I hoped to find my mother here."

"Adieu, mademoiselle; take my advice, and think no more about that; don't foster any such fancies in your head; and when you see Monsieur de Merval, tell him that he is mistaken, completely mistaken."

Violette went away, weeping bitterly; and in that condition she returned to Monsieur de Brévanne and told him of her interview with Madame de Grangeville.

The count pressed the young girl to his heart, saying:

" Poor child! the woman who gave you life is unworthy of your love, of your caresses; but if you have not found your mother, be comforted; I will take the place of your family, and I will never abandon you."

The count had been trying to comfort Violette but a few moments, when the door of his apartment was violently thrown open, and Georget appeared, out of breath, drenched with perspiration, and with joy gleaming in his eyes.

" She is here, isn't she, monsieur?" he cried; "yes, here she is! Rejoice, Violette! rejoice! No one now can have any doubt of your innocence; you are avenged! Monsieur de Roncherolle has fought a duel with Jéricourt. I wanted to fight in his place, but he wouldn't let me; we were his seconds. Oh! I ran at the top of my speed to your stand; I was in such a hurry to tell you about it."

Monsieur de Brévanne forced Georget to sit down, as he could say no more; when he had recovered his breath, he gave them an exact account of all that had taken place during the morning; of the duel and of its results. Violette listened with emotion; Monsieur de Roncherolle's devotion to her brought tears to her eyes. The count,

who had also listened to Georget with the deepest interest,
said to the girl:

"You see, my child, Heaven sends you a great consolation already: your innocence is fully established; no
doubt it is lamentable that a man should have had to pay
with his life for the slanders that he had circulated, but
while you may regret that calamity, you certainly cannot
accuse yourself of it. As for Monsieur de Roncherolle,
his behavior in this matter deserves nothing but praise;
he is entitled to all your gratitude; and before long he
will be well repaid for what he has done.—But didn't you
say, Georget, that he was wounded also?"

"Yes, monsieur, on the right side; the bullet made a
hole there; he says that it's nothing, but we put him to
bed, Chicotin and I, and my friend has gone to fetch the
doctor."

"I am going to take my place by his side, and be his
nurse," said Violette.

"Go, my child; devote yourself to Monsieur de Roncherolle; that is your duty, and I am quite certain that
it is also a pleasure to your heart."

When he saw the young flower girl enter his room,
Roncherolle sat up in bed, held out his hand with a smile,
and said to her:

"I was sure that my two chatterboxes would go at
once to tell you all about it. Well, yes, I fought for you,
my child; ten thousand devils! you are well worth the
trouble. The little fellow didn't want to let me do it; he
wanted to fight in my place. Ah! he has a stout heart,

he is a fine fellow; but he is too young as yet; and then it was much better to have it happen as it did."

"Oh! how can I express my gratitude, monsieur?"

"No gratitude; affection,—that is much better."

"Will you allow me to kiss you?"

"Will I allow you! I shouldn't have dared to suggest it, my child, but I accept with all my heart!"

And Roncherolle embraced Violette, whose eyes were moist with tears; but this time it was a pleasant emotion which caused them to flow.

Chicotin brought a doctor, who examined the wound, and ordered perfect rest. But in the evening the gout reappeared, and the wounded man said with a sigh:

"The doctor need have no fear, I fancy I shan't move for some time yet."

"I will stay with you faithfully," said Violette; "I will not leave you until you are cured."

"I don't propose to have that, my little neighbor; you will go to sell your flowers as usual, and come here in the evening; even that will be very kind of you."

Georget also asked Monsieur de Roncherolle's permission to come to see him, and he replied, pressing his hand:

"As often as you can, my young friend; a little bit for me, and a great deal for this child,—for whom you will be a pleasant companion, and who will not be sorry to have you."

The next morning the count called early to inquire for the wounded man's health, and told the concierge to tell Violette that someone wished to speak to her.

The girl ran downstairs and said to the count:

" You might have come up to my poor patient's room, monsieur, for he is asleep just now; and as he slept almost none during the night, I hope that he will not wake for some time."

" I thought that his wound amounted to nothing?"

" We thought so at first, monsieur; but he has had an attack of gout which has made him very feverish, and increased his pain."

" Well, my child, to give him some relief in his suffering, take this letter to him, and when he is calm, and you two are alone, give it to him."

" Very good, monsieur; and shall I say that it is from you?"

" Yes, yes, you may act without secrecy now. Au revoir, my child; I hope that the contents of this letter, bringing him good news, will restore your—your neighbor's health."

The count took his leave; Violette carefully bestowed in her bosom the letter which he had handed her, and returned to the sick man.

About noon, Roncherolle, his pain having subsided, felt more calm, and tried to smile at the girl who was nursing him, saying to her:

" You are alone, dear child; have our young men left you?"

" Yes, monsieur, they are at their work; but I am not sorry, for you are comfortable now and I have something to tell you—that is to say, something to give you."

"Something to give me? without their knowledge?"

"Yes, monsieur, this letter; and as I was told that it would give you pleasure, that it might perhaps contribute to restoring your health, I was in a hurry to be alone with you so that I might give it to you."

"A letter that will give me pleasure! From whom did you get it, my girl?"

"From—from Monsieur Malberg."

"From Monsieur Malberg? Georget's protector?"

"Himself, monsieur."

Roncherolle manifested such emotion, his face became so deathly pale, that the girl was terrified.

"What is the matter, monsieur? do you feel worse?"

"No, but what you've just told me surprised me so.— Do you know Monsieur Malberg, pray?"

"Yes, monsieur. Oh! he is very kind, I tell you! he took Georget and his mother into his house, he is interested in me, and he has tried to help me to find my parents."

"Your parents—but give me the letter, my child."

"Here it is, monsieur."

Roncherolle took the letter with a trembling hand and broke the seal. He instantly recognized the writing of the man who had been his friend, and his eyes, with feverish eagerness, read these lines:

"You were very guilty toward me. But God forgives the penitent man, and I should not be more inexorable than He. I give you your daughter; you have fought for her honor, and that act may well have earned pardon for your desertion of the child.

> " Comte de Brévanne."

As he read, Roncherolle became more excited; then he looked at Violette; and when he had finished the letter, his eyes rested upon the girl with an expression of such pure affection, that she was greatly moved, and faltered:

"What is it, monsieur? That letter was supposed to give you pleasure."

"Ah! it makes me very, very happy, my dear child; so happy that I dare not as yet believe in my happiness. It speaks to me of my daughter, whom I had lost, abandoned, and of whose fate I knew nothing!"

"You abandoned your daughter?"

"Yes.—Ah! I dared not confess that to you; one does not like to blush before those who show affection for one; but you, Violette, tell me, in pity's name, do you know nothing about your parents? Have you nothing of theirs, no token which might identify you?"

"Excuse me, monsieur; if I have not spoken to you about it before, it is because Monsieur Malberg forbade me to do so; but to-day he said to me: 'Have no more secrets from Monsieur de Roncherolle;' so I can tell you everything."

"Speak, speak!"

"In the first place, they gave me the name of Evelina de Paulausky; and then they kept this handkerchief for me, which belonged to my mother—see."

" Enough! enough! " murmured Roncherolle, holding out his arms to Violette. " Dear child, if you can forgive me for deserting you, come to your father's arms! "

" You, my father! my heart had divined it! " cried Violette, throwing herself into Roncherolle's arms, where he held her for a long time, against his heart.

But such violent emotion brought on a fresh attack, and the invalid, who longed to say a thousand things to his daughter, had not the strength to do it; she was obliged to entreat him to be calm and to rest.

After some time, Roncherolle, feeling more at ease, motioned to Violette to approach his bed, and bade her tell him all that he whom she still called Monsieur Malberg had done for her. The girl concealed nothing from her father, neither the bouquets which she had carried to Madame de Grangeville, nor the last interview she had had with that lady. And Roncherolle raised his eyes to heaven, murmuring:

" She told her that she did not know her mother! "

Then Violette informed her father that Georget's patron had come to see him during his last illness, when he was destitute; and she added:

" It was the very next day that you received that letter with money; I am very sure myself that it was he who sent it."

" Ah! this is too much! this is too much! " muttered Roncherolle, putting his hand to his eyes. " He has avenged himself more thoroughly than if he had killed me, for he has made me realize what a friend I have lost, and how often serious is a fault which men are accustomed to treat so slightingly ! "

Georget came very soon to inquire for the invalid's health. On learning that the girl he loved was Monsieur de Roncherolle's daughter, the poor boy was struck dumb; he feared at once that that discovery would interpose obstacles to his union with Violette; but Roncherolle, reading his thought in his eyes, held out his hand to him and said:

" My friend, I have no right to cherish prejudices; besides, I have allowed my daughter to sell flowers, so I may consistently allow her to marry an ex-messenger.— You love each other, my children, and I shall never oppose your happiness."

Chicotin appeared at that moment, and when he was told of all that had happened, he danced about the room, and attempted to make the furniture dance. To keep him quiet, they were obliged to remind him that he was in a sick room, whereupon he went out and skipped upon the boulevard.

Georget informed his patron of all that had happened at Roncherolle's room, and of the blessings which the father and the daughter had showered upon him; the count smiled as he said:

" Yes, I believe after all that one is happier in avenging himself as I have done."

Six days passed, during which Roncherolle was better and worse alternately. On the seventh day, he woke with a violent fever; his wound pained him terribly, and it

Copyright 1904 by G. Burrie & Sons

seemed from his general prostration and the faintness of his voice, that his strength was leaving him. But, still trying to conceal his suffering, especially from his daughter's eyes, he called her to his bedside about mid-day, and said, trying to smile:

" My dear love, do you want to make me very happy ? "

" Tell me what I must do, father ? "

" You must go to the Comte de Brévanne—for that is the real name of Georget's patron—and tell him yourself how grateful I am to him for giving me back my daughter, although I had inflicted such injury upon him. You must assure him again of my repentance, and beg him to repeat that he forgives me."

" But I should rather not leave you to-day, father; you seem very much depressed, and you are in greater pain."

" No, no, you are mistaken; I am in no more pain than usual; so do my errand; it seems to me that that will afford me great relief."

" Oh! then I will do what you say, father; I hear Chicotin now, and I will tell him not to leave you until I return."

The girl hastily put on what she needed to go out, then embraced her father. Roncherolle held her to his heart for a long time. She started toward the door, but he called her back, that he might kiss her once more; he strove to smile at her, and followed her with his eyes until she had left the room; then he let his head fall back on the pillow, saying;

"Dear love! I think that I have done well to send her away."

On leaving the house Violette met Georget, who was coming to inquire for her father, and who proposed to accompany his sweetheart to his patron's house. But the girl begged him to let her go alone, and to go up to her father; she was afraid that Chicotin might make a mistake about giving him what he asked for. Georget complied with Violette's request, and instead of accompanying her, he went up to Monsieur de Roncherolle.

When Violette arrived at Monsieur de Brévanne's, he was at home, but engaged with contractors, architects and men who were working upon some property of his in Paris; the girl waited until he was at liberty, for she was unwilling to return to her father without complying with his wishes and seeing the count. At last he was alone, and Violette was able to express to him all her gratitude for what she owed him, and to deliver her father's message.

Monsieur de Brévanne listened attentively to what Roncherolle had instructed his daughter to say to him. He took Violette's hands in his, and said to her:

"Yes, my dear love, I have forgiven your father, and he must know that I never speak except from the dictates of my heart."

"I will repeat your very words to him, monsieur," said Violette, "and I hope that it will do him good; for I saw plainly enough to-day that he was suffering more, although he tried to hide it from me; but this morning, when he looked at his wound, the doctor did not seem at all satisfied."

"I thought that his wound was a slight one?"

"So it was, monsieur, but a constant fever has prevented it from healing."

"If that is so, I will go with you, my child; I will take you back to your father, and see for myself how he is. Perhaps he should have another doctor."

"Oh! you are so kind, monsieur, and I am so grateful to you! Would you be willing to see my father, and to tell him what you have just told me? I have an idea that that would cure him at once."

The count at once led Violette away, saying:

"Come, my child; let us first find out how he is."

It was but a short distance from the count's house to Roncherolle's lodgings. Violette and Monsieur de Brévanne soon arrived. The concierge was not in her lodge, and Mirontaine received them, barking in most lugubrious fashion.

"That is strange!" murmured Violette; "this dog knows me perfectly well, so why does she make that noise? why does she howl like that? Mon Dieu! they say that that announces some calamity!"

And the girl ran rapidly up the stairs, while the count tried to reassure her. But when they reached the fifth floor, they saw Georget and Chicotin standing outside Roncherolle's door. Violette would have passed into the room, but Georget put his arms about her and detained her, and she saw that his eyes were filled with tears.

"O my God! my father is dead!" cried the girl.

Georget and his friend sadly hung their heads; there-upon Violette fell into Monsieur de Brévanne's arms, faltering:

"Oh! I have lost my father, monsieur! and it was so short a time since Heaven gave him back to me!"

"Courage, my poor child," said the count; "here-after I will take his place!"

XLV

CONCLUSION

After Roncherolle's death, Monsieur de Brévanne took Violette into his family and treated her as his daughter. He provided different masters for both Violette and Georget, who completed their education.

Study, Georget's love, and the count's affection, grad-ually changed Violette's grief into a melancholy souvenir. Sometimes she said to Monsieur de Brévanne:

"So you don't want me to sell flowers any more, mon-sieur?"

"No, my child," the count said with a smile. "You shall have flowers, you shall raise them, and pick as many as you please; but you no longer need to sell them, for I am wealthy, and when your mourning is at an end, I propose to marry you to Georget and share my fortune with you."

A few weeks after Roncherolle's death, of which the count informed Monsieur de Merval, the latter met Madame de Grangeville on the street, and she eagerly accosted him.

"At last I meet you, my sincere, my generous friend, and I am able to express my gratitude for what you are doing for me. No more mystery, my dear Merval, I know all; I recognized your handwriting; indeed, what other than yourself would have acted so delicately toward me? But I assure you that as to the little flower girl, you are mistaken, you are entirely wrong; it was simply some resemblance of feature which led you to think that."

Monsieur de Merval listened without interrupting, and when she had finished, he said to her in a very grave tone:

"Madame, it is time that you should be disabused concerning the error under which you are laboring. I am not entitled to your thanks, the money which you receive from an unknown hand is not sent to you by me, I tell you again; but I have a shrewd suspicion from whom it does come."

"Who is it, pray? For heaven's sake, give me the name of that generous friend."

"The Comte de Brévanne, madame."

Madame de Grangeville made a slight grimace and shut her lips together in annoyance, muttering:

"My husband! what an idea! how on earth could he have learned that I was in straitened circumstances?"

" It was I who told him, madame, after I had the honor to pay you a visit; I did not think that I did wrong in informing Monsieur de Brévanne that your situation was not—was not prosperous."

" I did not give you that commission, monsieur.—But in that case—the flower girl——"

" It was he who sent her also, madame."

" Really, monsieur, I utterly failed to understand the romance that that girl told me. Someone has believed, or imagined, things which are utterly absurd."

" It seems, madame, that Monsieur de Roncherolle understood better than you did, for he did not fail to acknowledge that young flower girl as his daughter."

" His daughter! Monsieur de Roncherolle acknowledged her as his daughter?"

" Yes, madame, before he died."

" What! Roncherolle is dead?"

" He is dead, madame, and he died asking forgiveness of the friend whom he had so deeply injured."

" Ah! poor Roncherolle! So he is dead! Well, after all, he was wise, for he was in a pitiable plight. And—and—the little flower girl?"

" She is living with the Comte de Brévanne, madame. He has adopted her, and *he* will never abandon her! Ah! there are few men like the count, and you should be very proud, madame, that you once bore his name!"

Madame de Grangeville could not repress a gesture of annoyance; but she restrained herself, bowed coldly to Monsieur de Merval and hurriedly left him.

Toward the close of the Carnival, which came shortly after, Madame de Grangeville, as the result of wearing a much too décolleté costume at a ball, was seized with inflammation of the lungs; and a week after taking to her bed, she realized that she would never leave it again.

Thereupon a maternal sentiment sprang up in that woman's heart for the first time; for thus far she had lived solely for herself. Hastily writing a few words in a trembling hand, she begged the count to be kind enough to send her daughter to her, as she would like to embrace her before she breathed her last.

But the count said to his wife's messenger:

" When a person has twice spurned her child, she must not hope that that child will close her eyes. It is too late now for Violette to know her mother."

A few days after Madame de Grangeville's death, the Comte de Brévanne resumed his name and his title, and there was an end of Monsieur Malberg.

The Glumeau family continues to give private theatricals in its little wood, but Chambourdin is not allowed to seat ladies on the branches of trees.

Little Saint-Arthur, having squandered his last sou with Mademoiselle Zizi Dutaillis, considered himself too fortunate to have found another place as clerk in a dry-goods shop, where he has resumed his own name and has become Benoît Canard as before. But the young actress is a good-hearted girl; she still allows her former friend to come to see her sometimes, and on those occasions it is she who invites him to breakfast.

As for Chicotin, he insists upon remaining a messenger. Witnessing the happiness of Georget and Violette, he says to himself:

"They owe it partly to me; but I am perfectly sure that if I were in hard luck they would give me a share of their good fortune."

LIST OF ILLUSTRATIONS

THE FLOWER GIRL OF THE CHÂTEAU D'EAU

——

VOLUME II

www.ingramcontent.com/pod-product-compliance
Lightning Source LLC
Chambersburg PA
CBHW030342020726
47493CB00003B/648